Mafia Prince
Vi Carter

DEDICATION

E mmaline this is for you, my twin flame. You will always be missed.

WARNING

T his book is a dark romance. This book contains scenes that may be triggering to some readers and should be read by those only 18 or older.

NEWSLETTER

JOIN MY NEWSLETTER AND NEVER MISS A NEW RELEASE OR GIVEAWAY.

Scan the QR Code to be taken to my newsletter page.

PROLOGUE

O'REAGAN
AN CHLANN

MAEVE

Memories.

Sometimes we build them up so high that they take on a life of their own. Sometimes they manifest into beasts that consume us from the inside out. Sometimes life loses its color, and we wait for the harsh reality that is to come. No one told me it would be this hard. Sometimes the power of a memory can either destroy us or lift us up.

CHAPTER ONE

O'REAGAN

AN CHLANN

MAEVE

PRESENT DAY

T he keys rattle in the door, and I press my foot to the base of the wood that normally gets jammed. Years of forcing the door open this way have damaged the base further; any day it could cave in. Pushing the door open, I hold my breath. I know the drill by now. Being away in college all week leaves my mother and brother alone, and they can barely keep themselves alive.

"Mom," I call as I force the door closed behind me. It takes three attempts before the lock slides into place, sealing me into the house. I step around the pile of cardboard that's being stacked against the skirting board. The yellow floor tiles are neglected and grubby.

The moment I step into the kitchen, I drop my bag on the floor. The table is flooded with plates with food caked onto them - the type that will take an hour of steeping to remove. I lift a pile of unopened mail and drop it back down as I scan all the empty vodka and wine bottles. Walking around the table, I force the window open and let some air filter in to try and get rid of the smell.

"Mom." I call louder as I open the back door and place a chair behind it to hold it open. My heart leaps as Sandy pounces off the counter and races out the back door. I don't even look at the counters to see what the cat's been doing. Takeaway bags and opened food are stacked high. It always looks like this when I get back from college. My weekend will be cleaning, working at the local grocery store, and trying to get some homework done.

Sandy's silver bowls are empty on the floor. I don't want to stay in the kitchen any longer, but I'm not cruel either. Opening the cupboard, I take out a moldy loaf of bread and place it on the counter. Pushing aside red sauce and some jam, I stare into emptiness. I close the cupboard and move onto the next, which holds a bag of sugar and some salt.

Sandy has re-entered the kitchen and cries up at me as she circles around my ankles.

"Yeah, I'm working on it." Kneeling down, I open the bottom cupboard and grin at the bag of cat food. Sandy leaps up on my knee, and I swipe her off.

"Here we go." I barely get the food into the bowl before Sandy's eating them. Filling up her water dish, I call my mother again before leaving the kitchen.

"Mom." She must be passed out somewhere. The sitting room door is closed, and I push it open. It takes my eyes a moment to adjust to the darkness, but once they do, I wish I could step out of the room—the air freezes in my lungs and the ground under me shifts. A man stands over my bleeding brother. My brother's gray t-shirt—that's nearly threadbare—is coated in flecks of his blood. His jeans hang off his thin frame. My gaze bounces around the scarcely furnished sitting room before landing on my mother. The air re-enters my system, and I try to control my racing heart. My mother is in a heap in the corner. Her wild eyes won't settle on anything. Mascara runs down her worn-out face. I'm tempted to step closer to her, but a shove to my back sends a shiver up my spine. The gun is nudged into my back again until I'm standing in the center of the room.

"What have we got here?"

I spin around at the voice. It's deep and holds an edge, like a sharp knife that nicks the skin. It makes me uncomfortable and cautious. Even without the gun, this man is dangerous. His bald head seems to absorb the light. Heavy brows curtain his blue eyes that assess me. He takes a step closer. The leather coat creaks as he reaches out a tattooed hand and lifts my blond plait before dropping it back down onto my bare shoulder. I want to yank my top up, but it's meant to hang off the shoulder, so I tighten my hands into fists.

"You're a pretty little thing." His grin is razor-sharp, and alarm bells start to ring as I take a step back.

"What do you want?" My voice sounds stronger than I actually feel.

"Leave her alone." Declan moans from the floor, and I'm relieved he's alive. His pale skin had me wonder if today was the day that I would find my brother dead. Now that I see he isn't dead, I wonder what mess he has gotten us into. I try to convey my question toward him with a stare that he meets briefly. His eyes slam closed as the man above him drives his black military-style boot into my brother's stomach. I'm moving, but a hand pulls on my arm and drags me back.

"Stay where you are, bitch."

"Just tell us what you want." I can't look away from Declan as he gasps for air. The man above him grins down with enjoyment. His gaze swings to me, and he spits on my brother like he's a dog.

"Declan here owes us twelve grand."

The earth beneath my feet shifts, and I need to sit down, but I don't move. I don't look at my brother any longer as he whimpers. I want to glance at my mother, who hasn't said a word, but she's alert and watching. I can hear her useless breaths from the corner of the room.

"And if he doesn't pay?" I ask the dreaded question.

Blue eyes roam across my chest, and he takes a step closer to me, his gaze fixes on my exposed shoulder. "I was going to send your mother to one of our brothels until the debt is cleared. But now that you are here, I think you would be a very good money-spinner." His fingers reach out and grip my chin, and I'm ready to step away from him, but I hold still, and his eyes gleam with approval that I don't want.

"I could take a test drive before we agree to anything," the guy standing over my brother sneers.

"Leave my sister alone, bro. I'll get your money." Declan tries to stand, but a large boot is pressed against his chest and pushes him back down. He holds out his thin arms, and I hate how faded he looks. He's a copy of what my brother once was.

"Your sister?" I take a step away from baldy as he speaks, and his fingers fall from my face. I didn't expect him to let me go so easily.

"This is the deal I'm going to make." He places the gun in the band of his trousers, and it's like the room sighs in relief. But I'm not fooled. This man would pull it out in a second. I'm keeping an eye on his friend, who I don't doubt is packing a gun as well.

"You have twenty-four hours to get me my money. If it's not here when I return, I'm taking you." His eyes bore into mine, and he takes a step towards me. This time when his fingers tighten on my arm, there is nothing gentle about it. I'm slammed against his chest as his other hand roughly dips into my pants. Terror grips me by the throat before I snap out of it, and I'm struggling. I'm trying to push him away as a deep-rooted fear starts to freeze me from the tips of my toes and travels quickly up my body. I don't want to freeze, I can't, or he will rape me. His fingers invade inside me, and then I'm free as he steps away and places his fingers in his mouth. Horror ripples through me, and my stomach lurches; It's over in a second.

"I'm nearly hoping you don't have the money. See you in twenty-four hours." His laughter floats out the door as his friend takes his foot off my brother's chest and follows him out. The moment they leave, my mother's cries grow by the second. I want to comfort her, but I'm on my knees, trying not to think about the invasion on my body.

"Declan." I'm searching his face. His soft brown eyes—the same as mine—smile up at me.

"Hi, Kiddo." His grin has always been a comfort when shit hit the fan, but now that I'm older and have taken a pounding from life, his grin doesn't comfort me; it just makes me sad, and it makes me remember what once was.

"Twelve thousand, Declan?" I shake my head, and he lies fully back. His top rises, and I hate how prominent his bones are.

"When did you last eat?" I take his arm in my hand, and he doesn't stop me as I turn it over. I expect the fresh needle marks, yet seeing them still dries up any hope that was about to flourish. Each week he makes me the same promise that he will get clean, and when I get back, he'll be a new man. The stupid part of me wants to dream that he will. I snort at my naive thoughts. Yeah, and maybe my mother will stop drinking, and my father will walk through the door. Why not go wild and let me quit my job that keeps the roof over our heads and food on the table.

"I'll get the money." Declan's smiling up at me through cracked lips that plead for water, that he doesn't even know his body is craving. I rise, and my mother continues to wail in the corner. She's managed to get her cigarettes and lighter out of her pink dressing gown pocket, so she's not that traumatized. I enter the kitchen, and the smell has me swallowing saliva. Taking down a mug, I fill it with water and return to the sitting room.

My brother drinks and slowly sits up.

"You remember that Christmas..." he's laughing at the memory that hasn't left his lips yet.

I examine his face; a cut above his eye is still bleeding.

"The one where mum knocked over the Christmas tree, or the one where she fell into the bath?" The list was endless, but none of them were funny. Not when you craved your father to walk through the door every Christmas, but he never did. Each year I grow harder until it doesn't matter. Nothing matters, only surviving.

"The one where you swore you saw Santa Claus." Declan finally says, and his long arm wraps around his waist like he can keep the laughter in that spills from his lips and fills the room. His laughter fills the room with a small amount of light that I bask in for just a moment. I'm smiling down at my brother. It reminds me of us under his blanket late at night after our mother had passed out from drinking. Declan had a way with words, a real natural storyteller. He would take me away from our home and bring me to the magical lands of Ireland where pots of gold sat at the end of rainbows, and banshees wailed about death. He made me believe for those brief moments that maybe there was something more to this existence than this.

"It was one of mum's boyfriends." He's still laughing, but his words sober me up.

The endless stream of men through the door never got old. Each one as much as a write-off as my mother, who still wails in the corner like a fucking banshee from one of Declan's stories.

I'm tempted to tell her to knock it off, but I don't waste my breath. I need to bandage Declan up.

"Can you stand?"

I hate how easily I lift Declan from the floor. It's like a light sack of tinder for the fire.

"Don't leave me." My mother whimpers from the corner. Anger bubbles in my veins, and if it could morph into something more, it would scorch her.

I leave with Declan. His room is a bare mess. His bed frame is long gone. The dirty mattress on the floor is covered by a sheet that I can not lie him on. He hobbles over, and I stop him.

"I need to change it, Declan. It has sick on it."

"It's my sick."

He's ready to lie down when I whip the sheet from under him. I don't meet my brother's eyes.

"How are you going to get the money?" I ask the stupid question as I throw the sheet onto the pile of clothes next to his chest of drawers.

He lies down and groans as I pull open his curtains and let some light flitter into his room.

"Come on, Maeve, close them." He slings an arm across his eyes. But I don't close the curtains. I force open a window to let in some air.

"Declan, this is serious," I say while staring out onto our lawn that died a long time ago. My gaze travels further as a group of young people huddles together while one jams to a beat that another makes.

"I don't know how I'll get the money."

I step away from the window at my brother's admission and leave him as I grab the first aid kit in the bathroom. My mother's cries have ceased as I re-enter my brother's room and kneel down on the floor beside his mattress.

"What about Lenny?" I ask and cringe. I hate even mentioning Lenny's name. But he is a local loan shark.

My brother turns his face towards me, and I hate the sadness I see in his eyes. It's like all his pain is swimming in circles and sucking the soul out of him. A force that I can't stop. My hand touches his dark hair, and I want to plead for my brother to come back to me and help me.

The weak thought has me focusing on his cut.

"Lenny broke my legs the last time," Declan says and hisses as I press down heavily on his cut.

"Yeah, well, I don't want to be raped over and over again." My words are harsh, and Declan's lanky frame goes rigid. He's five years older than me, twenty-nine, but most days, he reminds me of my little brother.

"I'll figure something out." He turns away from me onto his side. I sit with the bloodied cloth in my hand until his breathing evens out, and I know he's asleep. When he wakes, he might not even remember the threat that hangs over our heads. The bang from the hall has me freezing beside my brother. They changed their minds.

Chapter Two

O'REAGAN
AN CHLANN

JACK

The jeep sways as I cross the large steel bars that are laid at the entrance to the farmhouse. Rolling down the window, my lungs burn from the cold wind that whips its way inside the vehicle. The air pricks my skin and wakes me up a bit. How many hours had it been since I slept? Thirty-six? I had no idea. I had honestly lost count. I drive up to the red barriers that stop me from going any further. Knocking off the ignition, I reach into the back of the jeep and search for my coat. My hand skims across cold leather; I must have left my jacket in the club. Pulling the keys out, I get out reluctantly. The smell of steel and cut grass circles me as I stuff my hands into my jeans pockets and bend so I can get under the red barrier. The old farmhouse is derelict; the windows boarded up. More grass grows on the roof than in the small patch of dirt that would be considered the front lawn.

Walking along the side of the house, I make my way to a large shed that must have housed a hundred cattle at one time. It's empty. The livestock is outside on the green patches of grass in the distance—my breath dances in front of me as I spin around at the purr of an approaching vehicle.

The job I am doing today has nothing to do with my own work; this is for my father. I stay within the clubs, running them, and maintaining order. Other parts of our operations are run by one of my uncles; they all have their roles to play. But this job today is the start of my trials. I have to prove my worth before my father passes me the crown. A white jeep pulls up behind mine. I can't see the driver, but I know who it is.

Finn, my uncle, gets out, and I curse my fucking father. Finn is nice. He never says a bad word about anyone and is known as the peacekeeper. I wanted to work with my Uncle Shane or even my Uncle Darragh. They all had their hands in the jar that my father held the lid over, ready to close it when he saw fit.

Finn waves at me, his eyes crinkle at the corners. He opens the back door and pulls out a heavy gray jacket that he slings across his body. At least he had the common sense to bring a jacket. But I couldn't see Finn any other way, only sensible and prepared.

"Finn." I greet him with a jerk of my chin as he gets closer.

"It's a cold one." He pulls a pair of gloves out of his pocket and stuffs his hands inside them.

"Mighty cold. So, what's the job?" I hope he knows more than I do, but already the fact my father sent Finn, I'm assuming this is a simple pick up. He wouldn't send Finn to harm anyone. My uncle would release them or try to talk the rest of us out of hurting anyone.

He looks so much like my Uncle Darragh. They are twins, but they are both at the opposite ends of the spectrum. Darragh's a mad bastard, always was, as far as the stories go, that I've heard countless times about him.

Finn is always wrapped in a never-ending circle of pain. They say it's from losing his wife. I don't understand his pain. I honestly think if he got laid more, he'd be better off. Of course, I'm wise enough not to voice this; no matter what I think, I have to give my respect to my elders.

"I have no idea what he sent us here for." Finn glances around the farmyard while zipping up his coat.

I pull my hands out of my jeans, and the material burns my skin. Blowing into them does little to fight off the biting cold.

Finn shrugs snugly in his jacket, and I follow him into the shed. He leans over each small wall and checks out the stalls before moving to the next.

"So have you spoken to Cian?"

I move to the opposite side of the shed and start looking into the stalls to speed up the process. I am freezing my balls off here. "No." I keep it short, but I'm also very aware of my tone.

Finn isn't moving anymore, and I tuck my fingers under my armpits to keep them warm before turning to him.

"He's ..." I'm trying to think of the right words. I want to say a complete jackass, but once again, I know I need to be careful with my words.

"I know he isn't easy."

I can't stop the sneer that tugs at my lips. "He's a red-headed little fucker." Fuck it. I've said it now.

Finn tries to hide a grin by looking over the next wall. "Don't let Shane hear you say that."

"I'm not stupid," I mumble.

"I know. That's why you will lead us." Finn's confidence in me makes me uncomfortable. I've known all my life that I would lead as the head of our family. We control all the North-East of Ireland. Every drug trade, every brothel, every delivery of arms, we controlled. My dad and his brothers had built it up from nothing, and the empire that sat before me had hotels, clubs, restaurants, and an endless portfolio of property. I should be ecstatic to be inheriting everything, but it isn't that simple. Nothing good ever is.

"Found it." Finn's words drag me out of my thoughts, and I bounce across the shed towards him. He steps into the last stall. Of course, it's at the end, the furthest distance away from the jeeps. I pull back the green tarp, and I stare at the white blocks that are stacked nearly five feet high.

"That's a lot of coke. Are we expected to load this into the jeeps?"

"No. We just stare at it and then leave it here." Finn's sarcasm is unexpected, and when he glances at me, I can see he's ready to apologize. I don't want his apology.

I grab two blocks of white powder and turn to Finn. He still wears a grin—the air ripples before warm liquid splatters across my face. Finn hits the ground, and I'm standing frozen as I blink several times. The gurgling at my feet has me dropping the white blocks, and I join Finn on the ground.

He's trying to breathe, but he reminds me of a fish out of water, gasping for air. Blood pours from his neck. His hands grip the wound, but blood oozes out far too quickly. I'm waiting for more bullets to rain down on us, but the air is still. The shooter has ceased or has left. I want to find him and make him pay for spilling O'Reagan blood. Already I'm fuelled with thoughts of revenge.

Finn's blue eyes are fading, and there is a wild panic in them that I've seen before, in dying animals and people.

"You're not dying today." I push a hand down over the wound while getting out my phone.

My father doesn't answer, and I curse him before I ring Shane.

"Finn's been shot." I want to add 'and it's bad.'

"I'm on the way." Shane hangs up and doesn't ask where we are. They would all know since this was part of the trials. I rub my face into my shoulder to try to get rid of the blood that still coats my face.

My hand turns red, and Finn's skin pales even further. All I can think of is that he can't die on my watch. This wasn't part of the trials. The blood that runs from him is warm; this isn't a trick or a test. Someone just shot my uncle. Maybe he wasn't the target. Maybe I was. I raise my head slightly but can't see much over the wall.

"Shane is on his way," I speak to Finn, and his eyes flutter closed.

"Stay awake, Finn."

His eyes open, but he isn't with me at this moment. He's somewhere else.

"Don't you fucking stop fighting," I warn and press my hand down heavier on his neck. All I can do is talk shit to him, to keep him awake. I'm telling him anything I can think of. I'm ten again.

"I met your dad once. My grandfather."

I swear it looks like his eyes widen.

"He said he just wanted to meet me, get to know me. He looks like you all." I listen for the purr of a vehicle that I don't hear.

Where are you, Shane?

"He said I was part of An Chlann."

Finn gargles as he tries to speak.

14

"Shut the fuck up, Finn." Panic tears through me. I don't want to hear his dying words. I won't be the one to watch the light go out in his eyes. A car tears into the yard.

"See, everything is going to be fine. Shane's here."

Hope doesn't blossom in Finn's eyes.

A car door shuts.

"The last stall," I shout. Once again, I'm tempted to say how bad it is, but I don't. "The shot came from the west. The shooter could still be here."

"Is it bad?" Shane's voice is closer.

I want to growl and tell him to hurry up.

"It's a neck shot."

Shane curses, and he appears. He stares at his brother on the ground.

"Finn." He kneels down, and his eyes roam across Finn's face and neck.

Finn's still alert, and I don't know how. *You can't kill a bad thing*; that's what my father always said. Only Finn isn't a bad person. He was the only good in all of us.

"We lift him on the count of three."

I'm gripping his legs, and Shane takes his shoulders. I hate as we rise how blood puddles on the ground. We leave a trail through the shed and all the way to the car.

Once he's loaded into the back of Shane's car, I'm ready to climb in.

"Stay here. Darragh will be arriving to help you clean up."

"What about Finn?" I can't see him now because Shane has laid him flat in the backseat.

Shane pulls the door closed and reverses like the Gardaí are chasing him. I don't move from the spot for a moment until my phone starts to ring.

"Shane arrived. He's taking Finn to the hospital."

"Darragh and Cian are on their way," My father says. I didn't want to have to look at Cian, but right now wasn't the time to start mouthing off. I climb into the jeep, leaving bloodied handprints everywhere.

Any brother would ask how his brother is after he's been shot, but not my father.

"Did you get a look at the shooter?" His line of questioning is so typical of him. Find the threat and eliminate it. The rest is collateral damage. I wonder if it were me flapping around like a fucking fish on the ground, he would still react the same.

"No," I answer.

"Did you look around?"

I grit my teeth and stare down at my hands. "No, Shane just left."

"The moment Darragh and Cian arrive, scout the area. Find something, Jack."

"I will."

I glance in the rear-view mirror as Darragh's BMW pulls up. The red-headed fucker is so tall in the front that he's hunched over.

"Darragh is here."

"Okay, ring me if you find anything." My father's voice is so formal. I'm ready to hang up when he pauses, making me pause.

"Son, be careful."

Dread tightens around the base of my spine; my father never said anything like that before. I want to question him, but he hangs up. Darragh's at my window lighting a cigarette

I get out, and he moves back.

His eyes dance to my hands, and I see real fear in Darragh's eyes.

"He's gone to the hospital with Shane."

Cian steps around Darragh. He's nearly seven-foot-tall and towers over us all. He wears his normal snarl as he places a huge hand on Darragh's shoulder.

"He's in good hands."

I scratch the back of my neck and stop when wet liquid touches the sensitive skin.

"What can you tell us?" Cian's wearing a gray jacket with the collar standing up like some fucking golfer. He's a right prick.

His words irritate me. "Nothing." I start to walk before I punch him in the throat. Instead of focusing on him, I draw all my attention to Darragh, who chain smokes.

"One single shot was fired from the west. So I'm going to scout the area."

"Where was he shot?"

"The neck." I jerk my chin towards the last stall.

Darragh curses as he glances down at the trail of blood that leads to the last stall.

"I'll scout the area with Jack." Cian offers up, and I'm already walking away, hoping he'll pick up on my subtle way of saying fuck off. If he had been shot and was gargling on the ground, I think I would have stood on his neck.

"So, you saw nothing?"

I clench my jaw. "No."

A high bank rises, and I start to climb. Cian is right behind me. Once I reach the top, I look for tracks, something that will tell me where the shooter was. I keep walking and look up. I'm close to the shed, but he would have had to have been further down to take the shot. Cian pulls out a gun and moves in front of me. I don't stop him. If he wants to be a shield, by all means, be a fucking shield.

"You think he's still here?" He asks.

How was he so tall? Shane was over six feet, but his mother, Una, was five feet. He got her red hair.

"If he is, he would have shot us by now." The logical part of my brain tells me, but I'm still fine with Cian going first.

He stops at a spot, and I walk around him. The grass here has been flattened. I lie in the exact same spot and can see the last stall where Finn and I had stood. He could have shot either of us. He chose to shoot Finn. My fingers trace the grass, searching for anything, but there is nothing left. The area is cold. "He's gone."

My phone rings in my pocket, and I stand up and pull it out.

"It's really bad." Shane's words have me lowering myself to the ground as I wait for the final blow, as I wait for him to tell me that Finn is dead.

CHAPTER THREE

O'REAGAN
AN CHLANN

MAEVE

I'm staring at the bedroom door waiting for a group of men to barge in. My mother's cough has me exhaling all the air from my lungs. My heart slowly starts to settle back down and I turn to Declan's sleeping form. I drag a small blanket over his sharp shoulders. The beat of the rappers' words floats into the room. The words of shootings and watching someone die have me getting up off the floor and closing the window.

I leave Declan and close his door quietly, not wanting to wake him up. "Why do you care more for him than me?" My mother's voice rains down on me like a million tiny pins.

"Why do you care more about drink than us?" I fire back and fold my arms across my chest as I face her. My words hold no anger. I'm at the stage where this is what I have come to expect from her.

"That's not fair." Is her reply as she extracts a packet of cigarettes from her pocket.

I unfold my arms as I walk towards her. The breeze from the open back door reminds me of the mess in the kitchen.

"What's not fair is that mess in there." I point at the kitchen wall. "What else is not fair is the state of my brother."

"I don't force the drugs into his arms." She lights her cigarette, and I push the tips of my fingers into my eye sockets. This is an old fight, one I can't believe I'm getting involved in.

"It doesn't matter. Right now, I," I point at my chest. "need to figure out where I can get twelve grand."

My mother looks away as she blows smoke from the corner of her mouth. She's an advertisement in life for what not to do. I don't drink or smoke because she does. It's one thing I've pledged, never to turn into her.

"Don't jump up and down wanting to help me," I say as I pass through a cloud of smoke, knowing I won't get a response from her. There is a brief moment when I walk back into the kitchen that I consider picking my bag up off the floor and walking out the door. I should let her clean up this mess. The only reason I am still here is asleep in the next room.

Closing the back door, I start tidying up, picking up all the empty packages and empty bottles and placing them in the bin. Once I have all the plates stacked in the sink, I clean down all the counters and stop, leaning heavily on the counter.

I push away from the counter and go to my brother's room. I extract my phone and take down Lenny's number that's scrawled on his bedroom wall.

The last time my brother borrowed money from him and didn't pay him back in time, he broke both his legs. This time it would be my legs on the chopping block.

I return to the kitchen as the phone rings.

"What?" His gruff voice has me pausing.

"Lenny, it's Maeve Reilly, Declan's sister." I cringe at how low my voice is and clear my throat.

"What do you want?" He barks before speaking to someone else. His words are muffled like his hand might be covering the receiver.

"A loan." I wait, and when he doesn't answer me, I repeat myself, only this time I'm louder.

"How much?" Once again, his voice is muffled, but the fact we are still talking has hope flourishing in my chest, and my confidence grows. *I can do this.*

"Twelve grand."

His laughter has me holding the phone away from my ear. I wait until it ceases before bringing the phone back.

"There's two hundred percent interest."

"That's extortion."

"Then ring your fucking bank." He's ready to hang up, and I can't let that happen. I can't ring the bank because I've borrowed before to keep the roof over our heads and struggled with repayments.

"How quick would it have to be paid back?"

He exhales loudly. "Two months."

"Two months?" I repeat and turn away from the pile of plates in the sink.

"Thirty-six grand in two months," I repeat as my gaze meets my mothers. She leans against the door frame, a mug in her hand, as she watches me.

"Let me think about it," I say, but I already know that isn't possible.

"Yeah, you think about it." He sneers before hanging up.

"Well?" My mother's eyes dance with alcohol.

"Can you pay back thirty-six grand in two months?"

She holds the mug away from herself and tucks her chin into her chest. "It's not my debt."

I shake my head and stare at the phone before pushing it into my pocket. "Did you not hear what those men said? They'd put you in a brothel."

"Don't be daft." She relaxes her shoulders and drinks from her mug.

I can't have this conversation with her right now. It's useless. There are no other loan sharks in the area. My family has burnt too many bridges.

"What about your rich friend?"

My stomach tightens with guilt. I've thought of Dana too many times already. But I can't. She's in Italy with a group of friends.

"Who?" I pretend not to know and fill up the sink.

My mother pulls out a chair and sits down. I think for a moment that she has left after a brief amount of time has passed. Then I hear the click of her lighter.

"The O'Reagans." She spits out their name.

I sink my hands into the cold water and scrub the plates. "There's no hot water," I tell the suds.

"The one who gave you all the clothes."

I ball my hands into fists under the water. Dana had always given me clothes she no longer wanted. As I got older, I stopped accepting them. I felt like a charity case.

"You know her family owns 'The Viper.'" My mother continues hampering on from the table.

"How do you know that?" I glance at her over my shoulder and quickly look away. She makes me exhausted by just looking at her.

"I've been there a few times." She's up and takes a dirty plate off the counter and carries it back to the table.

I try to swat away the image of her grinding herself against unknown men.

"Dana's in Italy," I say, and immediately regret it. Time is ticking away. Washing plates and talking to my mother isn't going to get us out of this mess.

"Don't be so negative, Maeve. Her mother always liked you." I wipe my wet hands on my jeans and turn to my mother.

"Negative?" I question.

She extinguishes her cigarette on the plate. "Yeah, you're very negative. Even Declan thinks so."

Her words sting. I don't want her to mention his name. I don't answer her but scoop up my bag and leave the kitchen. Taking my bedroom key out of the side pocket of my bag, I unlock the door and enter my bedroom. The smell of incense and fresh air greets me. I left the window half-open but kept the curtains drawn. I couldn't leave my door open, or my mother would sell anything she could. I didn't really have much to sell. But my room is furnished and clean.

I try not to think as I take a black, tight top from my chest of drawers. It fits my body perfectly—like poured-on ink. After pulling out a fresh pair of black jeans, I slip them on before unplaiting my long blond hair and letting it fall down my back. If I wanted to get into 'The Viper,' I needed to look the part.

My stomach churns at the thought of seeing Jack O'Reagan, but I know he works there day and night, Dana told me—and his cousin Cian—who isn't an ass like him, told me also.

Fourteen years ago...

"Push me higher." Dana squeals like a princess on some adventure, and I want to be right there with her, so I push her higher, and her squeals of delight force a smile out of me.

"Higher, Maeve."

Her long dark hair whooshes towards me, and I turn my head to the side, avoiding the sting to my eyes that her long tendrils would inflict. Instead, it's a short-lived sting to my face as I push her higher. She soars into the sky, her white dress clinging to her ballerina frame, and she continues to laugh, drawing the attention of her mother.

Immediately, I ease down on my pushes. Svetlana smiles at Dana, with one hand on her hip. "Girls, that's too high." Her mother is beautiful, just like Dana. She has black hair and crystal blue eyes, which smile even when her mouth doesn't move. They both make me feel happy and at ease.

"Sorry, mom." Dana giggles.

Reaching out, I grip the rope in my hands and pull back until it burns my palms, but it slows Dana down, and her mother steps onto the manicured lawn.

"You girls thirsty?" Svetlana glances from me to her daughter. The red dress she wears doesn't billow in a breeze as I imagine it should with its long tail. It's as still as the air.

I lick my lips. The sun is high in the sky, and pushing Dana for so long has tired me out. "Yes, please."

"Maeve, your manners are wonderful," Svetlana speaks while staring at her daughter, who jumps off the swing and marches into her mother's outstretched arms. A pin pricks the back of my neck, and I don't understand the sensation fully, but it disappears when Dana steps out of her mother's embrace.

"I'll be just a minute." Svetlana smiles. Her words are spoken differently than Dana, and I speak. Dana says her mother is from the Czech Republic and is teaching her how to speak some Czech. I wish my mother taught me another language. I wish she taught me anything.

Dana turns to me with a huge smile on her face. "That was so fun." She's grinning as she pulls me into her for a hug. I like Dana's hugs, they are warm as sunshine, and she always smells of home baking.

"Dana, what has dad told you?"

My stomach curls in on itself, and unlike the pricking on the back of my neck, I understand this sensation. My cheeks heat as I look up at Jack, Dana's older brother.

Ice-blue eyes narrow on me, and my spine straightens. My stomach squirms as he glares at me, and I'm wondering what I've done wrong. Each time he looks at me like that, I want to ask why, but my courage fails me, and I'm sinking my heels into the lawn.

"Go away, Jack." Dana releases me and folds her arms across her chest. I notice her nails are painted a vibrant blue, and I wonder how I hadn't noticed that before.

Jack still glares at me, and I'm snared in his gaze. I want to snarl at him so he'll stop looking at me, but at the same time, I hope he never stops looking at me.

"She's an Outsider, and we don't mix with them." He takes a step closer, and my feet sink further into the grass. I want to be brave, but he's taller, so tall that I have to crane my neck back to look into his eyes.

"Shut your face." Dana steps closer, and she's like a warrior from one of her fairy tales. She's so strong, and sometimes I wish I was like she is.

He releases me from his hold and turns those crystal eyes on his sister. He sneers. "Make me, you little brat."

I move quicker than I thought possible. My hands reach out, and like I've pushed Dana a million times on the swing, they slam into Jack's chest, and I watch in horror as he stumbles back and he's falling. A look of utter shock covers his features but turns to anger; when he thuds heavily onto the lawn, he bounces back up and towers over me.

"You little shit."

I raise my head high. "Touch me, and my dad will kick the shit out of you."

"I wouldn't touch you." The way Jack looks me up and down makes me uncomfortable, and I frown. "I wouldn't piss on you if you were on fire."

"Mom!" Dana's scream pierces the air, making both Jack and I jump apart.

He swings around and steps closer to me, lowering his voice. "You're scum, and my father doesn't want you around Dana, and neither do I. We know your kind, and you're not welcome here. No one wants you here."

"What did dad tell you?" Jack grabs Dana's arm and drags her over to me.

I'm staring at my best friend in the world. She chews her lips, and her blue eyes waver. "She's my friend."

Jack shakes her, and I'm ready to knock him on his ass again when his sharp gaze pins me to the spot.

I see Svetlana come out the back door with a tray of drinks. Did she think I was scum?

"Tell her." Jack forces out.

"Dad said that I can't play with you anymore. That you are an Outsider."

"Drinks!" Dana's mother, none the wiser, steps onto the lawn, and Jack releases his sister before stepping into my personal space.

"Now fuck off and run home to your alcoholic mother."

It's like a slap to the face. My eyes sting, and when he starts to grin like a shark circling blood, I know I can't let as much as one tear fall. I'm running past Jack and Svetlana, I'm running home, and the worst part is, Dana doesn't call me back or follow me. She never tries to stop me.

I'm staring in the mirror as I come out of the memory, my brain not wanting to go to the part that happened after that. I'm already trying to talk myself out of this. If I have a chance of getting this money the decent way, it's with the O'Reagans. I could work at the club or clean something to pay them back. Dana had told me countless stories of how her family has helped people. If I ask her, she'll give me the money, but I know she won't let me pay her back, and that isn't the deal I want to make. I also don't want to pay back two hundred percent interest to Lenny.

As I continue to stare in the mirror I think of the two people who hurt me the most: one is Jack O'Reagan and the other my dear old daddy. Yeah, on the same day, these two men seemed to tear me to shreds, and I've never been able to put myself back together. I've tried. Trust me, I have, but it's like each time I try to swim, the water rages around my ankles, and its icy fingers tighten painfully as it drags me out to sea until I'm drowning. So, through life, I've learned to float.

I try not to think too much or feel too much. So far, I've gotten by just fine like that; until more moments build-up, and soon you are looking at a mountain of shit. The shit pile is so high that I can't see around it anymore. It blocks out all the light and plunges my world into darkness. The sad part is, the one person who might be able to help me is the one who started all this. The one who helped bury me knee-deep in all this pain and suffering.

The irony.

Looking away from the mirror and burying my depressing thoughts I pull out a leather jacket and take my purse from my bag before locking up my room again. I check my phone battery before slowing down at Declan's door. Pushing it open, I peek in; he's asleep. A heaviness that had clung to my chest loosens slightly as I leave our small bungalow and step out on the sidewalk past our dilapidated garden. A few guys cast glances at me. I nod in greeting and keep walking. Keep your mouth shut and head down. That's how I learned to survive in these parts.

I consider ringing a taxi but take the twenty-minute walk into town instead, to give myself time to talk myself out of this. The Viper rises above me; three stories of purple neon signs light up the street below. A queue has already started to form. It's still early, and I join them. We move at a steady pace, and when it's my turn, I'm ready to walk past the bouncer who has a face like a pit bull.

"ID," he speaks while looking over my head and onto the street. His gum isn't as white as his teeth. I take my ID out of my purse and hand it to him. He glares at it. The girl behind me clears her throat like I'm burning through daylight hours. Like somehow this is my fault.

I take my ID from the bouncer's outstretched hand, and he looks around me and motions the girl on with two fingers. I step in front of her, and his gaze zeroes in on me.

"No entry. Step aside."

Confusion grips me by the throat and erases any logical thoughts. The girl behind me walks past and grins. Her short purple hair bounces as she skips into the Viper. This is my only option. It's my best option, and I can't let it slip away so easily.

"Why?"

The bouncer blinks a few times while chewing his gum. I'm tempted to click my fingers in his face, but I can see from his pose that it's pointless. A drizzle of rain falls, and the bouncer takes a step back under the purple canopy. People pass me in an easy stream, and I'm stepping further back as I watch each passing second like the last train out of town.

I continue to move until I'm huddled at the side of the building. Pressing my back against the wall, I close my eyes and try to control my frenzied breaths. The memory of the invasive fingers from the bald man has me tightening my legs, trying to push away the feeling that the image conjures. The image crumbles, and I push off the wall. The rain has started to fall faster, and I tighten my jacket around me before moving further down the alleyway as I try to find shelter while I consider my next move.

A stream of light and noise pours out from an open door. The guy leaves with a garbage bag, and I make a split-second decision and slip through the door, but I don't go undetected.

Chapter Four

O'REAGAN
AN CHLANN

MAEVE

"**H**ey!" I move faster down the hallway. Empty bottle crates are lined up against the wall. The steel door behind me bangs, and I quicken my pace as I race towards a set of double doors that are slightly ajar. The undercurrent pulse of music is a beacon from the doors.

"Hey! You can't be in here." The guy's voice bounces around the empty hall, but as I move closer to the double doors, the music grows. I'm almost there.

I don't dare turn around but keep moving. The door opens under the slam of my palms, and I'm in the club. A few people close by look me up and down. I tug off my jacket as I enter the crowd. Lights dance across sweaty skin, and I take a moment to peek over my shoulder. The guy is still following me. A piercing in his ear catches the light. I shove quicker through the crowd of bodies. A few people cut me looks, but I can't get caught now that I've come this far.

I collide with a solid chest just as the guy reaches for me, grabbing my arm.

"Maeve." I know that voice.

I push away from Cian's solid chest as I'm spun around. "You can't be in here." I tug on my arm, but the grip is too strong.

"She's fine." Cian leans around me and peels the guy's fingers from my arm.

The guy looks at me again like it's the first time he's seeing me. He shrugs. "She came in the side door." His eyes slide back to me, and I relax my shoulders and tuck my leather jacket under my arm.

"I said she's fine." Cian turns away, dismissing the guy, and raises a brow at me. "The side door?" The grin on his face remains there as he pops peanuts in his mouth. "What are you doing here?" He leans in, and his breath fans across my ear.

Here is the perfect opportunity, yet I can't seem to say Jack's name. It lodges itself in my throat and refuses to leave.

Cian's brows draw down, and he tilts his head to the side. His long fingers run the length of my arm. "Why are you wet?" His eyes soften, and he pops two more peanuts into his mouth. I'm aware of how the crowd moves around us.

"I need to see Jack." I move my jacket to my other arm and take a quick peek around the club, expecting to meet ice-cold blue eyes. My stomach flips at the thought of seeing him. Emotions that I refuse to analyze swim way too close to the surface.

A girl nearly walks into me with drinks in both of her hands. I step out of her path and closer to Cian.

"I'm here." Cian grins, and I know that look; it's one he's given me many times. It's a 'come with me, and I'll give you what you want' kind of look. I put some distance between us. Cian's good-looking, but he's an O'Reagan, and that's enough for me to keep our relationship platonic.

"Can you help me or not?" My words are biting, and Cian stands straighter, towering over me again. His eyes never leave mine, and I wait as he pours the rest of the peanuts into his mouth.

"Follow me." He jerks his chin towards the back of the club, and I'm faced with his broad back. I could always leave, I remind myself, but I follow him. My jeans are damp from the rain, and I have no idea how I looked. I feel like a washed-up rat. Cian greets a few females, and each time he glances at me over his shoulder with a cheeky grin and winks. If I weren't in such a bad situation, maybe his flirting and looks would have some effect on me, but all I can think about is ice-blue eyes and helping my family.

We reach a set of red double doors, and Cian knocks three times. I don't hear anything from the other side with the pounding music. Cian pushes the door open.

"I have someone who's looking for you." Cian steps into the room, and I'm frozen for a moment. Dread and the unknown have a cold sweat claiming the skin on the back of my neck. On reflex, I scratch it as Cian looks at me expectantly.

My heart drums too fast as I step into the office. The lush carpet under my feet makes me want to remove my boots so as not to dirty it. The door closes, and all the sound is sucked from the room; all the air is vacuumed from my lungs as I slowly look up towards a large mahogany desk, and sitting behind it is Jack O'Reagan. He's older, angrier, but he still has the same effect on my heart.

Fury flames through my veins along with a longing that grips my throat. Every thought I have spins out of control. His crystal-blue eyes flash with a quick light before it fades. It's like a light bulb coming on only to burn out—a flash of recognition that gets swallowed up in a tornado of hostility.

"What do you want? I'm busy." His deep voice is like broken shards of glass, but I'm glad of it. It pulls me out of my frozen state.

Cian still stands beside me. He's watching me with amusement that I don't feel one bit of. "Just a quick word."

Silence.

His gaze cuts through me, and if it were a tangible thing, I would bleed out on his cream carpet.

"I don't think you remember me, but I'm Maeve. Hmmm... I'm friends with Dana." Any strength I had coming here dwindles away as Jack leans back in his chair.

"You can leave us, Cian." He doesn't take his eyes off me, but my gaze snaps to Cian, and I don't know what he sees on my face, but he hesitates.

"I said, leave." Jack's words are sharp, and Cian nods at me as if he's telling me it will be okay. I want to scream after that 'it won't.' The music pulsates at my back, and I think of hanging my head and following Cian out the door. I might even get a drink and fall into the abyss that my mother and brother seem to live in. The door closes, and the air grows thin.

My heart races as I turn to Jack, who's watching me. Too much blood all at once roars through my system, and I know if I don't calm down, I'll pass out on the floor.

"I'm looking for a loan," I blurt out, and Jack doesn't react. I step closer to his desk. There's still a good distance between us, but I try to use my legs, and it seems to relieve some of the panic that is clutching my throat. "I wouldn't have come here except I have nowhere else to go."

No reaction. He's just staring at me like I'm speaking a foreign language. I'm tempted once again to leave quickly, but I'm here now. "I'll pay it back, every penny. I can clean and work the bar..."

Jack finally responds by getting out of his chair. He's taller than I remember, his shoulders are broader, and I try not to shuffle as he walks around the desk and leans on it while folding his arms across his broad chest. The navy shirt stretches across his arms.

"What makes you think I'd give you money?" There is a sneer tangled in his words, and his cockiness has me biting the inside of my cheek. One thing hasn't changed about Jack O'Reagan; he still was an arrogant jerk.

"Dana told me you've helped people."

I can't hold his gaze, so I glance at the desk behind him before my attention gets pulled towards a trash can. A shirt peeks out, specks of blood are visible, and fear sends chills across my damp skin. "I wouldn't come here—only I have no choice."

"How much do you need?" He pushes off the desk and takes a step towards me. The room grows smaller by the second, and I could almost be convinced that the walls are closing in on me.

"Twelve thousand."

He nods and continues to advance on me. "And if I give you this twelve thousand, how are you going to pay me back?"

A glint of something close to enjoyment flashes in his eyes, and I force the image of my brother bleeding on the floor into my mind. It's the only thing that's keeping me here; otherwise, I'd tell him what to do with it.

"I can clean, work behind the bar. Office stuff. Anything."

He stops a foot away from me; the smell of his cologne and something else that's uniquely Jack wraps itself around me and causes a tightness to my stomach.

"Anything?"

A cruel glint sparks in his dangerous eyes, and I hold my head higher and wait for him to tell me what he wants. I wouldn't hurt anyone for him, that I couldn't do.

"Jack..."

His head snaps up, and a slow growl pulls at his lips. "Don't speak to me like you know me."

His reaction has me stepping back. He's always been volatile, but I've never feared him. Now the warning bells are ringing loudly.

"I'll give you the twelve grand."

Heat travels across the back of my eyes and nose, and all the adrenaline that is keeping me upright races towards my feet. Relief flows through me. I want to thank him, but the dangerous spark I've seen in his eyes is still there. My stomach curls and I ask the question that has my heart rate spiking again.

"How can I pay you back? I can work every weekend. I'm in college during the week."

"I want you for one night in my bed." He doesn't laugh or grin; there is nothing in his face that's telling me this is a joke.

"What? Why?"

A predatory sneer spreads across his face, and Jack steps in closer to me. "Come on, Maeve, you're not that naïve."

My breathing grows quick and shallow. "You want me to sleep with you?" Why?

"Yes."

Like some prostitute—he's making a point—belittling me. I want to scream at him that I'm not for sale.

"One night in my bed. You submit to me, and the debt is cleared."

My stomach churns, and I can't look at him. "If I say no?" I quickly look back at him while trying to hold the pleading note in my voice back.

He works a muscle in his jaw before his face relaxes. "You can say no." He shrugs and walks away from me. "But that's the deal. One night with me and I'll give you the twelve grand."

My options were; be used in a brothel by countless men or give myself for one night to Jack, and the debt is cleared.

Heat slowly creeps up my chest as I think of both scenarios. Jack sits back down behind his desk and starts writing. "Make up your mind quickly."

Anger accelerates my heart once again. He could have any girl in the world, so why me? I knew why— because he could—because his money is his power.

Hate heightens in my system, and I close my eyes briefly. "Fine."

He doesn't look up at me, even as my soul screams not to do this. He still keeps writing, and I wonder if he heard me.

"I agree," I say louder.

"I heard you the first time." He doesn't look up as he speaks, as if I'm not worth looking at anymore.

"Could I have a few drinks first?" I ask, glancing at the door. It has no lock. I need the money now, so it's better to get this done and over with.

When I look back at Jack, he's watching me. Anger flashes in his eyes, but he doesn't speak. I shuffle forward and try to gather some courage as I place my bag and jacket on a chair in front of his desk. There are no photos or anything personal on his desk, just a laptop, two files, and a three-tier holder that sits neatly.

"We can do it now." I can't even meet his eyes as I reach for my top. I hate how my hands tremble. The wet material I pull over my head comes away slowly. My cheeks burn as I place it on the chair. Am I really going to do this?

I glance up at Jack, and his gaze is fixed on my black bra before his blue eyes cut up to me.

"I'm not in the mood right now." He pushes a piece of paper across the desk towards me.

My face grows hotter. "I need the money now." My eyes and throat burn, and I swallow the humiliation. Why did he have to make me beg? Like this isn't bad enough.

He drops a silver pen on the table. "Read it over and sign."

I glance down at his piece of paper. "What is this?" I ask as my gaze skims over what looks like a contract.

Jack gets up from the desk and walks away.

I, Maeve Reilly. My heart jumps at my name. He knows who I am, and he remembers me even though he tried to pretend that he didn't know me. Why does that small amount of knowledge make me happy? What is wrong with me?

"Live with you?" I stand up straight and seek him out. He's kneeling down in front of a safe.

"Yes, until you fulfill your part of the deal, you'll stay with me." Jack straightens up and in his hands is a stack of money.

Money, the power it holds over all of us.

"I can do it now." I grit my teeth as Jack places the stacks of money on the table.

"I don't want you now." His grin is razor-sharp, and I hate him all over again. Angrily, I pull my wet top back on.

37

Jack sits back down and watches as I struggle with the material. It keeps rolling up, revealing my stomach that has caught his attention.

"Read it all. I want us both to be clear."

I snap my eyes to the piece of paper and continue reading it. I had to stay with him until I gave myself to him for just one night. Once I do, I can leave, and the debt is cleared.

The silver pen is sitting right beside it. How long would this take, a few days? I only had to sleep with him once.

You have to give him your virginity. A voice warns in the back of my mind.

I pick up the pen and think of Declan.

"I don't have all day, Maeve." Jack sounds bored, and I want to stab him with the pen. The ink races across the bottom of the page as I sign my soul over to the devil.

The moment I do, I reach for the money, and he pulls it away. "You said you'd give it to me." I hate the whine in my voice, but he's already breaking the contract. I should have known.

"Go home and pack. When you come back here, I'll hand you the money."

I grab my jacket and bag off the chair. He is going to make this slow and painful. I just know it.

"Maeve."

I want to tell him he has no right to use my name. When I look at him, he grins.

"One hour." His smug voice has me nodding.

I walk across the lush carpet as some part of me deep down knows that I have given away the best part of me to a man who will use it to destroy me all over again.

Like he had destroyed me fourteen years ago along with my Dad. The memory of that day assaults me and I can't stop the pain as I leave Jack's office.

My small fists pound the blue chipped front door, but no one answers. Jiggling the old handle, the door swings open, and I step into the hall. I'm ready to call for my mother when I hear raised voices coming from the bedroom. I close the door quietly. My brother's bike rests against the marked wall.

I advance down the hall, and my parents' bedroom door is open.

"So that's it, you're going to run." My mother snivels, the once pink nightgown is wrapped tightly around her tiny frame. She's thin, too thin. She blows smoke into my father's face. Seeing him, something in me softens and turns to goo. I'm ready to call out to him, tell him the horrible things Jack O'Reagan said to me, but something freezes me to the spot.

He stuffs shirts into a bag and glares at my mother. "I'm not running. I'm leaving. I can't do this anymore with you, Jane."

My mother grabs the bag with her free hand; the ashes from her burning cigarette landing on the worn-out brown carpet.

"Daddy." My heart pounds too fast, and I'm tempted to touch my chest. My parents freeze, and my father's shoulders fall forward like he can't hold his weight up any longer.

"Sweet Pea." His smile has all the moving parts slot back into their rightful place. His smile tells me that everything will be okay.

"Where are you going?" I ask.

My dad is so tall, but he bends and kneels before me. His soft brown eyes speak words that I don't comprehend at ten years of age.

"Daddy has to go away for a while." My dad reaches out and touches my arms, but I barely register his large hands on my skin.

"*Who will take care of me?*" The words are whispered because no matter what, I don't want to hurt my mother's feelings.

"*Your mother will.*" My father squeezes my arms and stands. What utter bullshit.

My eyes sting.

My mother takes my father's place, and the smoke assaults me. I cough, and she holds the cigarette behind her back. This close, I can see every crack around her lips. The gouges grow deeper when she smokes. "*I'll mind you since your father doesn't want us anymore.*"

"*Jesus, Jane.*" My father drags her to her feet and away from me.

"*Is there another woman? Who is she?*" My mother's words are barked.

"*What about Declan?*" I ask, and both my parents stop and stare at me.

My father shakes his head, and I hate the look of defeat I see in his eyes. "*I'm sorry, Sweet Pea.*" He turns and continues to pack his bag. The only person who wanted me doesn't want me anymore.

"*I promise. I'll be better.*" My lip trembles, and I want to grab my dad and stop him, but he continues packing.

He won't look at me. "*It's not you, kiddo.*"

"*No. It's me. It's always me.*" My mother stomps over to her vanity set and puts out a cigarette before picking up a mug.

"*What's in the mug, Jane?*" My father's angry words have my mother putting it back down, and she pushes dry blond hair behind her ear.

"*Coffee.*" I hear the lie; we all know what's in the mug.

"*Daddy,*" I call him again, and he steps away from my mother. "*Please. Don't leave.*" I start to beg as he drags the bag over his wide shoulder. A panic to keep him here has me running towards him, and I hug his torso with every ounce of strength I possess.

"Jack O'Reagan said nasty things to me; I need you to tell his dad. I need you to make him apologize." Tears stream down my face, and I have no idea if it's because of what just happened with Jack or the fact my dad wants to leave us.

"Jack O'Reagan, the rich kid, who thinks he's better than everyone else; keep away from them." My mother's order dries up my tears, and my father slowly untangles my hands from his waist.

"I have to go."

"Please don't leave me."

"Jesus, Jane, comfort her." My father's voice quivers as he launches himself into the hall with his favorite red cap pulled on his head. I know he would never leave that behind. He was actually leaving us. He was really leaving me.

I can't let him leave.

A scream erupts in the pit of my stomach and races up my throat. When it pours out of my mouth, my father swings around with tears in his eyes. It's a brief pause before he tugs the red cap further down and disappears out the front door.

"Stop it, Maeve." The smell of smoke and alcohol envelopes me as my mother drags me into her arms.

"He doesn't want us." Her words are the final nail in the coffin.

No one wants me.

Even the woman that holds me will only want me when she needs something.

"I hate you," I speak to her chest, and she drags me closer.

She cost me my father and my friendship with Dana. Everyone knows she is a drunk. I push her away, and her unbalanced frame lands heavily on the ground. Shock morphs into anger, and I'm running down the hall with her

41

on my heels. She's not fast on her feet, and I consider knocking Declan's bike into her path, but I don't want to hurt her. I dive into my room and lock the door. It rattles, and she screams at me from the other side of the door.

"You're such a brat. No wonder your father left."

My hands cover my ears, and her words become muffled as I lower myself to the bare floor beneath me—splatters of paint coat the boards from my attempt at painting my room. Closing my eyes doesn't cut off the pain. I never knew pain like this.

A part of me died at that very moment, in that room. A part of me that I didn't believe could ever be revived.

Chapter Five

O'REAGAN
AN CHLANN

JACK

The door closes, and I stare at it for a while. My cock is still hard. I hate how much I want her. I've always wanted her. And now, I could have her. Irritation crawls along my skin.

The moment she had stepped into my office, something old and buried inside me had sat up and paid too much fucking attention.

Maeve Reilly. She was one of those girls who got under your skin and refused to fucking leave. I glance down at the stacks of money before pushing them into an open drawer. The door opens, and I don't have to look up to know who it is.

"Why did you let her in here?" I ask while closing the drawer. An old part of me wants to thank him, but the larger part that hates him wants to take a dig.

"She's a friend."

I sit back and grin at Cian. He opens a pack of peanuts and starts to chew on them like this is his kingdom.

"Why are you here, again?" I sit forward.

He doesn't flinch at my tone. "I like hanging out with you. You make me feel all warm and fuzzy."

I rub my head, wanting the pain to ease. Since leaving the farmyard, my head has raged. Shane had rung and told me Finn is in surgery at the moment, and the doctors aren't hopeful. Having Maeve step into my office when I am knee-deep in anger wasn't wise. But I wasn't one to turn an opportunity away. Something close to guilt swells slowly inside me, but I push it back down. Her hand had trembled when she had pulled off her top. I had no intention of taking her anytime soon. She would wait and be obedient until she gave me the respect I deserved.

She always looked at me with hate, and I knew she thought she was better than me. Taking her down a peg or two would feel good. The thoughts of having her in my bed have me shifting in the chair. Cian's loud chewing has me putting away the contract that I had her sign.

"So, what did she want?"

His tone is delivered to sound bored, but the curiosity in his voice isn't lost on me.

"Why do you care?" I sit back. If he as much as touches her, I'd kill him.

He empties the pack of peanuts into his mouth before coming up to my desk and sitting down.

"You're not staying." I want him out, but he doesn't move.

"Like I said before, she's a friend."

Bullshit.

I'm ready to threaten him when the door opens, and Shay steps in. He's nodding his head while looking around my office. His suit doesn't hide the gangster he is. "Who do I have to fuck to get an office like this?"

Cian laughs. "That would be Jack."

"I've shagged worse." Shay grins.

I ignore Cian and get up. "Shay." He meets me halfway, and we hug. I don't ask why he's here. It's because of Finn; the whole family will come together when one of us has been hurt.

"You're some jammy cunt." His Northern Ireland accent is thick as he speaks. It turns the insult into a compliment.

I glance around me. "Yeah, it's not bad." I don't ever take a moment to appreciate what's around me. I'm too busy building it up.

"Ginger, what's the craic?" Shay swaggers towards my desk.

I grin as I return to my desk, also.

Cian isn't smiling at Shay's words. "Fuck you." Cian gets up. "I'll be out front."

"Leave the peanuts alone," I call after him, and he gives me the finger over his shoulder. Shay sits down in the chair that Cian just vacated. Dark, heavy eyes that smile at me don't make me relax. I don't see Shay very often, but I know how dangerous he and his people are. His dad had a history with mine. There is bad blood between them, so Shay and I always tread carefully around each other when it comes to business matters.

"Finn's in surgery." I sit back and run both hands down my face. I need to sleep.

"I might go and take a look at where it happened. You want to come?"

I remove my hands from my face and look at Shay. There is more to this than going to see where it happened.

"There's nothing to see. It's all cleaned up."

Shay tips the side of his nose with a finger. "I have a nose for things like this." He leans in closer, and any earlier joking is now erased from his dark eyes.

"We will get the cunt and gut him." He splays his ringed fingers out on the table like a promise for revenge. He's right. I will find out who did this and why. No one hurt my family and got away with it.

"Let's go." Shay drums his hands on my desk before getting up.

This time, I don't forget my coat as I leave the club with Shay. Cian spots us going out the back door. He's at the bar glaring after us while opening another pack of peanuts.

"So, you and Cian are tight now?" Shay asks while we get into my jeep.

"No. He came with Shane to help out. What could I say?"

Shay grins; it's disturbingly happy on his face. "I know what I'd say."

I close the door and start the jeep.

"I'd say 'fuck off Ginger. Go home to your mother's titty'."

"That's why no one likes you, Shay."

He sneers. "I'm not here to make friends."

I pull out onto the street. "Still doesn't mean you should make enemies." I glance at Shay; his intelligent eyes are on me. "What's this really about?"

"My Da stepped down."

That I didn't expect. His father, Connor, led the northern mafia with no interference from us. His father was my dad's half-brother—a complicated mess. My father wasn't gone on anyone who wasn't purely an O'Reagan, so he had a hang-up with Connor. Growing up, Connor attended my communion and confirmation, but he was the uncle that came late and left early.

"Is he ill?"

"Nah. He's just wanted to hand the reins to me."

I glance at Shay again.

His smile shows all his teeth. "The King of the North."

"Congratulations."

His tone grows serious. "I thought since you will take over the north-east that we should work closely together."

"We never have before. Why now?" We leave the town and make our way to the countryside.

"Things need to change. We need to open the border, have fairer trade."

Something heavy settles on my shoulders. "You're talking to the wrong person. My Father is still the king here."

"Yet, you've started your trials." Shay stares out the window.

"You sure know a lot for a Northerner."

His head snaps to me, and I give a nod, knowing I've overstepped. We might have been young kids once, but not anymore. No matter what you become part of, there will always be politics and rules. We might speak roughly to each other, but it's still wise rough words.

I pull up at the farmyard, and we get out.

"This is where it happened."

I take Shay up the side of the hill and show him the spot where the shooter lay. "A sniper?"

"Yeah, I felt it before it even happened." I stuff my hands in my pockets and look down at the large slatted shed. "He was aiming for Finn. He was aiming to kill."

Shay kneels down, and his hands sink into the grass. I have no idea what he's looking for. I've already searched.

"I didn't' know Finn well, but my Da always spoke highly of him."

"He's the good of the O'Reagans." I fight off the cold by shuffling. Jesus, I needed sleep.

"Who knew you would be here?"

Shay stands, and I know he's trying to help, but this isn't his jurisdiction, and Kings don't cross into each other's borders so easily.

"This isn't your fight." I'm waiting for the backlash. Shay was as wild as his father. He couldn't be controlled.

"My Da was shot two weeks ago."

All the pieces click into place. "That's why you are here. You think it's the same shooter."

A tightness strangles Shay's features. "A sniper too, only it wasn't a kill shot."

"A warning shot." I climb back down the bank with that knowledge, and Shay moves beside me.

"Why am I only hearing about this now?"

"My Da didn't want your Da knowing his business."

We get back into the jeep, and I turn it on to get the heat going.

"Your father was a warning," I growl. "You should have told us. We could have prevented this."

Shay shrugs like our uncle isn't fighting for his life right now. "It wasn't my call."

"Well, now it is. You have to tell everyone else."

Shay nods. "I will. I've arranged a meeting."

"When?" I back out of the farmyard with dread growing thicker by the second in my stomach.

"Tonight."

I hoped my father kept calm and didn't kill anyone, especially Shay. He had a tendency to say nothing and hunt you down and kill you later.

I glance at Shay. "Does your old man know you're here?"

His smile is sharp. "No. But I'm sure after tonight he will."

Chapter Six

O'REAGAN
AN CHLANN

MAEVE

I leave the club through the front door; the bouncer looks at me twice but doesn't say anything. It would do no good, anyway. It's raining, and I don't care that I'm getting drenched. I need the falling cold liquid to cool my burning heart. I need the air to re-inflate my lungs. I need the space that Jack robbed from me.

Jack O'Reagan.

Did that really happen? Did I really just ask him for money? Did he really just make me sign a contract to sleep with him? I'm tempted to take out my phone every few seconds and see how much time I have left before I have to return.

One Hour.

He had some neck. I take a deep calming breath. It's not a big deal. One night and that would be it. Declan would be safe, and I could return to my life. The lie leaves a bitter taste on my tongue that I don't believe any amount of drink could wash away.

I arrive home soaked right through.

"Maeve." My mother calls from the kitchen. She's drunk. That isn't something that normally happens. She can hold her liquor, so something must be wrong. Maybe they came back.

I pull my coat off as I enter the kitchen. She's alone. "Where's Declan?" Fear reignites the flames that I had just only doused.

"Out with friends." She puts out her cigarette. "He's fine." She rolls her eyes as she takes a large drink from her mug. "The angel is fine." Sarcasm drips from her lips like poison. I take a moment and inspect the kitchen. The sink is still filled with water from earlier. The bin that I had filled with their rubbish hasn't been taken out. At least no further mess has been made. I place my coat on the back of the chair. I grab the rubbish bag and take it out the back door. When I come back in, my mother is still sitting at the table watching me.

"I got the money." She doesn't ask me where I got it or where I was or why I'm soaked.

My mother rises, using the table to hold her small frame up. "A bit of good news." She pushes away from the table and wobbles to the cupboard. Opening it, she pulls out a full bottle of vodka and carries it back to the table.

"Let's drink to that." She refills her mug.

I swallow the bile that rises in my throat. Maybe getting away from this madness isn't such a bad thing. It's sad, when going to a man's house that paid for you, is more alluring than your own home.

"I'm going away for a few nights."

My mother snorts and lights up another cigarette. "Yeah." She blows smoke from the corner of her mouth. "Just don't forget to pay that bill before you go. I don't need men knocking on my door."

It's on the tip of my tongue to tell her what I have to do for that money— what I have to give. I swallow that knowledge. I wish she cared a little more, but she doesn't, so my words would be wasted. Would my father care? I close my eyes at the cruel memory that plays out before me. His voice is deep, his laughter real, his hands so large as he held my small ones. Standing on his feet, he had led me around the sitting room, dancing to music he hummed. I was floating. He was a giant, and I was safe.

The memory shatters across the kitchen floor as the front door opens. I grab the opportunity to get away from my thoughts and step into the hall. At least now I will get to say goodbye to Declan. He's not alone. He walks into the house with two other guys. Each of them is as thin as the other. Their sunken faces and over-delighted eyes have my heart sinking.

"Sis." Declan steps between them with open arms that I don't walk into. "What's with the long face?" Declan pulls down his lips like a child.

"Get out." My voice rises as I race forward and push both of the guys easily out the door. Their light frames and confused minds make the removal easy.

"Mae-ve," Declan whines behind me and laughs like I'm being unreasonable.

"Get out!" I push one of his friends, who wears a red superman t-shirt, hard in the chest. He falls backward but catches himself before his feet get tangled up, and he face-plants into the grass. I slam the door before they can retaliate and turn to Declan, who isn't in the hall any longer.

Marching into the kitchen, my mother hasn't moved. She shrugs. "He didn't come in here."

Useless.

Noise from his bedroom has me entering his room. A set of legs dangle out his window as laughter flows in. I move quickly across his floor and grab the band of his jeans, pulling him back in. His friends laugh like wild hyenas. I slam the window closed and draw his curtain.

"You are being very hostile, Sis." Declan smiles as he lies down on his mattress, and I'm standing here as a storm circles around me. I'm struggling to catch the calm in me.

"This has to stop."

Declan sits up, and for the first time in a long time, his gaze appears clearer. "I will."

Everything in me settles at his lie, and I walk over and sit down on the floor beside him. I exhale loudly.

"Why are you all wet?" He asks.

A laugh twists my lips. "It's a long story. Look." I glance up at Declan, who wears a goofy smile, but I see behind the curtain, I see my brother's pain. He wears it freely. That's what makes us different, and maybe that's why I ended up looking out for him, not that I've done a good job.

"I have to go away for a few days."

He's been watching me, but now he closes his eyes and exhales slowly. "Where are you going?"

"A friend's. But it will only be for a few days. You have to take care of yourself." I plead.

"Who's the older sibling here?" He grins while pointing at himself. I want to say 'Then act like it'. I think that phrase hangs on an invisible string between us, and we both feel it.

"I got the money."

Declan rises up on his elbow. "Really?" His smile lights up his eyes, and they dance with joy. Even if I wanted to, I can't stop the smile that erupts across my face at how happy he is.

"Yeah, really."

I'm in his arms, and slowly I wrap my arms around his waist. I close my eyes and let this brief moment of happiness grow and spread through my system. It feels good, and I smile into his shoulder.

"I'm going to really try this time, Maeve."

I push back; I have to see his face; I have to see he's as serious as his voice tells me he is. My heartbeat heightens. "Really?" I search his dark eyes.

I'm praying and hoping that this time is the real-time. All it takes is one time for him to stay clean, one intention to stay clean, one person to help him along the way.

"I'll be your sponsor." I know what that means because I've done it before. I've sat here while his body cried out for release from the agony. Release I refused to give, even as he begged and pleaded with me like a dying man. That's what it feels like— like your body is going to dry up and turn to nothing but ash. But I stayed here through his screams, his threats, his moments of lying on the floor and crying for a father who left us a long time ago—one who would never return. I had sat with him and held him until his sobs sent him into a restless sleep that he would rise from like a raging lunatic. Round and around and around it went until he slept more, and his threats decreased.

"We've done it before." I grip my brother's thin face.

His dancing eyes dwindle. "I failed then."

"Failing is only when we stop. We haven't failed yet."

His hands grip my face too. "I'm going to do this for you, Maeve."

Pride pours through me and burns the back of my throat. I lean my forehead against his; words aren't good enough right now.

Through my joy, the moving hands of time are ticking away slowly in my ear. I still need to show up to get that money. "I have to go now. But I'll ring each day."

Declan smiles, and when I release him, he lies back on his bed, and a look of peace settles on his face. I know as I leave his room and enter my own that I've made the right decision. Pulling off my wet clothes, I quickly re-dress into a pair of jeans and the red top I wore earlier. Re-plaiting my hair, I take a bag down from the top of my wardrobe and pack for a few days. I throw in what's clean. I don't have much, and my meager belongings fit into the one suitcase.

It's a few days, I tell myself again. That becomes my mantra. It's a few days, and this all ends. Declan will be debt-free, and now that he is going to get clean, maybe things can get better. I glance around my room and pick up my school bag. I don't know how many days I'll miss of college, so I stuff two books into my bag so I don't fall too far behind in classes. I had three more years before I would qualify as a social worker and help children like Declan and me.

Taking one final look around my room, I check the time. Five minutes left. I'd get a taxi back. Relocking my room, I pause at Declan's. The door is still ajar, and he's lying with his back to me. I'm ready to keep going, but I drop my bag and enter his room. His blanket is pushed down at his feet. He'll get cold, and I know my mother won't come and pull it up on him.

I grip the material, and my heart breaks as I drag it up his thin body—how time has reduced him to nothing more than flesh and bones. The air stills and all the blood is drawn down into my shoes. A plastic tube has been tightened around his forearm; the empty needle still hangs from his arm. I drop to the floor. He stirs at my movements.

"Just one last time." His words are slurred, and this time, I can't stop the tears that come. They silently trickle down my face as I remove the tube from his arm and withdraw the needle. A bubble of blood rises, and I drop the needle and tube to the floor. I sit for far too long, just staring at the needle mark. My mind conjures up memories of all the pain I've experienced and all the joy that has kept me standing. My body feels bruised—broken.

The twelve grand will fix things today, but not tomorrow. Hopelessness has me pulling my phone out of my jeans pockets, and I Google 'The Viper' through blurred vision. Pulling up the number, I hit the dial image and wait. I have no idea who answers, but I ask to speak to Jack. I keep my voice low as I stare at Declan.

I wait as music pours down the phone. Declan's still frame has me reaching for his neck. I sense the flicker of his pulse, and more tears fall.

"What is it?" Jack's voice has my spine stiffening.

I drag the blanket the rest of the way up to Declan's shoulders; the sad reality is I can't help him anymore.

"The deal is off," I say and hang up.

I know I have to go. I have to get away from here. Fear grips me by the throat and shakes me until I can't move. My hands grip onto Declan's back as my body shakes with a pain that's so deep it's all-consuming.

"I'm sorry." I peel my hands off him and get up.

You said we only fail when we give up. So don't give up on me. The voice of reason is a little too late.

Outside Declan's bedroom, I dial 999 and wait as the phone rings. I've never done this before, but I need to do something before I leave.

"Navan Garda Station."

"My brother is being hassled by men for money he owes. They've threatened to send me to a brothel." I swallow and close my eyes as I lean against the wall.

"Okay, what's your full name?" The Gardaí sounds bored like he's done this a million times. Maybe he has.

"Maeve Reilly."

"Address."

I rattle off my address.

"Your brother's name?"

"Declan Reilly."

There is a pause.

"Declan is known to us."

I open my eyes and push off the wall. "For petty theft, and that shouldn't matter. He's being threatened and harassed."

"Declan Reilly is under an investigation for the death of a homeless man."

Sickness pools in my mouth, and fear dances along my vision, darkening the edges. "What?" *No. Declan wouldn't hurt a fly.*

"When?"

"I'm sorry, but those details can't be given out."

"He's an addict." I'm trying to defend him already. "He's not in his right frame of mind." He wouldn't hurt anyone, I remind myself. I press myself against the wall, my breathing growing shallow.

"I can't discuss it with you, Miss. Now, what's the crime you want to report?"

"Who are you talking to?" My mother is in front of me. I take the phone away from my ear.

"Miss?"

I hang up. "The Gardaí."

"Why?" My mother doesn't react to 'the Gardaí' at all. She's too used to them banging on her door.

"Declan's being accused of murdering a homeless man."

Laughter bubbles from my mother's throat and makes its presence known in the silent hall.

"You knew?" Why am I not surprised?

"He didn't do that. Declan is a good boy. They are just trying to blame him because he's easy pickings. Those pigs have nothing better to do than pick on my sweet boy."

"I can't do this anymore." Those words ring true to me, but they are words I've heard before, words I've heard my father say. Was he pushed to the brink like me? No, I would never leave innocent children behind. He had a responsibility as an adult, as our father.

What about Declan?

"You can't do what? You're barely here."

"I'm ringing, Dad." I threaten.

My mother fixes a smile on her face. It's strained and exaggerated. "Good luck." Her gaze dances around the hall.

"What aren't you saying?" I have no idea what it is, but she's hiding something. "Is he dead?"

Her laughter is bitter as she pulls her fags and lighter from her pocket. "That son of bitch is very much alive with three kids."

I hold up my hands. "Don't tell me. I can't..." I'm shaking my head as I take the key from my pocket with trembling fingers. It's all too much. I enter my bedroom, and the room spins around me. I'm losing my mind.

Wood shattering and my mother's wails have me returning to the hall. I have no idea what I'm waiting for: an army of riot Gardaí to pour in, a SWAT team, or a group of gangsters— anyone but who's marching towards me with fire in his eyes.

Jack O'Reagan.

CHAPTER SEVEN

O'REAGAN
AN CHLANN

JACK

ONE HOUR BEFORE

I'm on the way back from the farmyard. My mind is still reeling with the new knowledge that Connor was shot—that we could have prevented Finn from being shot. We all would have been more vigilant if we knew there was a target on any of us.

Shay hasn't said anything else since his confession. My phone rings, distracting me, and I answer it. It's the club. Maeve is on the line. What was wrong with her now? Maybe she wanted more money. I'd give her more. It was only money, after all. I'd just have to make her pay it back in another way.

"Put her through."

She was making it a habit of appearing at the worst times possible. Shay is leaning slightly closer to me. The movement is subtle, but we've all been trained. My ears pick up the smallest of things. "What is it?" I bark into the phone, hoping she knows to make it quick and that I'm not in the mood.

There is a moment of dragged out silence that makes me grip the steering wheel with my free hand.

"The deal is off." Her soft voice has blood pumping around my body, and then she hangs up.

I put the phone down and press my foot harder on the accelerator.

"Something wrong?" Shay asks. He would have heard her voice. I'm not sure if he heard what she said. It doesn't matter.

I release my foot off the accelerator and search for control that my father would demand of me. He was the king of control, and I needed to exercise that.

"Nothing I can't handle." And I would handle it. I would go to Maeve and drag her to my home if that's what it took. No one walked away from me, especially not her.

"My father told me some history of our family. Did you know our Nan was gunned down by a gang?"

I nod and let my mind trail away from Maeve. "What? Do you think they are responsible? They got that gang and executed them." I'd heard the story.

"Yeah, I know." Shay rubs his lips with his forefinger. "It just didn't add up for me. Why did a gang gun her down?"

I glance at Shay and meet his gaze.

"You know what I mean?" He says.

"We have lots of enemies," I answer, but for the first time, I think about why Nan was gunned down. I never questioned it; I just assumed it was a rival gang, the wrong place at the wrong time.

"Enemies normally take out the Kings. Not the Queens."

Shay had a point. Our women were our Queens, and there was always that mutual agreement in place. We could hurt each other, but our women weren't to be harmed, and that has always been enforced.

"I'll ask my Father."

"I already did."

Nerves niggle at me at Shay's harsh words. "What did he say?"

"She wasn't the target; that she was in the wrong place."

I glance at Shay again as we enter the town. "You have your answer."

Shay taps his nose. "I have a nose for these things. My father said she was targeted. Your dad says she was in the wrong place. I wonder what Uncle Darragh or Shane would say."

I don't like the road Shay is walking down about our Nan. Her shooting isn't tied to this one, and it was a long time ago. My father had no reason to lie. If he didn't want to tell you something, he simply wouldn't.

I pull back into the club. "Let's say you're right, that something is off."

"I am." Shay corrects me, and I ignore it for the moment.

"Let's say you're right." I start again, and he doesn't interrupt me. "What do you think happened?"

"I don't know, but it must be big."

"I'm going to focus on Finn right now," I say.

Shay gets out. "Me too. I can multitask." I don't like the predatory glint in Shay's eyes. I return to the club and leave him with Cian at the bar. The moment Shay sits down, Cian gets up. I can't hear the words exchanged between them, but Cian looks pissed.

I need to sleep.

But first, I would take care of business. I take two of my security with me and ring Maeve's number back as I walk out to my jeep. I'm hoping she answers before I reach it. It rings out.

Her backing out of this deal is something I'd expect of her. Did she come into the club as a joke, knowing that I would give her the money? Did she do it just to shut me down?

She'd learn the hard way that you didn't play games with an O'Reagan.

I'd never been to her house, but I knew the estate she had grown up in. It was close to where we once lived.

The estate I drive into is a rundown kip. My Range Rover grabs the attention of every leech on the estate. None of these useless fuckers work. We drive slowly, but I have no idea which house is Maeve's. I pull up close to a group of youths and roll down the window. They are like flies to shit, moving around the vehicle. The first lad has his gray hood up; a black woolen sweater is wrapped around his neck.

I take a fifty out of my wallet and show it to him. "Where does Maeve Reilly live?" He ignores me and glances at Freddie, who sits in the front seat with a face as angry as a butcher's dog.

He juts his chin out and throws a look over his shoulder. "That one." He reaches for the money, and I pull it back. His eyes spring to mine. "Which one?" I speak clearly.

He looks back at his comrades, who all just continue to examine the jeep— none of these filthy bastards better touch my jeep. The guy finally points directly at a house. "That one." This time I let him take the money and start to drive. He jumps back before I roll over his feet. Pulling up outside the house, it's not what I expect. It's run-down; the small front yard, nearly non-existent.

"Lawlor, you stay with the jeep, any of them touch it: Shoot them." I glance at Lawlor in the back, and he nods. Freddie jumps out, and Lawlor takes his seat. I let Freddie go first.

Maeve needs to learn a lesson.

"Kick in the door," I say to Freddie, and he does as I say. Three slams of his large foot and the rotten door gives way. A woman wails from inside as Freddie enters, and my adrenaline accelerates as I march in behind him. This couldn't be Maeve's house. It's a dump. The smell has me wanting to leave. I look up, and my gaze clashes with Maeve's. I have a brief moment of wanting to step up to her and carry her out of this dive. But her gaze flares up, and I give her a grin that drips with a silent threat.

Her gaze dances around the hall, and she's moving to the wailing woman.

"Get out!" Her red eyes tell me she's been crying. A fresh flow of guilt filters through my veins, but I remember how brazen she was not long ago. She walked into my club, looking for money. Her eyes still held the same distaste they always did, ever since I can remember.

"Get your bags," I speak calmly, not allowing the fire to ignite in my words.

"What have you done?" The woman asks Maeve and shakes her head. Straight away, I get the urge to defend Maeve.

"Nothing," Maeve growls through clenched teeth.

I take another step towards her, and she stiffens.

"I said the deal is off." Like fuck it's off.

"Freddie here will pack your stuff." I threaten and tilt my head. This is her final warning before I carry her to my jeep. The thoughts of touching her have me stepping closer. "Or maybe you want me to?" I grin, and heat travels up her neck.

Maeve glances at the woman who must be her mother. I know an alcoholic when I see one and smell one. I want out of this hell-hole.

I click my fingers. "I've been patient enough."

"Fine, just... I'll get my bags now." Maeve's hands shake as she stops at a door to her right, where a suitcase and bag sit. She picks them up but stares at the door for far too long.

"Now, Maeve!" I bark, and she jumps. The look she fires at me shows her disgust. She stops at her mother's side.

With a lowered voice, she speaks hurried words, but I can hear them. "You take care of him. Promise me."

"He can take care of himself." Her mother speaks back while folding her arms across her chest.

Whatever comfort she was expecting from her mother, she isn't getting now. I nod at Freddie, and he pulls the bags from Maeve's hands.

"Stop, that's my stuff!" Her shouts don't stop Freddie, and she glares at me.

"Get in the vehicle now." I open a hand for her to move. She does, and the air ripples with her anger as she passes me. I give her mother one final look.

"I know you." Her lips twist into a snarl.

"No, you don't." I step over the destroyed door and follow Maeve out to the jeep. The group of lads watches closely. One of them calls to Maeve, but she doesn't respond. She pulls open the back door and gets in. I glare at the one who spoke to her, and he takes a step back.

I get in. Freddie's in the back with Maeve, who stares at her house. I look back at what isn't really a home; no one is standing at the door or window to see where she is going. I glance at her in the rear-view mirror, and our eyes clash. The brown in hers swirls with fury. That makes me feel better. I made the right decision.

I leave the estate and start the drive to my own home. I've never brought anyone here; I'm not sure what possessed me to make this agreement. To teach her a lesson, I remind myself.

My phone rings, and I take the call.

"I believe Shay has had a few words with you." My father's words are calm and clear— not a good sign.

"Yeah, Connor has stepped down, giving Shay the control of the north."

"What else did he say?"

"I know he called a meeting tonight." I am loyal to my father, yet Shay will make a good leader, too, and I don't want to take away from him telling everyone tonight about Connor being shot. I will give him this courtesy even against my father's disapproval. And he will disapprove.

"Did he say what the meeting will be about?"

I turn off the main road and start down a side road that took you to a few houses, all owned by the O'Reagans. My cousin Rachel, Darragh's daughter, myself and Cian, live down here.

"Yeah, about Finn."

"You aren't being completely forthcoming. So I am going to assume you are in a situation that won't warrant it."

I glance at Maeve in the rear-view mirror; she's glancing out the window. She isn't the reason I was with-holding information, but she would be a perfect excuse so I could answer honestly.

"Actually, I'm in the middle of transporting something."

Her head snaps up, and her eyes widen, while her nostrils flare with temper.

"Fine, I want you here before the meeting." My father hangs up, knowing I will be there.

"How long am I expected to be a prisoner?" Maeve's voice shakes, and I have been waiting for her explosion. I honestly thought she would wait until we were alone.

"You're not a prisoner. You are a guest."

She folds her arms across her chest, the image of her standing in my office in her black bra springs to mind. The soft tanned lumps of skin filled her bra perfectly.

"So, I can leave whenever I want?" Her angry words have me cutting her a look, and she wisely sits back.

"You leave when the contract is fulfilled."

Heat scorches her cheeks again, and it delights me.

I pull up at the large white gates and hit the buzzer as the gates open. I drive up to the front door.

"Freddie, get her bags." Freddie does as I say.

I take the keys out of the ignition and climb out of the jeep. Opening Maeve's door, she doesn't move. She shrinks back into the seat like a trapped animal, or like she might melt into the leather and disappear.

"Get out."

My words snap her out of her state, and she unbuckles her seatbelt before stepping out of the jeep. The smell of strawberry shampoo and something sweet has me stepping closer. She freezes and keeps her head down like she's afraid, but I know Maeve Reilly. She isn't a damsel in distress. Never was, never will be.

Freddie holds the front door open while holding her bags.

"You can take them up to my room." I don't look back at Maeve to see her reaction but step into the white hallway. The space is open, showcasing the large circular staircase that wraps around the first floor. I take to the stairs and glance back when Maeve doesn't follow immediately. She's looking around her, and instead of the awe I'm used to seeing, her eyes hold nothing but disgust. Those dark eyes move to me, and the disgust remains. I'm tempted to click my fingers at her, but she sensibly follows me up the stairs. I have several guest rooms that she can stay in, so why am I opening the door to my own bedroom?

Maeve enters my room and wraps her arms around her waist. The red top she wears hangs off one shoulder. Her skin appears soft and unblemished. The jeans she wears are tight, and each curve is emphasized. She's featured in so many of my fantasies. I hate her for infecting my mind like a plague. Her kind was a scourge on society, taking from the system and never working. It was also her kind that lined our pockets. I remind myself. She's glancing around my room, and I close the door loudly, making her jump.

She spins around and nods her head like she's come to some decision. "Fine." She runs her hands along her jeans. I don't say anything as I watch her struggle with her emotions. It's almost amusing. She reaches for the hem of her top, and I fold my arms across my chest, waiting to see what she's going to do.

She gives me one final piercing look before dragging her top off over her head. "Let's get this over with."

I clench my jaw, keeping the words in that want to pour out. She's acting like she can't bear me. The way she has always reacted to me.

"I'm not in the mood," I say with a smirk that I know will piss her off.

Her fingers curl around her top that hangs at her side. I don't pretend not to look at her breasts. Her cheeks burn, and she looks bewildered or like someone who is slowly coming out of a heavy sleep.

"What do you want from me?" Her voice is rising.

I uncross my arms and shake a finger at her. "There is no reason to raise your voice." I take a step towards her and love her reaction. She hugs her waist, and I drink in all her skin. One taste, one touch, one moment of having her might douse the flames she ignites in me.

Her chest rises and falls rapidly as I reach her. "I want you in my bed, naked, and I want to fuck you."

Her chest rises and stills. She's holding her breath.

"I want you on your knees. I want you to beg me for more."

She releases the breath and shakes her head, the defiance roaring to life in her eyes. "I'll never beg."

I grin at her. The temptation to touch her is too great, and I run my hand along her neck towards her breasts. She jumps away from my touch, and anger at her reaction has me stuffing my hands in my pockets. "You will beg. I'll make sure of it."

I don't let her respond, but calmly, just like my father, I walk to the door, pausing before I leave. "Don't leave this room. I'll come back for you later." I don't look back at the angry beauty as I leave her alone to fester and chew on my words.

CHAPTER EIGHT

O'REAGAN
AN CHLANN

MAEVE

I touch my neck, tracing along where his fingers touched. My core clenches again. What is wrong with me? How did one touch steal the air from my lungs? I shake out my top to distract myself from my deep-rooted and unhealthy attraction to Jack O'Reagan. He's a jerk who is going to take the best of me; I remind myself.

Dragging my top back on, I take in the room for the first time. A large queen-size bed dominates the room. The navy color is carried throughout the room, from the long curtains that hang from a set of double doors, to the armchair that sits in front of a large desk. I'm drawn to the doors and take in the view. If my heart wasn't so black and blue, it would sing right now. Mountains rise up in the distance; rolling green fields follow until it reaches a fence line that's been kept clear so as not to obstruct such a stunning view. The clear sky has darkened, but it doesn't take away the pure beauty.

Money.

Turning away, I focus on the desk and start opening the drawers. A fresh notepad and a stack of pens are in the top one. The second holds stationary, and the third is locked. I keep a mental note of that. I move to the door and try the knob. It doesn't budge.

How long has it been since I saw Jack? Years? After that day in his yard, when he told me I was scum, I had met with Dana when he wasn't around. I had avoided him, and whenever we did meet each other, it was always unpleasant. Each passing year he scared me more, until Dana and I drifted apart. We kept in contact, but we kept drifting. I lean my forehead against the oak door and allow the cold wood to knock some sense into me. What had I been thinking going to him for money? At some stage, Dana had convinced me with all her stories of Jack, that he wasn't such a bad guy. He had helped countless families, according to her. Now I wonder if she lied to me.

Declan. It was for Declan. Pressing my hand against the door, I picture my brother. The image of the syringe hanging from his arm will continue to break my heart. He once had been a healthy young man who loved biking and fast cars. He was clever and had a talent for art; to see him now, broke my heart.

A set of double doors opens up into a walk-in-wardrobe nearly as big as the room. I smell him from every piece of hanging fabric. It assaults me, and I want to pull everything onto the floor.

This is Jack's room. His bedroom. I glance back at the bed and hate the fire that flares up inside me. Stepping up to a row of shirts, I pick one up and smell it. His smell triggers my emotions. Heat blossoms in my chest while my fists tighten.

I keep walking deeper into his wardrobe and hold my breath. Even in college, when one of my classmates sat beside me during a lecture, and all I could smell was the aftermath of last night's party, I'd have to move, or else fury would consume me and worry for Declan.

Smells are as powerful as a picture— even more so, in my opinion. I hate the moments it creeps up on me as the smell invades my senses, a memory starts to build itself around me. Sometimes I wish to bottle up the smell so I can sniff it anytime, like the smell of my father's aftershave. Spicy and too strong, but it was his. Pain erupts at the back of my eyes, and I inhale Jack instead. It calms the pain that roars through me and ignites my hate.

Turning, I grip the marble knobs on the wardrobe door and drag them closed. The lights go out, and I don't mind. I walk as deep as I can and sink to the floor. My head rests on my knees, and I allow myself to be carried away with one of Declan's stories.

The light erupts, and his smiling face is there in front of me; I want to reach out and touch it. He appears so healthy.

"Then, the giant grabbed the princess and raised her in the air." Declan's hand rises, pushing the blanket higher. My heartbeat heightens as I stare at his hands that become the giants. Declan's dark eyes spring to me, and he lowers his voice. "And then he squeezed all her guts. They poured out of her eyes and ears."

I had pulled the blanket off us. "Yuck, Declan."

His roars of laughter had dragged dad into my room. Declan was given his marching orders while dad had tucked me in.

"Tell me a story."

Dad's large hand had run across the top of my head. "I think you've had too many stories already."

"Declan said the giant squeezed the princess's guts."

Dad can't hide the smile. "She tumbled to the ground..." Dad tightens the quilt around me.

'...-and was caught by a prince."

"Where did the prince come from? They are at sea." I narrow my eyes at my dad, wondering if he even knows this story.

"The prince had sneaked onto the ship to rescue the princess."

That made sense.

"He caught the princess and used his healing powers to fix her. They both dived off the side of the boat and swam to safety where they lived happily ever after."

"That ended quickly." I pout, but my dad bends down and places a kiss on my head. "Go to sleep."

His words dance around me, and like a command that I can't ignore, I fall asleep in the wardrobe.

When I wake, I have no idea where I am. All I smell is Jack. The club, the contract, the needle, Declan, everything assaults me at once. I pull myself up and slip out into an equally dark bedroom. Searching for a light, I manage to find one close to the door. The room is the same as I had left it. Nothing has changed. I try the door, but it's still locked.

This is madness. This isn't right.

I check the balcony doors, and they open. I hadn't expected them to be unlocked. Outside, a sharp wind races down the side of the mountain and blasts my face. Goosebumps break out across my flesh from the soft spray of the first signs of rain. Closing my eyes, I let it wake me up from my dream of my father, from this nightmare of Jack.

"What are you doing?" The voice is too close, and I spin around while moving back towards the rail.

Fear flashes in Jack's eyes, and I have no idea why. "Come inside." The command is said quietly.

"I want to go home." I need to go home. I shouldn't have left Declan.

"You think that's the way home?" His brows drag down too close to his ice-blue eyes.

"What? You think I'm going to jump?" The cold rain pelts my back as it increases in its force.

"Are you?"

I don't answer him because I like the fear I see there. It's the first time he's displayed anything other than dislike or disgust.

"Over you, Jack?" I step closer to the door. "Hardly." He doesn't move as I pass him. My body shivers from how close we are for a brief second.

The doors close behind me, and I wrap my arms around my waist as I wait to see if this is it. He had said I'd beg. That's one thing I would never do. No matter what happens, I will never, ever beg for Jack O'Reagan.

His arrogant walk towards me has my hate for him heightening to new heights that I didn't think existed.

"You either let me go or get this over with." My pulse pounds and pulsates in my neck.

"Are you going to give me another strip-tease?" Jack asks.

I don't answer him, and he tilts his head to the side like he's contemplated something.

He reaches for his waist-coat and unbuttons it, and I swallow as he takes it off and throws it on the bed. He moves closer, and I take a step back.

"I just want to go home." I keep my head high.

"That place I took you out of?" The disgust, in his words, is loud and clear.

I unwrap my hands from around my waist and match his step. "You might have lots of money and fancy things, but I bet no one truly loves you. You are a means to an end. A solution to a problem."

His eyes flash a warning that I ignore. "Just like you are to me. So yes, I want to go home to *that* place."

The warning in his eyes fades as he unbuttons his shirt.

Heat rises from my belly, and I push it back down.

"I didn't see much love in your mother's eyes." His cruel grin has me wanting to lash out.

"My relationship with my mother is none of your business."

His hand springs out like a snake and wraps around my neck. Fear shoots from deep in my gut and slams against my lungs, pushing out all the air.

"Everything about you is my business." He pushes me back until I hit the set of double doors. Jack towers over me, and when he leans in closer, I can't hold his gaze.

"Do you understand?" His anger has me nodding. His hand tightens on my neck. My gaze slams back into his. The coldness seeps out of him, and I fear he will keep squeezing.

"Say it." His thumb strokes my neck.

"I understand." The words are a croak, and he loosened his grip on me but didn't move away.

My throat burns, wanting to spill tears, but that's one thing I won't do. I will never show him weakness, the minute I do; he will swallow me whole. Or maybe like the princess and the giant, he will squeeze the life out of me.

His eyes roam my face. The coldness they once held seems to dim but not disappear. His nostrils flare like he smells something bad, and my stomach clenches as he leans in closer.

His lips brush mine, and the light touch robs me of the last bit of air I've been holding onto. His hand loosens further on my neck as he deepens the kiss. I don't respond as his warm lips move against mine. I tighten my legs together as every nerve and sensation in my system turns on full blast. He breaks the kiss, and I'm glad he did because I was on the brink of responding. I take a sharp breath at the hate I see in his eyes. He releases my neck but doesn't move away like I expect him to do. I'm waiting for him to turn and leave me in a puddle of confusion and want for him.

His gaze flickers to my lips, and my treacherous tongue wets them.

"You can hold back all you want." Jack grips my chin, forcing me to look at him. "I know you want me."

I muster up the best 'fuck you' grin I can without using my words. It works, but not necessarily in my favor. Once again, I'm expecting his pampered arse to march away, but he doesn't. He steps back and finishes unbuttoning his shirt.

Panic plummets my stomach into nothingness. Tanned flesh that's defined and muscular slowly comes into view. Tattoos peek out along his sides, but I can't make them out even as he pulls the shirt fully off. I wrap my hands around my middle as I envision his large frame on top of me. What would that feel like? I don't think anyone could walk away from Jack O'Reagan fully intact. The man was built like a god.

His sneer that says 'I see you turning to mush', outdoes any sneer I've ever seen, and I can't look at him any longer. He throws the shirt on the bed, and I'm tempted to glance at him, but I wrap my last shreds of decency around me like a frayed protective blanket.

When I hear water start to run, I take a shaky breath when I realize he's gone for a shower and I'm alone.

"You can join me if you want."

I can hear the smile in his words, and it irritates the crap out of me.

"I'd rather throw myself off the balcony." As soon as my words leave my mouth, I want to race after them and grip them and shove them back. I'm waiting for an angry and very naked Jack to emerge from the bathroom and threaten me. What I don't expect is the low chuckle that undoes me. I've never heard him laugh before, and thank God I hadn't.

Yeah, without a single doubt, I would never be the same again. I know one hundred percent I've made the biggest mistake by putting a foot inside 'The Viper.' I glance at the bedroom door before glancing back at the bathroom. It's now or never. I could run, maybe get Declan and leave. Go to England and find our dad.

To arrive at his door and say what? Hi, Dad. Remember us? The kids you abandoned.

All I know is I need to get away from here and now is my only chance. So I take it.

CHAPTER NINE

O'REAGAN
AN CHLANN

MAEVE

My fingers flutter along the white polished banister as I make my way down the carpeted stairs. I keep looking back, expecting to see Jack hanging over the rail with angry blue eyes, but it's empty each time. Golden lights over huge paintings cast a soft glow in the hallway and bounce off the gold bars that keep the carpet in place. I'm not surprised that Jack would decorate his house like this.

"And where do you think you are going?" My feet halt on the third last step. I'm so close to freedom only Freddie stands in the way. He glares at me, his legs spread like he's ready to take me down if I make one more move.

I move one space and stop on the second last step. "Jack said I could explore the house." I smile even as my heart threatens to tear from my chest.

"Did he now?" Freddie smiles widely, and he doesn't alter his stance. His smile tells me he isn't buying my lie for one second.

I nod. "Yeah, so could you move, please?" I try to leave the final step, and Freddie steps in closer until I'm level with his chest.

"Mr. O'Reagan doesn't let people like you wander around his house. The last time I checked, you were here to clear a debt." The look Freddie gives me suggests he knows exactly how I'll clear the debt in question. Heat blossoms in my cheeks and chases all my confidence away.

"Please, just move."

His hateful grin widens, and I turn on the step in defeat, knowing time is running out. I hear his low laughter like he just won. Spinning, I raise my knee hard and fast and drive it into his balls while gripping his shoulders.

I release him quickly. His face turns a funny shade of gray before he moves back a few steps and slowly descends to the white marble floor. I'm moving, racing for the front door. It's locked, and I can't see a key or way to open it. I need to calm down but can't. Adrenaline has me turning, and the marble floor squeaks under my boots as I race through the hallway and out into a kitchen that would make you stand and stare. It's a showroom: all chrome, all new, all shiny. A woman screams, and my own scream, I push down as I pass her like a trapped animal and tug on the door handle that leads to freedom. Nothing happens, and I pull it again. Wind and rain whip in, and I run out into a storm, not caring that I'm soaked within a second. I'm running up the fence line that I saw from the balcony window. It's five-feet high, and I scale it easily, using the meshed wire to push my feet into. I don't expect the decline on the other side and hit the ground hard. The impact knocks the air from my lungs. The lush green grass doesn't do much to cushion my fall.

I'm staring at an angry sky as I try to catch my breath. Something moves along the fence line, and fear that Freddie has recovered quickly has me trying to stand. Closing my eyes against the downpour, I brace myself to get up. Sucking in air is painful, and when I open my eyes, I'm no longer looking at an angry sky but an angry pair of ice-blue eyes. Rain pelts down on his bare chest, and all I can think of is how he looks like an angry, vengeful god, and God save the person who pissed him off. I remind myself that this angry god is here because of me. I'm scrambling backwards calmly, way too calmly. Jack stalks me like I'm real prey. He bends and blocks out the world with his wild shoulders. Hands grip my waist that burns into my cold skin, and I'm airborne. I have a moment where I'm trying to understand the image on his back. Black ink coats his skin and dips down into the waistband of his trousers. I get my senses back and wriggle against him. "Let me go! Now!"

He turns to the fence line, and I'm waiting for him to drop me across it. He pulls me from his shoulder, and I'm against his chest. I push as hard as I can. Narrowed eyes zero in on me, and I freeze.

Too Close.

The sensible part of my brain is ready to apologize and beg for forgiveness. But that part of my brain isn't working so well right now.

"Put me down, right this second." Jack takes the two steps to the fence line and, with grace and ease, lifts me over it before lowering me to the ground. I'm ready to bolt when his hand shoots out and grabs my wrist. With his other hand, that grips the post, he sails across the fence.

Show-off.

There is no victory in his eyes at the maneuver. He hasn't let me go as he walks us through the sheets of rain and back to the house.

Apologize. My self-preservation kicks in. I tighten my lips, not allowing myself to cave as we enter the kitchen like two drowned rats. The woman who had screamed when I ran through before, lets out a startled cry again but quickly grew quiet. Jack doesn't pause but drags me through the kitchen, leaving a stream of water behind us. I yank my arm again, and he throws me a warning look over his shoulder.

I pass Freddie in the hallway, and he doesn't smile in victory like I thought he might. Instead, he juts out his chin at Jack, who doesn't acknowledge it. I'm tripping over my own feet as I'm dragged up the stairs. Once we reach the top of the landing, I try to pull away again, but his iron grip has no weakness in it. I'm released and fall to my knees on the bedroom floor. The burn across my knees is instant. The door closes over, and I don't turn to look at him.

His legs appear in front of me, and I'm ready to get up.

"Stay on your knees. It suits you." His words are laced with menace. I've pushed him too far. I don't move.

"I think it's time you started begging."

I glare up at him. I won't beg. I shake my head even as my lips tremble from the cold, and the slight trickle of fear that drips down my spine should be my warning.

I anger the god further, and he moves three spaces back while a slow tug of his lips sets fire to my veins. I'm burning from the inside out.

What's going to happen? You walked into this.

Apologize.

I get to my feet and swallow my pride. "I'm sorry."

I don't know what I'm waiting for, for him to relent in his angry stance or for him to accept it, but what I don't expect is his next words.

"Take off your clothes."

81

I'm not ready.

"I said, sorry." My words are low and pointless.

He shakes his head as water drips from his dark hair and onto the floor and down his chest.

I shiver again. I could just get this done and over with, and I would be free. How many hours had I been here? I needed the money. I needed to clear that debt soon, or all of this will have been for nothing.

Don't think about it. I pull off my top, and it splashes at my feet. *You're alone in your room.* I unzip my boots and kick them off. *No one else is here.* I pull off my socks. *It will be over soon.* I open my jeans and painfully pull them down my legs. I have to stand on them to get them off. My skin is pinkish from the cold.

There. I don't look up but stand still. If I don't see him, then I can do this.

"Everything Maeve." His words make the hairs rise on my arms. I hate how he uses my name. It sounds too personal, and I hate that I like that.

I'm not ready.

I shiver and reach back for the clasp of my bra. I unhook it and let the straps slide down my arms before it sails to the ground. My breasts bounce free, and I'm tempted to reach up and cover them, but I clench my hands at my side. I pause and know I'm standing here prolonging the agony of this moment. This isn't how I thought it would happen. Am I meant to feel so humiliated? *No.* I reach for my black underwear and let them join my clothes on the floor. I stand straight, naked, and try to find my pride. I am more than him; I tell myself as I meet his gaze.

I can't decipher the look in his hooded eyes as his gaze touches every inch of my flesh, and when he moves, I flinch with fear, anticipation, and an overwhelming feeling to cover myself.

His gaze trails across my breasts, and heat flairs up along my chest. "How many men have you slept with?" His words come out angry, and I have no idea why. He circles me like a prized cow.

I want to tell him it's none of his business, but I can't find the words as his breath brushes the back of my neck. I hold still, so I don't lean into him. I hate how I crave his touch now. Closing my eyes, I try to picture something else. My eyes snap open as his hand grazes the side of my breast before brushing across my hard nipple.

"You're turned on."

Horror hijacks my body at the truth. His hand moves lower, leaving a burning path in its wake. When he pushes my lips apart and dips his fingers inside me, I gasp at the sensation. His hard wet chest presses against my back, and I lean into him. His erection presses against me, and my body thrills at the sensation, but the virgin in me shrivels up.

I gasp again as he pushes his finger inside me, his breath in my ear. "You're wet, Maeve."

I should tell him to stop, but I don't want to. I've never allowed anyone to touch me. His other hand skims up my side before his open palm runs across my breast. I shiver at the contact on my hard nipple. His index finger and thumb squeeze it, and pain and pleasure pool between my legs.

"You ever run again." His fingers inside me drag me closer to his body. His erection feels painfully large. "I will punish you severely." His promise, along with the removal of his hands from my body, has me slumping forward. He's no longer behind me. "Have a shower and get dressed."

My face grows redder by the second, and I want to turn and look at him, but I'm mortified as I attempt to scurry to the bathroom. I don't get far as his hand clamps down on my wrist.

CHAPTER TEN

O'REAGAN
AN CHLANN

JACK

She's petrified. I loosen my hold on her wrist and without looking at me she runs off into the bathroom. Water drips from my hair onto the wooden wardrobe floor. With a clenched fist, I lean against the wall. I should go into the bathroom and just fuck her, get it over with so I can focus on what's important. I didn't need someone like her distracting me. She's wormed her way under my skin, and I hate how I like the way it feels. Taking off my jeans, my cock painfully rubs on the denim material. It's still rock hard after seeing her body.

Beautiful things are normally dangerous things, just like Maeve. My hand grazes my cock, and I bite down as pain and pleasure shoots through me. Taking off my boxers, I stroke it, able to vividly picture her in the shower. Her tits were perfect, her nipples pink and begging to be sucked.

What the fuck am I doing?

I release my cock. I just needed to go in there and really fuck Maeve out of my system. *So why the fuck am I not moving?*

My phone rings on the desk, and I stomp across the room until I reach it. Cian's name lights up the screen; that's enough to make my hard-on die.

I'm tempted not to answer it, but it's probably about the meeting tonight.

"Yes, Cian." I keep my voice level and calm just like my father taught me, but with it, there is an air of irritation and the undercurrent of 'What-the-fuck-do-you-want' to my words.

"I'm picking up Dana from the airport."

I walk away from the desk and back into the wardrobe. I notice the water is no longer running in the bathroom, my cock starts to grow, but Cian's voice kills it completely.

"Just thought you would want to know."

I pull out a black suit. "Is that it?"

He's a moron, but even morons have their uses.

"Do you know, you're even more delightful on the phone than in real life." Cian hangs up. Very fucking brave when time and space divides us. I wonder if he will be as brave at the meeting tonight.

I knew Dana would return home with Finn being in the hospital. He's telling me something I already know. I'm aware of soft footsteps along the floor. Looking up, Maeve freezes; a large navy towel surrounds her fuckable body. Her blond hair pours across her shoulder, and my cock starts to grow. Her eyes widen as she stares at it.

She doesn't move, and I can see something play out behind her eyes. She's weighing up something. I want her to drop her towel, I want her to want me as much as I want her, yet I don't want her to drop the towel—if she does— then the deal is done.

Maeve clears her throat and looks away. "Since we are actually doing this. I need to get the money to someone. My time is nearly up."

She pushes her head high, and I recognize that as her defensive mechanism. I take a step towards her, and she fights to keep her gaze on my face.

I let a slow grin capture my lips, and the subtle but slow drip of pink that enters her cheeks has me wanting to touch her. "Who do you owe money to?"

She tightens her hands on her towel. "A man."

"Here, I thought it was a woman." Her eyes drop, and she bites her lip before they bounce back up to my eyes.

I grin wider, letting her know I saw that slip-up.

"I'll need to meet him in person," she says.

Every ounce of my teasing leaves me, and I stop walking. "No. That's not happening."

"I have to. I have no choice." Her panicked voice has me clearing the rest of the distance between us.

"Yes, you do have a choice. I'll send Freddie, you tell us who you owe the money to, and he'll hand the money over."

Defiance flickers in her stunning eyes. "I am going, or this deal won't work."

"I won't risk you."

Her eyes widen at my confession, and I quickly recover. "Don't get the wrong idea, Maeve." Her cheeks redden. "I won't lose twelve grand. You've already cost me enough aggravation."

"I'll go with Freddie, then."

Her pulse flickers under my hand as I grip her neck and push her head back. "Why do you think you can negotiate?" Her defiance is making my cock rock hard.

Her pulse quickens, and her tongue flicks out, wetting her red lips. I can't hold back any longer, and my mouth slams down on hers, and she freezes under me. Forcing my tongue into her mouth, I tighten my hold on her neck, and she gasps, opening her mouth, giving me entry. When she responds to my kiss, I push my tongue deeper into her warm mouth and drag her closer to my naked body. The towel is the only thing separating us. I pull it off, and her flesh is against mine. She moans into my mouth, and I lift her off the ground without breaking the kiss. Her ass fills my hands, and her legs instantly wrap around my waist. I pull her cheeks wide. She smells of my shower gel and something soft underneath it all. Her hard nipples brush against my chest as I lie her on the bed. The shift in her stature has me breaking the kiss. She's panting. Her wide brown eyes swim with lust and fear. Instantly, I glance at her neck to see if I hurt her.

"Jack." Her voice is strangled, and she's starting to look panicked. "I'm a virgin."

My cock grows harder and pushes against her stomach. Her three words elate me. No one has touched her. I'd be the first.

The last.

"I'll be gentle." I don't give in to her vulnerable words. I had no intentions of taking her now. She wasn't getting away from me that easily. I press a kiss to her intoxicating lips; I'm getting high on her arousal and have to hold back the want in me to take her right now. Her hands don't touch my flesh; instead, they curl around the quilt under us.

I move down her body until I'm between her legs. I push them apart, and she tries to get up.

"What are you doing?" Her voice quivers.

She falls back as I suck on her clitoris. My fingers dip inside her tight pussy, and it squeezes around me. Running my tongue across her pussy, has her squirming under me. Her long fingers grip my hair, and I move my fingers deeper, fucking what will be mine. She groans and tightens her hold on my hair. She tastes sweet as I lap up all the wetness that pools from her. Her body jerks, and her back arched under me. She's close to coming. Her panting grows more frantic, her groans louder, and I move quicker until she cries out her release. Her juices pour from her pussy as I pump hard while sucking her clitoris. Slowing down, I remove my fingers before I press one final kiss to her and come up to see her face.

The satisfaction has me crawling back up her perfect body. "Was that a first?" Her gaze darts to me as she fights for composure, but right now, she's still too high as she nods her head in acknowledgment.

Just take her now. My cock rests close to her opening, and the temptation has me leaning back down and pressing my lips to her neck. Her hands rest on my shoulders, but this time they are unsure about touching me. Leaning out, I look down at Maeve.

"What are you waiting for?" The irritation in her voice has me allowing a grin to spread across my face.

"I have a meeting." I get off her, and with all my willpower, I enter the wardrobe and start to get dressed for the meeting. I wasn't lying; I would be late if I didn't get there soon. She moves around the room, and when I step back in, she's wrapped up in my nightshirt. Her cheeks are still pink, and she crosses her arms over her chest.

"I'd like my bags, please." Her clipped words are delivered without looking at me.

I fix my tie and don't answer her.

She finally looks at me. Turning away from her, I pull on my jacket and leave her alone. I don't lock the bedroom door.

Freddie is in the hallway, where I had told him to wait. "I want you to bring up her bags and then guard the door."

Freddie nods and gets ready to carry out my orders.

"Freddie."

He pauses and glances at me over his shoulder.

"If she so much as puts a toe outside my bedroom door, I'll break your fucking hands."

His jaw tightens.

"I hate incompetence."

"Yes, boss."

I tap his face with two fingers before leaving the house.

The meeting is in my father's house; it once was my grandfather's, but when the power was handed to my father, so was the family estate. I pull up to the large black gates and wait for the gates to open. I'm left waiting a little longer than usual and roll down the window of my jeep while grinning up at the camera that's pointed down on me.

The gates start to part, and I drive up the driveway. It appears that every light is on in the estate house. Cars line the driveway. I spot Shay outside smoking with Niall, who was Shane's youngest son. His gaze is shifty, and it trails to my jeep when I pull up close to the front door. My father won't appreciate the parking, but I want to make a statement. I'm not like the rest of them in any way, shape, or form. That's why I will be King.

The moment I'm out, Shay jerks his chin out towards me while lowering his brows. "Who have I got to fuck to get one of those jeeps?" He crushes a cigarette under his heavy brown boot.

"Things must be tight across the border."

Niall hasn't moved a muscle as he takes our words in. His hair is gelled to the side; the white sports t-shirt is buttoned up to his neck—my gaze trails down to the white runners.

"You can pass some across since you seem to be flush."

"Did your father see you?" I ask Niall, stopping a foot away from the kid.

"Nah, why?" His tone has his lip raising, and the attitude has me stepping closer until he shrinks back.

"I'm going to give you a little bit of advice. If you want this family to take you seriously. Don't dress like the thugs that work for us. I see them on every street corner."

He keeps shrugging and glancing at Shay, not liking being pulled up in front of someone else.

"You look like a cunt," Shay says and winks at me as he enters the house.

Niall shrugs again like it's the only signal his brain is sending out. "The next time you're in my presence, you will dress appropriately."

I'm ready to enter the house when he decides to give lip back.

"You're not my da."

I don't turn to him but face forward, my hand still on the door handle. "No. I'm not. But I'll be your King soon." I don't say it with smugness, but it's a fact. That's what I will become to all the members of the Irish Mafia.

King.

CHAPTER ELEVEN

O'REAGAN
AN CHLANN

JACK

A lot of people say I'm the perfect mix of my mother and father. Standing shoulder to shoulder with the man in question, I never feel I actually measure up to him. He has a way in which he conducts himself, a way which I can never master. A deadly calm always flows around my father. It wouldn't matter if a bomb went off or the house burst into flames; he would assess the situation and always make the correct call. How the fuck could anyone measure up to that?

He wanted me to take a walk with him before the meeting, so right now, we are walking through the gardens that I grew up in. I didn't play much. My father used every opportunity to train me in our ways, and I soaked it up. I'm grateful to him for everything he taught me.

"I don't trust Shay."

"You don't trust anyone," I remark, hoping to lighten this conversation before it lifted itself entirely off the ground and took flight. Lanterns light the path we walk down; it leads to a large gazebo where my mother often hosted our evening tea. She was the fun one, the one who tickled me at bedtime and allowed me to be a child. With my parents, it was a perfect mix.

"With good reason." My father glances at me for the first time. "He's been asking questions about your nan. What has he said to you?"

The topic makes me uncomfortable. The fact my father is asking me about it means that Shay may have stumbled onto something he shouldn't have.

"He doesn't think you are telling the truth about her death."

My father's hands hang relaxed at his side. I'm checking for 'tells' that something is amiss, but it's hard to spot anything with him. His face is stoic, impassive, and I wait a beat to see if he will defend himself. Instead, he starts walking again.

"She was a good mother to us all. When she died, a piece of us all died with her." I don't hear pain in my father's voice or longing, but I notice his hands are behind his back now, one hand gripping the other.

He cares.

"I don't need the likes of Shay, digging up old bones that need to be laid to rest." My father stops walking again, and so do I. "Do you understand what I'm telling you?"

I hear my father loud and clear, but what he's saying can't be done. "He's King of the north. Killing him would cause a war." *I don't want to kill him.* I keep that fact hidden, but I'm sure he sees it in my eyes.

My father pauses before speaking. "It wouldn't be the first time we took down a king of the north."

My father's words cause ripples of shock to course through me. I had known that a raid had cost Shay his grandfather, who was not only once the leader of the north but also the Republican Army. To lead the Republican Army gave you tens of thousands of foot soldiers who would fight for you without an explanation. They just knew it was for the Irish, and that's all that mattered. It's been dismantled since Connor took over, but now I wonder if it really ever was.

I'm looking at my father again. Is he really saying I'm looking at the person responsible for this? My own father?

"What about the treaty?" I ask, trying to grasp and hold on to some rituals that were driven into me.

"The treaty has always been upheld." My father turns, and we start walking back to the house. "As far as anyone knows, that is."

Is that joy I hear in his voice? This time I stop walking and my father does, too. "On what grounds would you take down a King?" Didn't this change everything about what we stand for? Taking each other out is a slippery slope that I don't want to go down.

"If Shay keeps digging, that's grounds enough for me." My father walks away, and I'm stunned. Shay asking questions wasn't enough for me to consider killing him. Was this part of my trials? Was my father testing my understanding of our history, of our ways?

As I walk back to the house, all I can wonder is what really happened to Nan that could cause Kings to turn on each other.

I trail slowly back to the house. Taghd, another one of Shane's sons, meets me in the hallway. A nod of his head is all I get. He's quiet and reserved. He never says much, and I don't ask. Now I'm looking at everyone differently. If my father can kill a King, what else can he do? What else can his brothers do?

Everyone is here. The room I step into holds a large mahogany dining table that seats twelve people. The plaque above my father's head had always gained my respect. 'An Chlann' is carved into it. It's been in our family for generations. It held the importance of family, of loyalty, of respect. My gaze drops down to my father, who sits at the head of the table—his brother Shane on his right side and Darragh on his left. Beside Shane is an empty seat that I fill. Across from me is where Finn sits, but not tonight, and beside him is always empty. It's Connor's seat, but he's never filled it, and I don't question why. Now too many questions bounce around my head. Is there a reason for his absence; does he know my father took down his father?

Shay sits beside the empty seat that was reserved for his father. *Does Shay know?* If I failed, Cian, Niall, Eoin, Taghd, and finally Collin are the five that are next in line for the crown. That gave us a full table. The meeting would commence now.

"Finn was shot by a sniper. We don't have much information on it, but we will find out who did this. Everyone needs to be extra vigilant from now on." My father's gaze touches everyone before he continues. "There has been speculation about earlier shootings in the family that may be connected to this one." I look to Shay, his beard covers most of his face, but I see a slight grin there.

"They aren't. So rule it out and don't waste any more of my time on it." My father swings his dark eyes to Shay. "Thank you for joining us, Shay."

Shay nods his head.

I'm still watching my father, thinking how he has already given me the go-ahead to kill Shay; how his body language holds none of that threat.

Shay pushes out his chair and stands, gaining everyone's attention. "Thank you, Liam." Shay addresses the rest of us as he speaks. "My father was shot two weeks ago. It wasn't a kill shot, but a warning. I think it's the same shooter as Finn, only this time the warning was more serious."

I feel my father's gaze on me, but I don't look at him, knowing I will pay the price for withholding this information. I had to give Shay the respect as a King; that's what I was raised on, the belief that kings were to be treated as such.

"My father has handed over the power of the north to me." Shay's smug smile is directed to my father. "So from one King to another, we will track down this son-of-a-bitch who has caused both of us great pain."

My father rubs invisible dust off the table. 'Temporarily.' My father draws out the one word.

Shay expels a loud breath before he grins at my father. "Temporarily or not, right at this moment, I am the King of the north. Every command goes through me."

He's been acting in his father's stead since he was injured. He kept that part quiet.

"When that power is revoked, Shay..." My father gives a pause. "And it will be. Make sure you don't leave your father too much to clean up."

Shay stays standing, and no one moves. Darragh grins up at Shay, and I see some respect there in his eyes. No one stands up to my father, especially not one of his nephews, but Shay is a different breed. The northerners have different ethics than us.

"Since your father was shot by most likely the same man who shot Finn, I'll grant you permission to stay and help with the investigation, but all information must come to me first."

Shay nods and sits down. "I'll make sure of it." His word sounds more like fuck you. Shay scratches his beard before he sits back in his chair. My father wouldn't appreciate his scruffy appearance. I never really see my father in anything but a suit, so when we are having meetings, I always do the same.

"I've put Cian on this case with you, Jack." It's Shane who speaks up, my father's right-hand man, his brother. They better not think that when I'm King that Cian will be my right-hand man. I have a brother who isn't here, and he won't take part in what we do. He's off with a group of friends exploring my mother's country. At times I wish I had picked the same road as he, but the blood of the Irish Mafia is what pumps through my veins. I nod at Shane.

"Everyone else resumes their normal roles," My father says.

Shay raises two fingers like he's ready to order a drink. "A question." He says, and I'm waiting for a grin that doesn't cross his face. "Are Jack's trials over?" His question sounds so innocent, but it's not.

"No, they are still going ahead."

This time Shay glances at me and winks. "I'm glad to hear it."

He's making it look like we have some agreement, the two new Kings. He'll get himself killed if he doesn't tone it down, or maybe me too.

"Any more questions?" My father glances at everyone, and Taghd speaks up.

There is only a year between him and Cian, but to me, he's more fitting to rule. "How is Finn?"

The question that we all should have asked.

My father nods, and I know that's his approval of the question. "He's breathing for now."

My father's words don't drive much hope into us. I'm sure they are said to drive fear into every man's heart around the table.

"I've had contact from an old informant who gave me the name of a place where you might start your search." My father takes a piece of paper out of his pocket and places it on the table. His fingers hold it down. Shay and I move in at the same time because we are both on this case, but my father doesn't lift his fingers. "This isn't a safe place, so when you go there, tread carefully." My father speaks clearly as he picks up the paper and looks at Cian, who half rises and takes the outstretched piece of paper from my father, while I'm starting to wonder what exactly it is that he's playing at.

"Cian will lead the search. Both of you will help him." My father's eyes dance between Shay and me. I nod stiffly, and Shay gives a short smile that carries his signature word 'cunt' with it.

"What information did your informant give you?" Shay asks like Cian leading us isn't a problem. I don't look to Cian— he's fucking gloating— I know it.

"A man from out of town had inquired about a specific gun that could have done this kind of damage, so see if he spoke to anyone. If he is still here, we are all targets now." My father lets his final words settle on us before he rises.

"Dismissed."

"Guess you'll have to follow my lead." Cian doesn't waste any time.

"I'm sure you'll fuck it up," I whisper back before getting up. Shay is leaving the room, and I want a word with him.

"How are you holding up?" Darragh—my uncle—and Finn's twin, stops me outside the door. I watch Shay disappear into the kitchen.

"Fine, why?"

"After seeing Finn."

I shake my head and focus on Darragh. "Yeah, it was hard, but I'm sure he'll make a full recovery." Darragh is still watching me, and I have no idea why.

"You coming out for a smoke?" He asks, taking a packet out of his pocket.

"Sure, I'll come with you." I glance back at the kitchen and watch my father disappear. We didn't ask each other out for smokes, Darragh wanted to say something, and I was wise enough to listen rather than run after Shay.

"He's having Cian keep tabs on Shay. It's nothing personal." Darragh says the moment we are outside. He smirks. "I saw your face fall when he handed Cian that piece of paper."

I don't deny that he bothered me. "He should have told me."

"Nah. He needed your reaction to be genuine."

It's cold out, and some stars start to sprinkle the sky. I wonder what Maeve is doing. The thoughts of her back home in my room make me want to return. I'm usually not eager to go home to a big empty house, but it's not empty anymore.

"Well, he got it." I don't like being lied to.

"What's his hang-up with Shay, anyway? Apart from the kid thinking he's a God." More smoke spills from Darragh's mouth.

To our uncles, we were all kids. Shay is nearly thirty, so he's a man, but I don't correct Darragh. "He's been asking questions," I say.

Darragh gives a short laugh. "He should be shot."

I'm not sure if he's jesting or not. He's a loose cannon, but he's close to Connor, so I don't think he would hurt his brother like that.

"What kind of questions?" A more serious tone enters Darragh's voice.

I'm sure my father would tell them. They didn't keep secrets from each other. "About your mother."

Darragh's brows drag down, and his mouth forms a thin line. "Like what?" He's holding his cigarette, watching the smoke leave it, and now I know something is off. I'm watching him carefully.

"Just that he doesn't believe she was gunned down."

Darragh nods before forcing a smile. "What does he think happened?"

I can see the tension in his jaw and shoulders. What secrets are they keeping from the rest of us? "Did something else happen?" I ask a question instead.

Darragh drops the cigarette, and no matter what look he's trying to produce, it won't cover up the weariness I see in his eyes. He looks me straight in the eyes now. "For your own sake, lad. Let it go." He walks back into the house, and I know one thing for sure.

I can't let this go.

CHAPTER TWELVE

O'REAGAN
AN CHLANN

MAEVE

I'm trying to study, but my mind won't focus on anything, only the thing Jack just did to me with his tongue. The memory of his large hands on my body has me slamming the book closed. I shouldn't have enjoyed it; I shouldn't have allowed him to go down on me. My cheeks flame, and I push away from the desk. "This is silly." I get up and empty my bag onto the bed for the third time. I had searched it for my phone, but of course, he had removed it. I stack my clothes neatly; only this time, I do it by color. I don't have much, and only four colors are actually in my wardrobe, red, black, gray, and green.

I fold a red sweater as I stare at the door. I've opened it a total of seven times since Jack had left hours ago, each time Freddie is there. He has to take a break, eventually. I put all the clothes back into the bag. It's nice to be in my own clothes. The yoga pants and huge black t-shirt are what I normally wear to bed. I know it's late, but I can't crawl into Jack's bed. It feels wrong. Too tempting. I always knew—even from a young age—that I was attracted to him, but now that I'm in proximity to him, I'm starting to see this attraction like an obsession. I can't seem to get him out of my head. It's not good. It's really not good.

I open the door, and Freddie growls before dragging it out of my hands and slamming it shut. Yeah, I wasn't getting out of this room too easy this time. Turning, I take my bags off the bed and place them alongside the desk that I sit down at again and open my book. I wish I had my phone to see how Declan is. I had twenty-four hours to get that money, which was tomorrow evening. I felt like I'd been trapped here longer than a few hours. I try to refocus on my psychology lessons, but my mind refuses to take anything in. Closing the book for God knows how many times, I leave the desk.

In Jack's wardrobe at the very back, I find what I am searching for. A fresh robe. His smell surrounds me, and I inhale intentionally, my stomach wriggling with the memory of his hands on me. What way would I be after having him completely? He'd discard me like I'm the dirt under his shoe. That's what he really saw when he looked at me, scum. He'd said it before to my face. My heart starts to race, and shame snakes its way into my heart. I enjoyed him touching me, and I shouldn't have. I couldn't control my body's reaction to him, but I could control everything else, I tell myself. It gives me some comfort as I leave the wardrobe with his robe in tow.

I sit down on the large navy armchair and drag the robe over me. I've slept in some questionable places in my time, so this was more comfortable than most places.

"Where have you been?" My mother crushes a cigarette out on the linoleum, the hole starts to grow, and my father stamps on the melting plastic stopping the hole from progressing any further.

"Jesus, Jane. I didn't put that down for you to fucking burn it."

I move back into the hall and huddle against the wall. My dad normally never curses.

A plate smashes, and I cover my ears. The floor is cold under my bare feet, and I glance at Declan's door. Should I wake him up?

More things smash. Then I hear a sound I've heard before, but I'm not sure what it is until my dad speaks.

"Hit me again, Jane…"

"You'll what? Hit me back?" My mother's voice vibrates with emotions she can't control. "Who was it this time? Pauline? Lisa? Which one kept you out all night?"

The kitchen door closes, and I hear my dad's voice hiss quietly, "Don't wake up the kids."

I open my eyes as they burn, and I rub the dream right out of my head. *Was that a memory?* My mind slingshots back to our kitchen, and as if I'm holding a magnifying glass, the burn mark on the linoleum is there. I just thought it was one of her drunken nights, and she fell asleep. I run my hands across my face and roll over in my bed, only to catch myself at the last second. I'm not in my bed. I'm not alone. I'm not home.

He's asleep on his stomach. One hand is under his head, and he's facing me. He has no top on, and I can see the flames of the black ink flow across his tanned and solid back. I bite hard on my lip as I will my body to relax. I'm trying to remember how the hell I got here. I glance at the armchair; the robe is thrown across the high back.

My gaze springs back to Jack. Dark eyelashes rest on his high cheeks. I curl my fingers into fists so I don't do something like touch his face. Squeezing my eyes tightly, I try to force my heart rate to slow before opening my eyes again. I shift slightly and wait. Nothing happens. I move until I'm up on my knees, bending over his huge frame. God, even lying down, he looks so big. I'm careful with the quilts so as not to pull them down too far on him.

His back is in full view now. I study his back until the image becomes clear. It's a lion wearing a crown, he's on his hind legs like a man. The image is stunning, and I'm tempted again to touch it. My hand reaches out, and my pulse pounds in my ears. The tips of my fingers touch the image. Muscles clench, and I withdraw my hand. I can't move as the horror at being caught has everything in me freezing. Jack doesn't move. His eyes are still closed, his body relaxed. I look to the ceiling and question what the hell I'm doing. Taking one final look at his back, the only color in the whole image is the lion's eye that is red.

I slowly and carefully lie back down and shuffle as far away from Jack as I can. He's not good for me. He's not good for my heart. The feeling that he's going to destroy me all over again, keeps me awake for hours. Each time I try to close my eyes, my heart flutters like it's missing a beat. The sensation is uncomfortable. I move slowly out of bed and go to the bathroom to relieve myself. Returning to the room, I see the first signs of morning coming with the rising sun behind the mountains. Grabbing the robe, I throw it over my shoulders and try the balcony doors. They open. Taking one final look, I step outside and close the doors behind me. It's really stunning, and I envy Jack for having the luxury to see this every morning. I think I'd put a small table and chairs out here to have my breakfast every morning. I wrap the robe around me and tie it. This morning there is no wind, the fields are still, and there is something majestic about the red flaming ball that rises behind the peak of the mountain. I stay outside until the cold drives me back in. My nose is numb, and I push it into the shoulder of the robe before stepping inside. The bed is empty, and my gaze darts around the room, looking for him.

Noise in the wardrobe has me closing the balcony door behind me. Jack steps out and pauses when he sees me. I have no idea what to do or say.

"Did you put me in the bed?" The question flies from my lips.

My voice has him moving to a bedside table. "No, Freddie did."

The thoughts of Freddie's hands on me have my spine straightening.

"Today, Freddie will go with you to deliver the money, and then he will bring you straight back."

A thank you is on the tip of my tongue, but I swallow it fast. "Can I have my phone?"

"No." He slides a gold watch onto his wrist without looking at me.

"Can I use your phone?"

"No." He picks up his phone and puts it in his trousers pocket. "When you behave, I will give you privileges; otherwise, you will be punished."

My cheeks redden at how he says punished. I hate how my core tightens with delight.

"I know you tried to leave your room several times last night."

Freddie did a full report. "I was hungry."

Jack steps closer. "Next time, tell him that you are hungry, and he'll have Liz fix you some food."

Liz must be the woman who was in his kitchen, his chef. He's staring at me like he's waiting for something, and I tighten my arms around my waist. When I remember I'm in his robe, I quickly unwrap it and take it off. Holding it out to him, I don't meet his eyes. "I was cold last night," I explain, but I'm still holding it out when I glance up at him.

"I'm going out for a few hours. So go with Freddie and behave." My arm drops down to my side as he leaves with a tightened jaw. He's always hostile, but this morning there is a different feeling in the air, and I have no idea what it is.

I do tell Freddie I'm hungry, and he grumbles at me before he closes my door. I hear a key turn in the lock. I put my ear to the door and hear his heavy footsteps pound down the stairs. While he's gone, I shower and get dressed for my meeting today. I am excited to see Declan so I can reassure myself that he's okay. Then when I return here, I hope Jack takes what he wants so I can leave.

After breakfast, I'm still locked in my room. The day drags by, and I try to study again, but I can't. Once I get the money handed over, I might be able to breathe a bit better, knowing no one will harass Declan or my mother.

Tea and sandwiches arrive in the middle of the day, and I'm locked in the room again. I spend most of my day out on the balcony, tortured by memories that I had forgotten. Being here has forced me to face all the forgotten ones. I think I wanted to forget them. They didn't paint my father in the best light. Each memory is my mother accusing him of having an affair, and now it makes me question if it's why she drinks—why she has always drunk. Guilt clenches my gut and throat, and I quickly go back into my room. I'm ready to demand Freddie to get me out of this room, when the door opens like he knows I'm at my breaking point.

"It's time," Is all he says.

Freddie takes me out to a waiting car. He holds the back door open, and I slide into the back. A bag is sitting beside me. Freddie slips into the driver's seat. "Your money is in there."

I touch the bag, and I'm tempted to zip it down, but I don't have to question if Jack has the money. I am, after all, being chauffeur driven in a Range Rover. I fix the black shirt on me, it's see-through, but I have a cami underneath. I feel like I'm going for an interview. Nerves niggle under my skin, making me itchy. Sweat makes an appearance on the back of my neck. I lift my hair and fan it. Freddie's watching me, but I don't speak to him.

As promised, I'm driven to my house. I'm eager to get out of the car, but when I reach for the handle, the door doesn't open.

"Unlock the door," I demand with one hand on the bag. Freddie doesn't; instead, he takes off his seat belt and faces me.

"I'm not fucking Jack. I don't have a hard-on for you. If you try to run, I'm going to hurt you."

I sink into the seat, wondering if I just heard him right.

"I'll fuck you up if you cross me." He's glaring at me. "Got it?"

"Crystal clear." I exhale a shaky breath.

"Let's go."

"You don't have to come in."

He gets out, and I know arguing with the giant is pointless.

The door has been boarded up, and more guilt ripples through me. I had left without even considering how either of them would fix the door. I knock a few times before it opens, and my mother's glazed-over eyes start at my toes and work their way up to my face. "I thought you left us here to rot."

I reach in to touch her face. The side is swollen, a purple bruise blossoms along the skin.

She flinches away from my touch, and I won't lie and say that it doesn't hurt.

"Just like your father." Her words are like a slap to the face.

"I'm here, aren't I?" My defense is weak.

Her gaze trails down to the bag in my hand. "Is that the money?"

"Yes. What happened to your face?" She steps into the hall, and I follow her into the kitchen with Freddie on my heels.

"Those bastards came back for their money. Slapped me around."

My mother sits down, and under the light, her face looks bad. "Jesus, mom. Did you ring the Gardaí?"

She takes the cigarette and lighter out of her nightgown pocket. "Yep. That was hours ago. They still haven't arrived."

I drop the bag and go to the freezer; there's no ice or food in it. I close the door and run the cold tap.

"What did they say?" I ask as I run a towel under the cold water.

"They were looking for you, so I told them Jack O'Reagan took you."

Every cell in my body goes rigid, and I'm paralyzed for a moment. What would that mean? "Why did you tell them that?"

My mother growls and points at her face. "I wanted the bald one to stop hitting me." I bring the towel over and try to put it on her cheek, but she swipes my hand away.

"Where is Declan?"

My mother's laugh is bitter and twists her lips. "That's all you care about."

"Where is he?" My voice rises and bounces around the space.

"They took him."

"Why didn't you say that when I came in?" I'm picking up the bag, but I have no idea where they are.

"Calm down." She takes a slip of paper out of her pocket. "They said to meet them here if you want Declan back."

I snatch it out of my mother's fingers, and I'm ready to march out of the house, but Freddie is in the way.

"Boss told me to bring you here and bring you back. That's it."

"Freddie, they are going to kill my brother." I try to reach out to his compassionate side, but by the look on his face, he has none.

"Ring Jack," I demand, but everything in me wants to go right now. I need to get to Declan.

"No."

"Ring him!" My shouts don't make Freddie flinch. My mother's screams behind me have me swinging around. She's falling from the chair.

I'm trying to bend down and help her when she grabs me. "Go." She whispers before she starts to scream again.

"Help me," I beg Freddie, and he steps in to pick my mother off the ground. I use that moment with his back to me to spring from the kitchen.

CHAPTER THIRTEEN

O'REAGAN
AN CHLANN

MAEVE

I don't dare look back as I shoot out of the side gate of the yard. I lean out around the black and green bin as I dash down the side of the house and emerge along the front garden. My focus zeroes in on the group of lads who hang out on the large patch of grass rapping.

The air feels as swollen as my lungs as I scream Lee's name. The words that had flowed freely from his mouth cease, and he turns to me, dragging down his gray hood that always covers his head. I glance at the house as the front door opens, and Freddie bursts from my house. His head swings right and left, and when he spots me, his large frame makes a beeline in my direction.

"He's going to hurt me," I scream at Lee, who stares. I've grabbed everyone's attention now as I hit the grass heavily. I nearly fall but drag the bag closer to my chest. I race past the group, and Lee nods at me. Freddie is heavy on my heels, and if something doesn't slow him down, I won't get away.

"Hey, you, dickhead." Lee's words are followed by the abuse from the other lads; their shouts erupt like a popping blister behind me. I keep running until I'm across the large expanse of grass. The grass gives way to tarmac before I hit the sidewalk again and race into grass that's nearly up to my knees. A wooden fence line that surrounds the estate comes into view. I take a peek back and see the group has circled Freddie. Freddie swings first, and one of the lads hits the ground hard.

Freddie glances up like he senses my thoughts, and his gaze narrows on me. I face forward and push my body harder as I hit the fence line. Freddie's roar has me racing along the fence while I search for a way out. I push in the loose panel that's been damaged since I was a kid. I bend down and push the bag out first before squeezing my no longer childlike frame through the hole. My top snags, and I don't pause but yank. Hearing the tear of fabric allows me to get free as I climb up to my feet and grab the bag off the ground.

On the other side, I half walk, half run down the sidewalk as cars zoom by. My lungs burn, and I open the piece of paper again. Overhead, street lights buzz to life as they prepare for the impending darkness that isn't far away.

Fulham's Car Repairs. That's the address that Declan is being held at. It's a ten-minute walk away. Once I feel like my chest won't cave in, I start to jog again, but it's not the easiest in boots. I leave the sidewalk and take one of the back streets to Fulham's. I can't imagine Freddie knowing these shortcuts. We don't see his kind around here. I can only hope I'm right. I'm too close to get caught now. Once Declan is out of harm's way, I don't care what happens.

I come out to a small row of bungalows that sit behind a row of shops. I can see the main street through small gaps between the houses. I'm looking for a Range Rover. It will be easy to spot. The sound of cars revving and voices ahead of me capture my attention. I walk into a cul-de-sac where Fulham's Garage sits. Two large roller doors are open, and the noise from inside sounds like there's a lot of people inside. My stomach squeezes painfully, and I pray that Declan is okay. Two guys sitting outside on the backseat of a car that has been ripped out, stand as I approach.

"I'm here for my brother, Declan." One stands up holding a can of Tenants, one of the cheapest beers you can get. His eyes dance the dance that only alcohol can achieve.

"What's your name, pretty lady?" He tugs up his navy tracksuit bottoms as he walks towards me.

"Maeve Reilly."

He nods his head. "Ah, Reilly. Yep. Declan is here. He's hanging out." His sneer has the other guy laughing too, and worry worms its way into my stomach.

I'm waiting for them to take me in, but they continue to stare at me. The other guy, who was still seated, stands now. His denim jeans are painted onto his long legs, and streaks of oil coat his thighs.

"What do you want with Declan? He's a little high right now." More laughter follows.

Someone else steps out of the darkened shed, and I focus on him. Both men's laughter dies as the bald guy that had been in my house steps up to me. He holds his hands out wide; he's wearing the same leather jacket. Anger rises as I think of my mother's poor face. It's a tide that I try to push down.

"I have your money."

His grin is wide. Blue eyes flicker to the bag in my hand. He clicks his fingers, and the guy who had spoken to me removes it from my hand and takes it inside the shed.

"I want my brother."

"Making demands, are we?" I hate the smile on his face. "Come on in. Your brother's in here." He opens out his arms, and I peer into the darkened shed, but I can't make out much. Sparks fly from an angle grinder that's pressed against a car door. It hits the ground and bounces a few spaces away from the car. My eyes adjust slowly. There are a lot of men in here, all aware of my presence.

"Where is he?" I ask. My heart slams against my chest as I continue to search for him. The guy who had taken the bag of money has all of it stacked on a table and is starting to count it.

"Look up." The words are whispered into my ear. Dread curls around the base of my spine, and I slowly look with trepidation above me. My stomach recoils like I've swallowed something acidic.

"Let him down." Panic tears through me, and I spin around. "Let him down. Please." My body stretches painfully as I crane my neck back and gaze back up to Declan. Large steel chains wrap around his arms that hold him suspended from the ceiling. His face is a bloody mess. The earlier jokes outside about him hanging and being high, have red hot anger pouring through me until I feel like it's scorched my skin.

"Please," I beg.

The hook that holds the chains starts to lower, bringing Declan to the ground. I'm running towards him, and no one stops me. My fingers reach up, seeking to touch him. I graze his shoes with the tips of my outstretched fingers when he stops moving towards me.

I spin around again.

"See, we rechecked the books, and Declan owes a lot more than we first thought." The bald man nods his head and forces a sympathetic look onto his face that doesn't pass the test.

I'm ready to cry. What utter bullshit. This was all because of my mother telling them about Jack O'Reagan. The two people that constantly bring everything down around me.

"Let him down." My voice is low, but the bald man takes a step towards me. I'm aware that everyone is watching. I keep a hand on Declan's shoe, terrified that he might be taken from me.

"Enough of your demands, little girl." His words are growled, and when he reaches me, my skin crawls. His hand whips out. The impact of the slap he gives me sends me sailing downward; the floor rises up to meet me.

My face burns, and my eyes roll back in my head until my vision turns dark. I'm airborne, and slowly Declan's shoes come into view as I'm dragged off the ground and back up onto my feet. I can see Declan being pulled away back into the air. I'm reaching for him, trying uselessly to stop this. Warm liquid fills my mouth, and I blink the stars back to the skies.

I'm moving through a maze of cars. I can't draw my focus away from Declan as he rises into the air again. A groan has my knees giving way, and I'm tripping over my feet only to be dragged back up again.

"It's all there, Butcher." The guy who had been counting the money appears at my side. I flinch at his toothy grin. Trying to look over my shoulder, hurts my neck as I'm pushed into a small room. Declan's legs disappear, and a cry leaves my lips. The room that I'm pushed into has an old block TV on a wooden table. I stumble as the reality keeps pounding my system, and I stop the fall that has come from my weakened knees. I trip into the wall instead as I fight to catch my balance. I'm reaching for order to the chaos of my mind, like trying to reach for a helium balloon that's already too far out of my reach.

The slam of the door has every thought dispersing across the room. I'm standing up and facing Butcher. I try not to let my mind go to why he's called that.

"Your brother's mounting debt is nearly one hundred thousand."

I'm shaking my head while swallowing the words that I know he won't like to hear. My fingers run across the un-plastered wall. The rough stone keeps me alert and present; it keeps my mind away from Declan. All I want to do is find a way out of this room and to my brother.

"I know you don't have that kind of money." Butcher picks up a steel chair that's been folded against the wall that's covered in graffiti. He opens it out and places it in the middle of the room. "Sit." I swallow the blood in my mouth and my stomach rebels. I'm shaking my head again. If I do sit on the chair, it feels like a one-way ticket to the bottom of the ocean.

He's moving towards me. I'm anticipating another slap, but my scalp screams as he yanks me over to the chair. My back slams against it and my weight has the chair tipping over. I can't stop the descent or the impact with the solid concrete ground. I keep my head upright, avoiding hitting the floor. I'm scrambling along the floor, my frantic mind like a freight train with one thought—I need to get out of here before he kills me. No calm comes as I'm put back on the chair with rough hands.

"Me and your mother had a little conversation, and I learned that you are riding Jack O'Reagan's cock." He grabs his own private parts, and I try to focus and still my mind even as it screams at me that death is breathing down my neck, and I need to run.

"So I know you have a source. I want my one hundred grand, or I'll gut your brother where he hangs."

My frantic mind calms. He wants money. It's money. There's a way out. "I can get it." I force a smile that feels like it has been carved into my face by a surgeon's scalpel.

"Do I look fucking stupid to you?"

I'm shaking my head until stars bloom behind my eyes. "I can get it; I know where the safe is. I can get … it." I'm still nodding as tears blur my vision.

"You tell Jack O'Reagan who the money's for, and your brother and mother die."

He kneels down close to me, and I fight with everything in me to hold still as he reaches for my face. "I'm glad we understand each other." Every fiber in my body shakes, and a numbness overtakes my panic.

"You can go." He stands up. I rise, and my knees don't give me support; they feel like sponges that have absorbed too much water.

"Your brother stays here until you return."

Jack isn't going to give me one hundred grand. I have nothing left to bargain with. My head hangs as I step up to the door. Once I get out of here, I can think. I'm no good to Declan being kept in this room. That thought has me reaching for the door handle.

"Oh, one thing before you go."

I turn to find Butcher right behind me. "Ride my cock."

At his words, I want to curl into a fetal position and close my eyes, but the speed of the fear that rockets into my mind, has me going into a panic that drives my hands high until I'm clawing his face with a viciousness that I feel I have no part in. Something else feral has taken over as I claw and spit.

Butcher's screams drive me further, and my thumbs sink into his eyes. Terror eggs me on from the corner of my mind telling me if I stop, I'll be raped, so I don't until I'm plowed into the ground. The impact steals the air from my lungs, and my mind flips a switch, and I'm in flight mode, but as Butcher drags me along the floor, I know it's a little too late.

I should have tried to run. I should have tried to run.

CHAPTER
FOURTEEN

O'REAGAN

AN CHLANN

JACK

"I'll drive." Cian swings his keys around his thumb, and I hope it grinds into the flesh and cuts it off, but that doesn't happen.

"No," Both Shay and I say at the same time. I meet Shay's gaze as I unlock my jeep. He climbs into the passenger seat. Cian slams his car door and walks back to us. He glares at me as he gets in the back. He's fucking lucky he's Shane's son.

Once we are all in, Cian grips both front seats and sticks his head in-between me and Shay. It's a dangerous position he's put himself in.

"Just a fucking reminder that Liam put me in charge." He's glancing from me to Shay like he can run this show. Someone needs to tell him this isn't a sideshow at the fucking circus.

I start the jeep and grin, allowing Shay to take this one, which I know he will, beautifully.

"Ginger, sit the fuck back before I unleash my anger on you." Shay straps in, and Cian sits back. But Shay's seat jerks forward when Cian kicks it.

"Kick the seat again, and you're walking." I adjust the mirror so he can see how serious I am. That ends his assault on the car seat.

"So, where is this place?" I ask.

Cian puts on his seat belt. "Brews Hill. From the outside, it looks closed up. But it's always open."

I keep the mirror adjusted so I can see Cian. "How do you know so much about it?"

"I mix with the locals, Jack." Cian grins and starts chewing on what? Who the fuck knows.

"It's smart," Shay speaks from the front, and I ignore them both. I wasn't mixing with the locals, no matter how smart Shay thought it was. Kings didn't walk amongst their followers. It's like a giant walking with men. It isn't happening.

My phone rings and Freddie's name flashes across the screen. I'm tempted to hang up on him, but he's with Maeve. I've been trying to avoid thinking about her since this morning, but it's like trying not to breathe in through your mouth–it's uncomfortable, and eventually, you suck in a lungful of air. She had been intrigued by my tattoo this morning. The sensation of her hands on my back has me answering the phone.

"Yes, Freddie."

Freddie's panting has me grateful that I don't have the phone up to my ear and that it's on speaker. "What are you panting for?"

"She got away."

I glance at Cian; he's staring out the window. I don't want him knowing my business. I take the phone off the speaker.

"She tricked me and ran off. I had to get the information out of her mother. She's gone to Fulham's Garage to finish the deal. A man called Butcher has her brother."

The phone doesn't crush under the force of my hand as I squeeze it, wanting it to be Freddie's fucking moronic neck.

"Fulham's Garage." I glance at Cian in the mirror, keeping a calmness attached to my words that I no more fucking feel. "You know where it is?"

Cian grins, and I'm ready to pull over and kick ten colors of shit out of him, but he must sense the undercurrent of violence that moves across my skin in waves.

He speaks up. "It's on Brews Hill too, not far from the pub. It's not a legit garage but run by a group of local lads who think they rule the area."

I put the phone down, and my foot hits the pedal hard. "Do we not own them?" I ask. We should.

"No. It's a small drug ring that runs independently. I think you might be their supplier."

"Think and might; two useless words, Cian. You should know this. It's not my department."

Shay turns and looks out the back window. "Are we being chased?"

I hit Brews Hill and slow down. "Where do I go now?"

"Go down to the roundabout and take the first left, then another left, and it's down the road." Cian undoes his seat belt and moves too fucking close to me. "These guys won't like you dropping in on them."

I follow Cian's directions, and a large garage comes into view.

"You want to tell us what's going on?" Cian asks as I pull up at the garage doors. Two men stand as I get out of the Range Rover. One of them starts moving backward, nearly tripping over his feet to run into the shed. He must be warning whoever is in charge.

Good.

The jeep doors close, and I don't look to see who has followed me.

"Where is Maeve Reilly?" I ask the first guy who is stupid enough not to run.

"With Butcher." He points inside, and I grip him by the back of the neck and heave him into the shed. "Show me."

We step into a dimly lit space that's filled with cars. The men stop what they are doing and stare at me.

"Which one of you clowns is Butcher?" I push the man in my grasp ahead of me. He falls but recovers quickly.

No one speaks.

"The man asked you cunts a question." Shay steps up beside me with a gun in his hand. I'm aware that a man is suspended from the ceiling. His white skin and thin frame suggest he's been up there for a long time rotting away.

"In there." One of them wearing overalls points at a closed door, and real fear that I've never felt, has me moving.

"Be smart." Shay is on my heels, and all I can see is that fucking door. The knob turns under my hand, and I open it.

"No one move." Cian's voice booms behind us, and I don't turn to see who he is talking to.

Fury licks along my skin as I take in the scene before me. Inside me, everything rattles. A deranged animal fights to get out of his cage inside me.

Butcher is on top of Maeve, who's screaming; his trousers are around his ankles as he tears at her clothes.

My sanity starts to slip.

It snaps.

My steps are driven by a need to spill as much blood as possible. I'm behind the fucking animal before he even knows we've stepped into the room. My arms tighten around his thick neck. He's twice my size, but nothing could match the adrenaline that roars through my body. I drag him off Maeve and throw both of us back until my back slams against the floor. He's on top of me; my arm tightens around his neck.

His fists rise and swing at my face, but I keep my head out of his reach as I continue to squeeze. A savage roar leaves my lips as I tighten my hold further, feeling his thumps reduce to slaps. I want him to die.

My gaze clashes with Maeve's, and the horror in her brown eyes don't make me loosen my death grip on him. I keep tugging until he gives up his hold on this earth, and the bones give way under my forearm. The satisfying snap has me releasing his body and dumping it to the side. Violence still pounds inside me, and I try to tame it as I get up and walk over to Maeve.

A whimper leaves her mouth as she tries to gather the shreds of her top to her chest. I'm assessing too much damage and loosen my fist before kneeling down and scooping her up off the ground. Shay stands at the door and holds the gun at half-mast.

"Are we good to go?"

"Yes," I answer, carrying Maeve out of the room. Cian takes one look at her and steps towards us, but he pauses when he looks at me. I can't control myself right now, and I don't want him near her.

"My brother," Maeve speaks like she's waking up from a dream.

"I need to get you looked at first." We move through the men, and Maeve starts to become alert in my arms.

"No, my brother." She's wriggling, trying to get free, but I tighten my hold on her.

"We need to get you seen to."

She doesn't hear my words as her hysteria starts to grow. She's pushing against me, trying to get out of my arms, and I won't stop walking. I won't let her go.

I can't.

She continues to cry and scream as I leave the shed. "Jack, I'll never forgive you."

I glance down at her as I fight with the feral animal inside who still hasn't settled. Outside in the light, her face is swollen, blood drips from the side of her mouth. It looks so much fucking worse than it did inside. Seeing her wounds is like a physical pain, like a knife being dragged along my skin.

"I don't give a fuck about your brother," I speak through gritted teeth.

"Don't you dare leave him." Her hands connect with my face, and I struggle to keep her in my arms while stopping her from hitting me.

Cian jogs up beside us. He's focused on Maeve and not me. "I promise I'll get him down and to a hospital."

Maeve's heaves reduce, and she stops her attack on me. She's nodding at Cian like if she stops, he won't really do it. "Give me your word."

"I wouldn't lie to you," Cian says.

I grit my teeth as Shay passes us. "All done?" He asks with a flash of teeth. I have no idea what the fuck he's smiling at.

Maeve holds herself as far away from me as she possibly can. The moment I place her in the back, she scurries away from me like I'm the one who fucking attacked her.

"Shay, you drive."

Shay stops at the passenger door and closes it before dancing around to the driver's side and climbing in. I get in the back with Maeve.

"I don't want you near me." Tears flow from her eyes and into her mouth.

"Calm down." I get in and close the door. I don't move close to her as she pushes back against the far door like I might hurt her.

She's forgotten about her torn top, her breasts almost spilling out of her bra, so I shrug out of my jacket and hand it to her. She turns her head to the side, and I move closer to wrap it around her.

The slap she leaves on my face stings.

"Don't do that again, Maeve," I warn.

Weariness fills her eyes, but it's washed away quickly by a tidal wave of anger and pain.

"You left him." She frowns angrily at me. "You left him."

Her brother looked dead to me. I did her a favor.

"Was he the one that got you into all this trouble?" I question now. Since he was hanging from a fucking ceiling, he must have really pissed those people off.

I'm not ready for the second slap she delivers, and I move away from her as she curls further into the corner.

I meet Shay's eyes in the rear-view mirror, and he grins at me.

I ring Liz at the house, she answers on the third ring.

"Hello, O'Reagan residence."

"Liz, it's Jack," I speak low as I glance at Maeve, who's watching me with hate in her eyes. Cian will be the fucking hero.

"Have Doctor Coffee there. I'm on my way home."

"Are you okay?" Her concern isn't wanted.

"Yes, Liz. Just have the doctor there."

"Of course."

The moment I hang up, Maeve speaks. "I don't need a doctor." She's barking.

Shay's laughter isn't subtle in the front. "No, love, you need an exorcist." His gaze flashes to me. "She's like a woman possessed."

"Shay, she's none of your concern." My voice is low as I try to control my temper. Shay's grin leaves his face, and he gives me a nod.

"I hear you," he says as he turns off the main road.

I exhale loudly before turning to Maeve. "You do need a doctor."

"No, I don't. I need to get as far away from you as I can."

My sanity slips again, and I move across the seat, ready to grip her, but fear has me pausing. Her fear is good. It means she might behave, but I can't justify touching her right after what she just went through. "The doctor will examine you Maeve, if you don't allow her, then I will." The threat isn't idle, and she must notice that as she folds her arms across her chest. She glances down at her herself and quickly snaps up my jacket and drags it across all her flesh. I sit back, but I don't move far from her.

My phone rings, and I glance at it. I smile, like a shark that spots a drop of blood in the ocean.

"You're fired. If you ever come near my home again, I'll fucking shoot you." I hang up on Freddie. Shay's watching me again, and I try to seek out the control my father has, but I can't fucking find it right now.

I'm twisted and squeezed and wound up so tightly that I'm too close to snapping again.

Chapter Fifteen

O'REAGAN
AN CHLANN

MAEVE

I know I should be crying or wailing or breaking down, but that's not happening to me. Right now, all I feel is pure anger. I don't want to cry or heal or do anything else I'm meant to do. I keep my focus out the window as my body screams at me with pain. There's pain everywhere. I tighten the jacket around me until I remember who it belongs to. I loosen it but don't take it off. My half nakedness is a reminder of what happened, what could have happened if Jack hadn't arrived. Butcher had lived up to his name. He had torn my top like it was a piece of paper. His hands had greedily groped my breasts, his prodding fingers painfully bruising my skin. My back had taken the brunt of the abuse. Each time he had slammed me into the ground, it did a bit more damage. I think he was trying to knock me out as I fought to keep my trousers on. The moment he had pulled his own down, my flight mode reverted back to fight mode. If Jack hadn't come in at that moment, I don't think I would have stayed conscious for long. Butcher would have eventually overpowered me. I drag my feet up onto the seat and hug them against my chest.

I'm staring at my reflection in the glass, wondering where the tears are, but no burning sensation assaults my throat or nose, the normal warning signs that I'm about to cry. The jeep continues to move, and I sense Jack beside me. He's too close, and I want him to sit on the other side of the jeep, but telling him that means acknowledging him. The gates to his home appear, and my stomach tightens. I don't know what I expected, to be dropped home, maybe. To be brought to a hospital?

The jeep slows down at the door, and Jack shifts beside me. I swing around as he reaches for me.

"Don't touch me." His inhumanity at leaving my brother to die is eating away at any good thoughts I had about him. I meet his ice-blue eyes. I want to lash out at him again. How could he? He continues to stare at me.

"I want to speak to Cian." At least **he** had a heart.

Jack doesn't answer. His jaw clenches, otherwise he shows nothing else as he leans away from me and gets out of the jeep.

"Answer me," I shout after him, but he closes the door behind him.

When the door closes, I take a calming breath, trying to keep myself together, but the stitching that has been holding me together my whole life is frayed and tearing slowly. Someone clears their throat, and I remember the driver. I don't like him. He seems to have a permanent grin on his face. He's an O'Reagan; there's no doubt about that. They all have that smugness about them that pours off this one.

"Are you staying in the back? Love?" His Northern Ireland accent is heavy, and the way he says love sounds like an insult. I don't get to answer as the door opens before I can even reach for the handle. Jack opens it slowly so as not to startle me and stands back to let me out. "I want to speak to Cian," I repeat, but my voice is weak.

"Soon." One word passes between gritted teeth, and I will accept it for now. It is better than his angry silence.

I'm surprised that my legs hold me up as I step out of the jeep. I keep the jacket held tightly around me as I go into the house. I don't speak as I start to climb the stairs. My movements are stiff, and pain laces across my back. I stop halfway up to try to ease some of the pressure off my lower spine. I hear his heavy footsteps behind me before I'm airborne as Jack scoops me up. His hands are surprisingly gentle, but I want nothing from him.

"Put me down." My voice sounds strange to my ears.

Jack won't look at me as he faces forward. He doesn't put me down until we are in his room. I'm lowered onto the bed. I scurry away from him; my anger repelling him from me.

His gaze is trained on me. "Doctor Coffee is going to examine you."

Pain like nails being dragged down my stomach has my vision blurring. "So what? You want to make sure I'm not soiled?" My words rise high and lash out like a whip at him.

He doesn't answer me but walks over to the double doors that look out onto the balcony. I stay huddled at the top of the bed, wondering if this really happened to me. If someone actually tried to rape me. If my brother had been really suspended from the ceiling. These things happened in movies, not to normal people like we are. Declan didn't deserve this fate. He just got messed up with the wrong people.

Footsteps on the stairs draw my attention to the bedroom door. A woman with pixie short brown hair and white framed glasses steps into the room. She's holding a black bag and gives me a warm smile. She's in her sixties and has a motherly warmth about her.

"I'm Doctor Coffee." She's tall, and the white woolen sweater that swallows her neck, looks itchy.

"I want her checked." Jack doesn't turn as he speaks.

Bitterness fills my mouth and twists my lips. "He wants you to make sure I'm not soiled," I speak up to Doctor Coffee.

She glances at Jack before taking instruments out of her bag like she didn't just hear me speak. How many people had she patched up for him? How many situations had she given her warm motherly smile? It made her almost as bad as he is.

"Don't worry. He didn't rape me." I'm speaking to Jack's back—what he did felt worse. My breasts ache from his rough hands. The fear of what was going to happen makes me almost feel like it did. Like Butcher took a part of me that he had no right to take. "He just made sure he had a good feel."

Jack turns to Dr. Coffee. "I want a full report."

"Of course, Mr. O'Reagan."

Both of them are ignoring me like I'm a chipped cup to be assessed. Am I worth gluing back together or not?

Am I not good enough anymore to even speak to? He's leaving, and fear grips my throat and propels me off the bed.

"Look at me." My voice rises, and Jack stops at the door, but he doesn't turn. His hands grip the door frame.

"What's wrong, Jack? You don't like to share your toys?" I prod and want him to lash out at me so I can strike back.

"Let the doctor check you, Maeve." His voice is a low growl.

I step up closer to his back that's heaving. "I saw it in your eyes." My vision blurs, and my throat burns. "You didn't kill Butcher because he was hurting me; you did because you enjoyed the power." Jack releases the doorframe, and I'm expecting him to leave, only he turns around and looks past my shoulder.

"Give us a minute." He speaks to the doctor and steps aside to allow her to leave the room; she doesn't pause as she passes me. Jack takes a step towards me, and I take one back. My survival mode kicks in, and I close my mouth. He snapped Butcher's neck. The look of madness in Jack's eyes at that moment, I don't think I will ever forget, even as I take my final breath while on this earth.

"I enjoyed it. I enjoyed every second of it." Jack's eyes gleam like melted steel, and I take another step back.

"I only wish that I had taken my time, that I spilled as much of that animal's blood as possible."

Goosebumps break across my skin. The door is still open, and I'm sure the doctor can hear his words. How many secrets will she carry to her grave?

"I'd do it all over again." Jack's words are harsh, and he reaches out, touching my neck. His fingers are like butterfly wings, soft and gentle, but the impact sinks under my skin and has me closing my eyes, allowing my tears to spill.

We are suspended in this moment. I'm okay to stay here for a while, where my warmth comes from Jack's flesh, where the safety comes from his touch, where the air comes from his lungs. Yeah, I'm okay to stay here.

His hand is withdrawn far too quickly, taking everything with it. It's like the plug being pulled on life support, and something in me cracks as I open my eyes.

"I had warned you not to run, and you broke my rule, so you will be punished."

Blood burns up my veins, and heat scorches my face and neck. I remember him choking Butcher, the feral roar that had left his lips. The air in the room is dragged from the ceiling all the way to the floor, and spots break out in front of me.

"What will you do to me?" *Now that I know what you are capable of.*

Beg. Throw yourself at him. My mind keeps firing solutions that my broken body can't even begin to comprehend.

"I haven't decided. Right now, Doctor Coffee will return to this room and examine you." His jaw is tight like one more wind of a spanner, and it would snap.

But the thoughts of him leaving me are driving fear that's so much worse deep into my heart. I have no idea why, but I'm shaking my head.

"This isn't part of the agreement. I can't be kept here, Jack. I need to see my brother."

"Your agreement isn't fulfilled."

"Fulfill it already." My voice rises, and he takes a threatening step towards me, but I'm at the breaking point. I need to know my brother is okay.

"Watch your tone." His voice is controlled, and I hate it so much. I have no control. Everything screams and roars inside me.

"I hate you." I'm moving this time, and my hand strikes his face. An iron grip tightens around my wrists painfully, and I'm moving until my back is against the wall.

"Get off me." I push both my hands against his chest, but he doesn't release me.

"Hate me all you want, but no matter what, you aren't leaving this place until you fulfill the agreement."

He lets me go and turns, leaving me panting and shaking. Doctor Coffee steps in and gives me the same warm smile she had the first time.

"Why don't you remove your garments and let me take a look." She closes the door, and my mind is still stuck on a loop that I'm going to be punished. *What would he do?*

I shiver out of his jacket, and my cami is wrapped around my waist, torn and tattered. My body seems to be losing its anger, and something deep-rooted takes over, causing my hands to tremble.

"Let me help." Doctor Coffee steps forward with the scissors. I hold my hands out at my side as she cuts the top from my waist. I focus on her chocolate brown cords. She places the scissors on the bed and assesses my chest; I focus on the door over her shoulder.

Her fingers touch my chest, and I hiss. "I'm just checking to make sure nothing is broken."

"I don't think there is anything broken," I answer honestly, just wanting her away from me. I feel more bruised and battered than anything else.

She continues to check my stomach before I turn around. My back aches with every touch. "Your back is badly bruised, but it's all superficial; it will heal." She spins me back around.

"Why don't you take off your trousers and lie down."

"I'm okay." I fold my arms across my chest.

"Mr. O' Reagan has requested a full examination."

"What about what I want? Someone just tried to rape me, and I'm being treated like a criminal. Nothing happened down there."

Doctor Coffee nods and touches my arm, leading me to the bed as if I hadn't spoken one shaky word. "It's best we just check. It will only take a second."

I open my jeans and push them down my legs, knowing arguing is pointless. "And your panties."

She's a doctor. I say that mantra in my head as I remove my panties and lie down. The noise of the rubber gloves being placed on her hands has me closing my eyes.

"I'm going to just take a quick look."

I nod, unable to say anything.

She keeps to her word and doesn't stay long between my legs. After checking me, she stands up and removes the gloves. She disappears into the bathroom, and I hear the water running. I sit up, but my back screams in pain, but I'm not lying here naked any longer than necessary. I cover my private area with my hands. "Could you pass me that bag beside the desk?"

The doctor does as I ask and places the bag on the bed. As she goes back to her own bag, I pull out my yoga pants and large bed shirt. It takes me a few minutes to get them on. The rattle of tablets lands on the bedside table.

"Take two tablets three times a day. They will help with the pain."

Anything for wiping away the memory? I want to ask. Instead, I nod at her, just wanting her to leave. She seems to hesitate at the side of the bed, but whatever she was waiting for passes, and she gathers up her equipment and leaves me alone.

I feel like a broken-down car abandoned at the side of the road. I lie back and drag my knees up to my chest. I'm ready to let the pain leak from my eyes, but I'm too broken right now to cry.

CHAPTER SIXTEEN

O'REAGAN
AN CHLANN

MAEVE

Three days.

Three days I have been locked in this god forsaken bedroom.

Food comes and goes.

Light turns to dark.

Opening my eyes, I enter another day and sit up. The room is the same way as it was last night. Another no show on Jack's part. How long does he think he can keep me locked in here? The balcony doors were locked on the first morning I woke up; that was the only sign I had that Jack had been in here. That was the last sign of anyone entering the room without my knowledge.

I get out of bed and rattle the door handle. Lawlor locked it after the third time I had opened it on the first day that I'd been locked in here. He was meaner than Freddie. The first time I'd opened the door, he had threatened to hurt me if I didn't step back in.

I believed him.

I had tried twice more when I thought he had left. The punishment was a locked door, which was unlocked when the food arrived or was taken away.

I couldn't stay here one more day without knowing what happened to my brother. I get dressed in jeans and a black sweater before plaiting my hair. I make the bed out of habit, out of boredom, and out of guilt. I had never struck anyone in my life. No matter what situation I was in, violence isn't something I reach for. The fact I had hit Jack multiple times weighs heavily on my conscience. Each night I seem to be plagued with memories of my mother putting her hands on my father. I'm not sure if it's memories or my own guilt and embarrassment, but all I know is that no matter what, I will never do it again. No matter how far I'm pushed, I'll reach for an alternative. I've spent too much of my life trying not to be my mother. Not drinking or smoking, and now I'm doing the worst thing of all, putting my hands on someone.

I have no clock or indication of what time it is, but soon I know Liz's heavily clogged shoes will beat up the stairs, and this time I'm not letting her out without taking me with her.

My stomach somersaults when the door handle turns. I hadn't heard her footsteps. I stay standing at the end of the bed with my hands behind my back, waiting to see who it is. Maybe one of the other servants is bringing my food, one who has lighter steps. They could be easier to convince to help me.

The door opens, and ice-blue eyes land on me. The air switches gear in the room, and it's like I'm sucking in too much oxygen; I feel funny like I'm not actually here as Jack steps into the room. His white shirt is crumpled, and three buttons are opened at the top, showing off his tanned skin. I swallow when I note the flecks of blood on the front of the shirt. My gaze trails down to the cuffs that look like they've sat in blood and soaked it up like a sponge. I'm walking towards him. His head snaps away from me, and he steps into the wardrobe. I'm aware the bedroom door is open, so why am I following him into the wardrobe?

"What happened?" My pulse picks up pace as he peels off the shirt.

He drops it on the floor before reaching for a fresh shirt; he turns to me as he pulls it off the hanger. I'm examining every inch of his perfect torso, looking for the cause of the blood, but he seems unmarked.

Perfection, that's all I see. A perfect six-pack that dips down into his jeans.

"Are you hurt?" My voice is high-pitched.

Jack unbuttons the fresh shirt while watching me. "No."

I nod slowly, and my heart-rate starts to lower slightly. Of course, it isn't his blood. I'm a little stunned that my first reaction was to follow him in here instead of my freedom.

"My brother?"

He exhales loudly as he puts the shirt on and starts to button it up. The dark circles under his eyes are stark, like he hasn't slept in days.

"I just need to know he's okay." I take a step towards Jack. He's so big, and I feel weak and inadequate to him. I have no idea why I ever thought I might win against Jack O'Reagan.

"He's recovering in Navan Hospital." His words are as cold as a December morning.

I reach out and hold on to the shelf with relief. "Thank you."

Jack kicks off his shoes, and I'm ready to leave as he opens the belt of his trousers.

"Dana is home. She's going to stay here for a few days."

Humiliation hammers itself into my body, and heat rises along my chest as its scorching flames consume my face. "Please, Jack…" I take a step towards him, and he swings around. The anger that flashes in his eyes has me stepping away from him until my back hits a shelf.

"Don't tell her," I whisper. The humiliation of her knowing I sold my body for money is too much right now.

"She thinks you're here with me." Jack takes off his trousers, and I try to keep my focus above his waist.

I can't.

His large muscular thighs seem to ripple with each movement.

I want to cover my burning face. "You told her?" I grit my teeth.

Once Jack has a fresh pair of jeans on him, he walks over to me without zipping them up. "I told my sister that we are together. So when she sees you, you better act like it."

His words have an odd impact on me. "Together? Like I'm here of my own free will?"

Jack's gaze drops to my lips.

I can't stop the laughter that bubbles up to my throat. "She won't believe that."

His hand is quick as he grips the shelf at the side of my head. "Maybe I should tell her the truth then." He leans in; his breath fans across my face. "How you came to me and agreed to fuck me for money."

The air halts in my lungs at his crude words.

He dips his head so I can no longer see his eyes. "You want her to know that about you?" His voice sounds gleeful. He's found a sore spot, and now he'll poke at it.

"No." The word comes out on a shiver as I close my eyes. His lips touch the base of my earlobe, and I swear he inhales deeply.

"Then be a good girl and pretend that we are fucking for real."

The laughter in his voice tells me he would never fuck me willingly. Shame once again slams into me, and I reach behind me, touching a lower wooden shelf as I try to steady myself.

His body seems to lean closer to me, and my eyes shoot open at the large erection that pushes against my stomach. My mind trips and falters over the fact he's aroused right now. When his fingers trail along the side of my face, a shiver pours down through me like liquid lava. It fills my shoes and turns solid. I can't move or even breathe with him this close. His wet lips graze the side of my face, and my stomach erupts and sparks fire through my body. On instinct, my hands reach out and touch his sides—the muscles bunch under my touch.

Jack's lips leave my cheek, and he leans back until I'm being sucked into the depths of his ice-blue eyes. His jaw is set, his fingers dance along my jawline as he leans in and kisses me. I can't stop the reaction that overtakes me, and I'm responding to him. Like when a light goes green to cross the road, or you open a door before walking into a room, it's so automatic only hunger for him has me devouring his kisses.

My hands leave his sides, and I'm clawing at his shoulders. Large hands grip my thighs, and he lifts me. Wrapping my legs around him, he deepens the kiss sinking his warm tongue into my mouth, his cock is pressed against me, and my body is fully aware of every inch that we touch. My back rebels, still not fully healed, but Jack's touch overrides any pain. My hold tightens on his wide shoulders as he sits my ass on a shelf. I groan into his mouth as his hand grazes the side of my top. My nipples pebble inside my bra, and I've never wanted anyone to touch me so badly.

My own fingers seek his shirt, wanting to feel his hard, warm flesh. My fingers work on the buttons of his shirt, but I stop as he fills his hand with one of my breasts and squeezes. I groan into the kiss that I break to catch my breath. Jack's not ready to lose the kiss and recaptures my mouth in his.

I push his shirt down his shoulders; the warm skin ripples and muscles tighten under my touch. I feel powerful to have gained such a reaction from him. His hands slip down until he dips under my top and runs them along my stomach. It's my turn to inhale deeply at the contact. A shiver assaults me. Jack pushes his cock harder against me, and my core tightens, and wetness pools between my legs. My body is telling me it's ready.

I let my hands roam across his shoulders before dropping lower; once my fingers dance close to his open jeans, his kisses cease. His hot breath puffs against my swollen lips. I've never touched a man like this. I quickly peek up at Jack to find him watching me. My heart starts to race. I push his jeans down his hips. I lean in and place a soft kiss on his lips. My kiss seems to jumpstart Jack into action, and he grips the back of my neck almost painfully as he pushes us together. Our teeth clang and his kisses are frantic and almost savage. It's a domino effect: all that lust pours into me, and I sink my hand into his boxers and touch his cock.

It jerks at the contact, and Jack's loud groan has me gripping it tighter. Its wide head jerks again, and I move my hand down before slowly stroking back up. Jack's hands leave me, and the material that covered him is gone as he pushes down his boxers and steps back slightly. I look down to see his cock. It's huge and intimidating, and I have a moment of not knowing what to do.

Jack keeps his body slightly away, giving me room while he dips his head back down to me and starts a slow rhythm against my lips. I move my hand up and down his cock as each groan has me feeling powerful and more in control; my pace grows faster. Jack's hands grip my face, and his shallow breaths continuously brush my lips in between half kisses that break on groans and moans.

I move faster, and it's like his cock swells in my hand. Some part of me considers stopping and telling him to finish this inside me, but having Jack bent over me fighting for his breath, has me stroking it faster and faster. His hands dig into my arms, and his body stiffens before he groans long and hard. Thick, warm cum pours from the tip of his cock all over my hand. His grip on me loosens, but his breathing doesn't return to normal as he buries his head in my neck. I slow my pace until I stop. I'm still holding his meaty cock; my hand covered in his semen.

The wardrobe around us comes into focus, sharpening my senses. I'm very aware of what I just did. I wanted to touch Jack O'Reagan.

His hands touch my neck, and he presses a kiss to my jawline. So much confusion assaults me. I love how he feels against me, but as he said, he's paying me for this. Does this make me a slut?

Heat travels quickly along my neck, and I try to salvage what I just did. My heart pounds.

"I think I can convince Dana that this charade is real." Words that aren't mine leave my mouth.

Jack doesn't move, but I swear he is holding his breath. I hate how I love his smell and his large frame protectively around me.

"I think that earned me a phone call to my brother." I sound like a brazen slut.

Stop it, Maeve.

I can't ever let Jack know what this meant to me. He's a means to an end for me; he shouldn't mean so much to me. I shouldn't allow these types of feelings for him to grow.

I release his cock, and he pushes away from me. His hard gaze travels painfully slowly across my face. A cruel grin spreads out, and I feel the bite of it before he speaks.

"You sure have."

I feel like dirt. *Scum.*

Jack pulls up his boxers and jeans but doesn't close them. He doesn't look at me as he picks his shirt up off the floor and puts it back on. His smell surrounds me as he moves past me and out of the wardrobe. I'm expecting him to leave, but he's at the bedroom door. He's speaking to someone. Once it's closed, I hear the turn of the key. Jack stops at the wardrobe door, and my heart stills in my chest.

"I'm going for a shower. Since I know what you can do, you can join me if you want." His words end in a sneer as he leaves me in the wardrobe.

CHAPTER SEVENTEEN

O'REAGAN
AN CHLANN

JACK

I've stripped down. Some of my cum still clings to my boxers as I take them off. My fists clench at her tone. She didn't give one flying fuck. All she saw when she looked at me was a way to fix her fucking problems. I'm holding myself back from going back out there and telling her she can't speak to her brother. A smile crawls across my face at the thought of doing just that. It would piss her off, but nothing would come close to how pissed off I am.

I turn on the water and remove the rest of my clothes before getting in. Her soft hand on me nearly undid me at the start; I had to hold back, so I didn't come. I've had plenty of women, and none of them had that effect on me. My cock starts to grow again as I think of her hands on me, her intoxicating scent, her bewitching brown eyes.

Fuck.

How did I let this happen? I'm out of the shower, water dripping all over the floor. I need to fuck her and let her go. I need my life back. I'm ready to leave the bathroom and throw her on the bed so I can finish what she started.

She's standing at the door. Her cheeks are pink as she stares at me. Her gaze dances across my wet flesh; she opens her mouth, but nothing comes out. She closes it and looks away. "I need to wash my hands."

Her hand is still sticky with my cum. My cock continues to grow. She hasn't moved, and I know I need to take this opportunity, give her one good fucking and let her leave. She half looks up as I step closer to her. She swallows before glancing up fully, fear and something deep sparks in her eyes. I reach out and grip the back of her neck, dragging her to me before pressing her mouth against mine. Her arms instantly reach for my shoulders, and my cock gets thicker with each passing second. Her lips are still swollen under mine, and I'm wondering what it would feel like to have them wrapped around my cock. I groan as the thick head of my penis twitches.

I catch the bottom of her top and break the kiss so I can pull it off over her head. I don't wait but press my lips back to hers as I pull it down her arms and let it sail to the floor. Her body is perfect against mine. I run my fingers down her spine, and she pushes closer to me. Her hands trail up until they sink into my wet hair; she tightens her hold painfully as she pulls my face closer to hers; her tongue enters my mouth, and I'm working on unbuttoning her jeans.

I grip her panties along with her jeans and push them down. Lifting her without breaking the kiss, I carry her to the bed. Her eyes pop open as I stay standing and take off her boots and her trousers. The black panties join everything on my floor. Separating her legs, I crawl up her body. Her eyes flash with fear, but she squeezes them closed.

Anger has me gripping her thighs, and her eyes pop open. "I want you to look at me."

Her chest rises and falls rapidly as I move up her body. My cock throbs at her entrance. She nods like she's gearing herself up for the grand finale. Bending down, I push her bra aside and take one of her hard nipples in my mouth. Her hiss of pleasure has me nipping on it. My cock throbs between my legs and I release her breast and move onto the other one.

"Oh, God." Her words have me smiling against her nipple. Running my hand along her stomach, she inhales sharply. I run my fingers all the way down to her entrance, where my cock sits. Moving back, I slide my fingers inside her, and she arches up. Her breast fills my mouth, and I suck while plunging my fingers into her wet, tight pussy.

"Jack." My name is released on a breath. I let go of her breast but don't stop fucking her pussy with my fingers. I want to see her face.

The look of awe as she moves her head from side to side has me dragging my thumb across her clitoris.

"Oh, God." Her hands leave the quilt that she had gripped and sank into my shoulders. I've never wanted to fuck someone so badly. My cock swells painfully, and I want nothing more than to find my release inside her sweet pussy.

"I'm going to cum." Her eyes shoot open. Her words sound almost panicked or tinged with disbelief.

I pump harder, my thumb rubbing her clit, and I can't take my eyes off her as she takes in three sharp breaths before she slams her eyes shut. Her nails sink into my shoulders as she cries out her release. She's loud and my fingers are being drenched in her juices. I slow down but kiss her lips. Just small, quick kisses as she continues to call out her release. When she's done, I remove my fingers from her, and her gaze swings to me as she tries to catch her breath.

My stomach flips as I know I need to just do it— fuck her. She's here, wet, naked, and ready, so why am I getting off the bed and walking back to the bathroom?

The water is still running, and I step into the shower and try to push the image of the beauty lying on my bed out of my mind. My enlarged cock aches and cries for release, but I won't. I know why I won't, but I don't want to admit that to myself.

When I'm finished showering, I grab a towel and start to dry myself as I enter the bedroom. Maeve isn't lying on the bed as I had envisioned. She's in the wardrobe, getting dressed with a troubled expression on her face.

When she notices me, she quickly finishes buttoning her jeans. I should have taken her, I had the chance, but I didn't.

She bends down, her breasts nearly falling out of the bra as she takes out a green top from her bag.

A knock at the bedroom door has her tightening her hold on her top. She looks startled, as if it's the first time she hears that sound.

I step out of the wardrobe and answer the door. I'm expecting it to be Lawlor since I put him at the door.

"Why is your door locked from the outside?" Dana's voice penetrates the wood.

The key turns in the lock, and I can hear Lawlor trying to stop her, but that's not going to happen. The door opens, and Dana grins at me.

"Why is the door locked?" She keeps grinning as she tries to look over my shoulder.

I tighten my towel around my waist. "I'm trying to get dressed."

Her gaze travels back to me. "Alone?" She presses her lips together like she's trying to stop the smile.

"No," I answer.

Her smile widens. "Maeve," She calls over my shoulder.

I grip the door and try to close it. "She'll be out in a minute."

She's smiling and shaking her head in disbelief. "I don't believe you." She's moving past me, and I could stop her, but I don't. "Where is she?" She's glancing around the room.

"I'm in here." Maeve's voice shakes.

Dana's smile dissolves as she glances at me. "She's really here?"

I close the bedroom door, not answering her.

Maeve steps out of the wardrobe. The plain green top hugs her curves and emphasizes her breasts. The braid that's flung over her shoulder is now messy, and her cheeks are still flushed. She looks perfect.

"Hi." She sounds breathless, and the pulse pounds in her neck with nerves.

"Now, you saw her. Let us get dressed."

Dana keeps looking between us like she's trying to piece it together. She ignores me and steps into the wardrobe, dragging Maeve into a hug. "Why the hell haven't you been answering your phone? This is where you've been holed up?"

Maeve looks at me, and I take a moment and enjoy watching her squirm. "I lost my phone, and yeah, I've been staying with Jack." Maeve's words sound like misery. Jesus, she isn't selling this.

"Out now, Dana. You're making Maeve uncomfortable." I step into the wardrobe, and Dana rolls her eyes.

"Hardly. Anyway, mom and I are cooking a meal tonight." The smile returns to Dana's face, and she leans into Maeve. "You have to come."

Before Maeve answers, Dana turns to me. "You're bringing her." Her authoritative tone is just like Mom's.

"I was hoping to introduce Maeve to Shay." Dana places her hand over her heart. "He's a big friendly giant. A kitten, really."

She had no idea, but that's what happened when you shield someone from our world. Mum wanted Dana to have a normal life.

Shay's a savage, but he turns on the charm when he has to. "Well, she's with me."

Dana widens her eyes and grins while looking at Maeve. "You hear that? He's jealous."

"Okay, Dana, out now." I wasn't jealous; my sister had no idea what she was talking about.

She holds up her hands. "I'll see you tonight?" She asks Maeve, who tries to smile, but she looks like someone who is in pain.

"Yeah. We will be there." If mom is cooking, then there is no way to say no.

Dana's still grinning as she leaves my room. I'm ready to slam the door when she puts her foot in the threshold, stopping me. "What, Dana?"

"Have you spoken to Richard?"

The change in topic is welcome. "No. Have you?"

She removes her foot, and her face grows serious. "He won't answer his phone. I want him to come home. He always liked Uncle Finn."

I hate seeing my sister upset. "Why don't I give him a ring?"

Her smile is instant as if she was hoping that would happen. "You're the best." She spins and jogs off. Lawlor is still at the door. I remove the key.

"You can go now." I close the door, but this time I don't lock it. I have something else that can keep Maeve here.

If she tries to run, I can threaten her by telling Dana the truth. Maybe having Dana here isn't such a bad thing.

"I can't do this." Maeve's voice comes from behind me.

"Do what?"

She's waving her hands between us. "This... with us. Lie to Dana."

Irritation has me stepping closer to her. She makes it sound hard to pretend she likes me. "You didn't do too badly earlier when you were screaming out my name."

Her lips form a thin line, and she folds her arms across her chest.

"Maybe you need more practice." Without her permission, I capture her mouth with mine, and she pushes me away. There isn't much force behind it, but I stop.

"Do you want me to tell Dana the truth?" I dip my head as she lowers her gaze. I won't let her get away that easy.

"No," she whispered, and she raises her head so I can look into her eyes.

I've never craved anything in my life. I've always had money, power, women. Anything I wanted, I got. I take Maeve's face in my hands and imagine if this was real. If for one moment I could truly have Maeve as mine.

I lean in and press my lips softly against her lips. "You're so beautiful." Her eyes widen, and her nostrils flare. Warm breath brushed across my lips, and I give her another kiss. "You always had my attention, even when you didn't want it." I smile into the next kiss, remembering picking on her when we were young. Even then, she was beautiful and defiant but off-limits to me.

When I release her face, she looks panicked for a moment. "You need to work on that. I didn't quite believe it." Her hands curl into fists at her sides.

I grin at her. "I'll practice." I walk around her and get dressed.

I had meant every fucking word.

That's why she's off-limits. She's too beautiful, and she isn't like us. She would be the ruin of me.

After tonight, I would fuck her and let her go.

CHAPTER EIGHTEEN

O'REAGAN
AN CHLANN

MAEVE

I can't go to dinner with him. I'm staring at myself in the bathroom mirror, wondering when this situation turned into this state of confusion.

I can't go.

I can't do this.

I march back into the bedroom. He's fully clothed in jeans and a blue sweater that is dyed the same color as his eyes. He's sitting on the bed, lacing up a pair of brown boots. My stomach tightens when his gaze travels up my legs to my face. I fold my arms across my chest.

149

"I have nothing to wear." I nod my head in agreement. It's a good argument as to why I can't go. I can't show up at his house in jeans and a plain top. It isn't appropriate for dinner.

"What's on you is fine."

I hated the word 'fine.' I unfold my arms. "I want to speak to my brother."

Jack exhales loudly. "You can't."

Trepidation drips like a broken tap, and the worst thought enters my mind. He's dead. I let him die.

Jack's standing. "He's fine." Jack walks to me and grips my arms, bending his large frame, so he meets my eye. "Maeve, he's fine. He's just recovering, so you can't ring him. But I'll take you to him."

Shivers race up and down my arm as feeling returns to my body. I swallow. "Thank you."

Jack releases me and goes to his desk, where he retrieves his phone and wallet. I store that information away for another time when I might need it, which I'm sure I will.

"Am I going now?" I'm moving to my bag to get my leather jacket.

"Yeah." Jack straightens and gives me a final look over as I pull on the jacket.

It's odd being out of the house with Jack. It's even odder climbing into the front of his jeep. In the light of day, he's even more handsome. I focus on the scenery that moves quickly past the window instead of him.

"You are studying psychology?"

Jack's question throws me for a loop. The way he says it, makes it sound conversational. Since when do we have conversations? I glance at him to gauge where he is going with this, but he's focused on the road.

"Yeah. But I've missed a few days now."

A muscle ticks in his jaw.

"I want to be a social worker."

"You'd be really good." Jack glances at me now, and I have no idea what to do with his compliment. "You never really talk about yourself." His gaze prods at me, to take advantage of this moment and to talk about myself.

"What is this? A practice run for tonight?" I bark a little too loud. He's making this normal, like this could be real, like he and I are a possibility. It's a mind game, so that he can smash me to fucking pieces at the end. He's always been crafty and cruel, and I've already fallen too far. I need to protect myself.

Everyone hurts you at the end.

His hands tighten around the steering wheel. I'm waiting for him to threaten me, lash out at me, or even laugh at me for getting so wound up.

"I'm just trying to get to know you, Maeve." He glances at me from the corner of his eye.

He could force me to answer or threaten me, and it's more disturbing when he doesn't. He falls silent, and now I'm feeling like a bitch.

I swallow the confusion and guilt and stare out the window as we drive onto the hospital grounds. A few scattered cars take up residence in the parking lot. A pot that's large enough to hold a tree has one lone leaf clinging on for life; that one brown leaf bends like the weight of the world is on it. Jack parks the furthest possible spot away from all the other vehicles, and I'm ready to tell him I can go in myself, but that's not going to happen. I can see it in how he takes the keys out of the ignition and unbuckles his seatbelt. Once he finishes, he doesn't move.

Neither do I.

"What's wrong?" His words are sharp.

"I'm sorry for putting my hands on you." I face him. "I should have never slapped you the other day. No matter how mad I was. I'm sorry." I need to get it off my chest.

I'm waiting for him to either accept my apology or say something smart. What I don't expect is for him to reach across the space between us and take my face in his hands. The kiss is harsh but softens swiftly. It's over far too quickly, but he still holds my face in his hands.

My heart beats wildly. I have no idea what this is. But when he touches me, I'm not so strong. I want to ask him what this is, but I'm the one moving and pressing my lips against his. I break the kiss and reach up, running my finger along his bottom lip. It's soft and warm, and when his tongue flicks out and licks my thumb, my gaze jumps to his—my heart slams against my chest. One look, and he can melt me so easily.

"Jack," I whisper his name against his lips. I don't know why I do it. It's odd to spend your life wanting someone and to have them now, but I know this is as false as all my dreams. I pull away, and his hands fall from my face. I unclip my belt, and without a word, I get out of the jeep.

Declan's asleep. He's ghastly white against the white bed sheets, and it's frightening. I'm beside him, holding his limp hand. Tears make a pathway down my face as I try to control the pain that eats away at me.

"Declan," I say his name, nearly afraid to wake him.

He stirs.

When he slowly opens his eyes, he smiles. "There she is. I knew you'd come."

I laugh through my tears. "You couldn't keep me away. How are you feeling?"

He exhales and closes his eyes before sinking back into the pillow. "Do you remember when you were like twelve? You and I were practicing kickboxing close to the radiator in the sitting room?"

"Yep, when I hit my toe off the corner and split the nail in half. Pure agony." I don't think I'll ever forget the pain.

Declan smiles. "You remember trying to wear socks over the cracked nail?"

I nod. Every time the sock got caught, I was waiting for it to rip off the toenail. I remember complaining about it for a week.

"I feel like that."

I release Declan's hand and drag a green chair over to his bedside before reclaiming his fingers in mine. I'm all too aware of Jack staring in the window outside the hospital room. He's on the phone, but he watches me as he speaks.

"So you feel like a cracked toenail," I clarify with a smile and push the tears away. He didn't need sadness right now. He needs to know that someone cares. We all do sometimes.

"Yeah." His cracked lips beg for water. I get up and pour him out a cup before putting a straw in it. Bringing it to my brother's mouth, the humor in his brown eyes never leaves. It's funny. It's always there no matter what. Maybe that's what draws me to him. No matter how bad things are, he always finds something to smile at.

"So, your boyfriend is very protective of you."

I know he's referring to Jack. I'm tempted to turn and look at Jack, but I focus on Declan. "He's not my boyfriend."

Declan smiles around the straw. "He's the one paying for the hospital bed, so you mean **something** to him." It was funny when Jack had led me to this room. My first thought was, *why does he have a room to himself?. Why isn't he in the general men's ward?* Now my question is answered like I feared it would be.

The hairs rise along my arms at Declan's words, and I take a look at Jack over my shoulder. He's still on the phone, his jaw set, but his gaze holds me in place. What would he want me to do to pay him back for this? I had nothing else to give.

I turn back to Declan and force a smile. "So are they taking care of you?" I ask, sitting back down.

"Three days, I've been clean."

I want to squeeze Declan's hand. He looks so good for day three.

"I'm getting methadone, but my head is clear."

"I'm so proud of you." I tighten my hold on his hand. His other hand is wired up to an IV drip.

"Mom?" Declan bites his bottom lip that's already suffered far too much abuse. His eyes grow sad, and I hate seeing him like this.

"I haven't seen her in a few days," I confess. "But don't worry, I'll swing by that way."

Declan's thin shoulders sink into the bed. "She hasn't come to see me." His voice is childlike.

"Maybe she doesn't know you're here, Declan. I never told her."

He's already shaking his head. "I rang her. She knows."

What the hell could I say to that?

"You focus on getting better. I need you."

Declan's gaze grows determined, and he nods. "I will. I promise, Maeve."

I smile at his promise that he has broken so many times. I sit back in the chair, and we just talk like we used to. I talk about college; he talks about his latest girlfriend, who he can't even remember her name. He has me laughing, just like he always does.

A tap to the window brings me right back to reality. My time is up.

"I have to go."

Declan licks his dry lips. "Can I have a bit more water?"

I hate leaving him. I think he hates me leaving him too. He's stalling, and that makes this harder. I retrieve the water from the bedside table and bring it to his lips. He's still so frail. He shouldn't be alone like this. He takes a sip from the straw and releases it.

"I'll come back as soon as I can." I'm struggling to keep it together as I place the cup back on the table and stand up.

The door opens, and I don't know how I feel when Jack steps into the room. I want to protect Declan from him. The room seems to shrink in size. I want to hide Declan from him. It reminds me of how Jack would have left him to die.

He nods at Declan.

"Cian told me you were paying for my bed." Declan tries to sit up, and I step in, helping him with the pillows. I wonder if Declan remembers being in the shed. Does he remember Jack carrying me away and leaving him there? I hope not. I'd hate for him to think that someone thought he was disposable.

"Don't worry about it." Jack's voice sounds strange. Strangled.

"No, once I'm on my feet, I'll pay you back."

I know that won't happen. When Declan's more propped up, I take a step back.

"Don't worry. I've got it," I smile at Declan, not wanting him to even worry about something like that. He just needed to focus on getting better.

Declan's shaking his head, and I hate the serious expression on his face. "I said, I'll pay it back."

"Okay." There is something different in his voice that I've never heard before, so I agree.

Declan looks beyond me towards Jack. "And the twelve grand. That's my debt, not hers."

Panic infiltrates my system, and I'm looking at Jack, pleading with him not to tell my brother about our agreement.

"Fair enough." Jack stands tall, and I'm so grateful that he would allow Declan to believe he was repaying all the money. No matter what, it meant the world to me. I stuff my hands in my leather jacket pockets, so I don't step over to Jack and hug him.

"Now, will you get some rest?" I smile at Declan, and there is a look of peace on his face.

"Yes." He closes his eyes. "I'll see you soon?"

I lean in and press a kiss to his hollow cheek. "Yeah. I'll see you soon." I'm grateful his eyes are closed, so he can't see the pain in my eyes. I give his hand one final squeeze and leave without looking at Jack.

The moment Jack joins me, I give my thanks. "Thank you."

Jack just nods.

"I know I'll pay it back, but thank you for letting him believe he can."

Jack pauses, and I stop walking too.

"You can thank me tonight."

My heart palpitates. Tonight? Tonight would be the night. I nod even as my cheeks burn. I'm nervous. I'm scared. I'm excited. That last thought has me walking fast while tucking my chin into my chest so he can't see my burning face.

He's already chipped away at the barrier I had put up around my heart.

No, it's not chipped.

He's smashed it.

After tonight, I might be able to leave his home, but I'd never truly leave, Jack.

I never have.

CHAPTER NINETEEN

O'REAGAN

AN CHLANN

JACK

She's not saying much in the jeep. For the first time, I don't want to prod. Seeing her in the hospital with her brother made me feel like a monster. She loved him. I had been willing to let him die.

I glance at Maeve, and she tightens her arms around her waist. The heat in the jeep is instant once I turn it on, and Maeve loosens her deadly hold on her waist.

"Was your mother okay?"

Maeve's eyes are filled with mistrust, but I don't blame her. I haven't given her a reason to trust me or to think my questions weren't genuine.

After we had left her brother, I had given her my phone to ring her mother; their conversation had seemed brief, and Maeve had been withdrawn ever since.

"Yeah." She turns her head, so she's facing the window and making sure I can't see any of her face.

"Are you sure?" I pull up outside my parents' house. I notice the stiffness in Maeve's shoulders as she glares at the gates that open slowly.

"Thank you for allowing me to use your phone. But don't pretend you care about my family."

I continue up the drive, and I want to tell her I don't give two flying fucks about them. She's right. But what I do care about is Maeve and how they affect her. So, in a really fucked up, roundabout way, I do care. Once I pull up close to the door, Maeve doesn't get out straight away. Knowing her, she's preparing an apology. She can't seem to help herself.

"You're right. I don't." I answer, honestly.

She shakes her head while unclipping her seatbelt.

The front door opens, splashing light onto the large steps that rise up to the front door. Maeve is out before I can finish explaining myself. Taking the keys out, I get out of the car.

The moment Dana spots Maeve, she drags her into a hug. Mom is hovering in the hall. She keeps glancing at Maeve with a soft smile on her face. She's always been fond of her.

Once Dana releases Maeve, my mother swallows her up in a hug. "We haven't seen you in a long time." She kisses Maeve on both cheeks. "It's so great to have you over for dinner."

"Thanks for inviting me."

My mother waves it off before leaving Maeve and stepping up to me. Dana and I have our mother's blue eyes and dark hair.

"Why am I only seeing you now?" Her tone isn't as friendly as it had been with Maeve, and I bend and hug her tightly.

"I'm sorry, mom, I've been busy." When she leans out, she smiles and lowers her voice as Dana takes Maeve by the arm and leads her into the kitchen.

"I'm glad it's with Maeve." She's always encouraged Dana's friendship with Maeve. "She's a good girl."

If my mother ever knew what I'd done, she wouldn't be happy. She'd be furious. I hate where my mind goes, so I drag it back to someone who wouldn't judge me. "So, where's Dad?"

"Out the back with Shay and Cian."

That's enough to piss me off. "Who invited them?"

"Your sister wanted her cousins here. You know how she loves a full house."

I try to hide my hostility as I move into the kitchen with my mother in tow. The double doors are opened onto the patio where a large table has been set up. Laughter floats from the table and into the kitchen. Dana's introducing Maeve to Shay, and he's smiling like he works for Santa Claus.

"Aren't you worried Dana will learn something from them?" I keep my voice low.

The horror in my mother's eyes is naïve of her. Dana couldn't be kept in the dark forever. It made no sense in our world.

"She won't." My mother has paused in placing drinks on a tray, and now she continues. She hands me the tray. "Take these out like a good lad."

I take the tray and press a kiss against my mother's cheek, hating seeing her upset. She relaxes instantly.

I step out onto the patio. The small lights that circle the large pillars are the main source of light. Maeve is still standing as I pause beside her.

Without looking at anyone, I place a kiss along her jawline. She tenses before looking at me; our lips are so close that I'm tempted to kiss her. Her smell seems to float on the warm breeze and entices me to lean a little closer.

"Let the girl take a breath," Shay speaks up, and I plant a light kiss on her lips before sitting the tray down on the table.

"Shay, so great to see you." He takes a bottle of Bud, and with a grin, he raises it before taking a long swallow.

My mother arrives, wiping her hands on her apron. "Shay was telling us about the job you are both working on."

What the fuck had he said?

"It's only plans to merge and open a pub. A pipe dream at the moment." Shay smiles as my mother sits down beside him. He really has the power to make anyone see him for whatever he wants at that moment. He's attentive, and his voice is gentle. Everything he says comes with a smile, and Dana and my mother lap it up.

Cian, of course, doesn't hide his hate for Shay.

I pull out a chair for Maeve, and she plops into it like she's unable to keep standing. Once I'm seated, I finally look at my father, whom I have been avoiding. He's watching my mother like I've seen him do a million times before. There is always that look of contentment in his eyes that never really settles, but when he looks at my mother, it's like she's a calming hand. I've never seen him look at anyone like that, not Dana or me. Only my mother seems to have that impact on him.

"Well, you are merging with the right person. You know Jack owns the Viper, and it's doing so well." My mother's words are filled with pride. I pick up a bottle of Bud and fill a glass. Placing the glass beside Maeve, I glare at Shay.

"I might stick around for a while and learn the tricks of the trade." Dana flicks her hair across her shoulder, and my father sits up straight, no longer captivated with my mother. He wants Dana to know what we do. He always has. But my mother said no, and this is one thing he hasn't dared go against her on. The strain is visible on my mother's shoulders as she waits for me to answer.

"Yeah, I've room for another bartender," I tell Dana.

"I'm more of an office kind of girl."

My mother relaxes. "I'm sure Jack can find something for you in the office. There must be stock control, or accounts, or even filing. Oh, maybe you could answer the phone."

I drink from the bottle and nod. "Yeah, I can find something."

Dana squeals and I know she won't be happy when she arrives at a boring job. Dana didn't settle. This time would be no different, but if it made my mother happy for just one moment, that's all that mattered.

"How's your brother?" Cian asks Maeve, and she stiffens beside me.

"We just visited him. He's doing great." I fill in before turning to my mother. "He fell at work and broke his leg."

The lie is quick, and my mother gives her condolences to Maeve.

"Declan got a job?" Dana smirks, and I quickly glance at Maeve, smirking back like they share a secret joke. I'm sure Dana knows all about Maeve's family.

"It was short-lived, in a garage," Maeve answers Dana while trying to hide a smile.

Cian keeps stealing glances at Maeve, and it's pissing me off. I want to drag her chair closer to me.

"Who's ready for food?" My mother gets up.

"Do you need any help?" Maeve looks ready to bolt.

"No, you sit and enjoy, sweetheart. Dana can help me." My sister obediently follows my mother away from the table. My father hasn't spoken one word, and that doesn't sit too well with me.

"Any word on how Finn is?" I ask him. He's sitting back, taking it all in. What my father is doing with that information is anyone's guess.

"He's still the same." My father leans forward, unbuttoning his suit jacket. Maeve seems to have gained all his attention. "Aren't you going to introduce me?"

It's automatic that I reach out and take Maeve's hand. Her fingers are stiff, and it takes a few seconds before she wraps her fingers around mine. "Maeve, this is my father."

"I know." Maeve's voice is harsh, and that surprises me. I give her hand a little squeeze but don't look at her.

"Girlfriend?" My father asks while sitting back; he's assessing everything between us.

My gaze trails to Shay as he smirks at my discomfort.

I refocus on my father. "Yes, she is."

My father nods. "Welcome to the family, Maeve."

Maeve is still beside me. "Thank you." She doesn't sound very pleased. "Can I use the bathroom?"

I release her hand reluctantly. "Yeah. I'll show you."

She rises and waves me off. "Dana can."

We all half rise as she leaves the table, and I watch her leave. Once she disappears through the double doors, my father speaks. "Does she know what you do?"

"I think her family is in a similar line of business." Shay offers up like anyone fucking asked him.

"Sort of," I admit.

"You need to tell her everything, or it will never work." I'm surprised by my father's words. I thought he would be trying to convince me to get rid of her. It's also odd for him to talk about anything that's within our family with other people here. He's extremely private.

I nod, unsure how to answer and pick up my drink, but it pauses at my lips as he continues.

"She'll need to know that her whole family is a target once she's with you." His side jab is heard loud and clear.

I take a large drink and place the bottle back on the table. "I'll make sure to tell her that."

My mother comes back with her hands full and places plates of barbecued food on the table, Dana follows behind, and Shay is smiling up at them as he starts to fill his plate. Cian, on the other hand, is eating as he stacks his plate sky high. He's like a fucking savage. I can sense my father's eyes still on me, but I get up and excuse myself.

The downstairs bathroom door opens as I approach it. Maeve pauses with her foot halfway out, and I gently steer her back inside and lock the door behind us.

Alarm flashes across her face and the worry widens her brown eyes. "I'm sorry about your dad..."

I stop her. "I know he can be intimidating."

Maeve focuses on a light over a wide mirror and folds her arms across her chest. I hate how closed off she is.

"But he's one of the good guys."

Her gaze is on fire when it snaps to me. "Just like you," she says, and the smile that slowly develops on her lips is raw and carries a note of pain. "Do you remember the things you said to me as a child? The things your father said about me?" She frowns, and lines appear on her forehead.

Her anger is clinging to her like a second skin, and I want to peel it off. I have no idea what she's talking about.

"No, I don't."

She unfolds her arms. "Of course, you don't. What am I to you?"

A knock at the bathroom door has me pausing. I don't know how to answer her, anyway. What is she to me? A craving. A want. A longing. She's all of those things and so much more.

The knock gets louder, and I swing the door open. Why the fuck am I not surprised. It's Cian, and he's too busy looking over my shoulder at Maeve. I step in front of her.

"What the fuck do you want?"

Maeve inhales sharply behind me.

"So fucking charming," Cian says. "I need to take a piss."

I reach back to take Maeve's hand, and when her fingers slide into mine, I feel a sense of relief. I had thought she wouldn't take it. Cian glances at her as we move past. Before going back outside, I stop her in the kitchen. I want her to make my family believe this is real. The look in my mother's and Dana's eyes is really something, and how this is making me feel like it could be real.

I pull Maeve slowly into my arms. She's hesitant, but when she's against my chest, she seems to relax.

"Remember, you promised to sell this. So far, you really aren't doing so well." I'm a bastard for my words, and she stiffens in my arms, but I want this.

"Don't worry, Jack." Maeve smiles as she steps out of my arms. "You'll get your pound of flesh." She keeps smiling as she goes back out to the table, and I feel like a fucking monster.

Cian stops beside me, and I'm in no mood. "Say anything, and I don't care who's watching. I'll smash your fucking face in."

Silence.

I glance at Cian. "Got it?"

He nods with a clenched jaw. "Loud and clear."

Chapter Twenty

O'REAGAN
AN CHLANN

MAEVE

He is worse than I thought. It's moments, it's glimpses that I think I see something more in his eyes for me, and then he goes and reminds me of our contract—of what is hanging over my head. I pick up the beer; I don't drink, but right now, I'm not doing so well, so I partake in something I hate. When Jack sits beside me and drags my chair closer like I'm a possession, I drink more and focus on the red and white tablecloth. The liquor has a funny effect on my system. I shrug out of my leather jacket as heat that I hadn't felt before starts to fill my body.

Cian returns, and everyone starts to eat. Dana and her mother keep the chat flowing. All the men seem to smile and nod at whatever they say. I love their relationship. Everything Dana says about college and her trip to Italy, Svetlana's excitement for her daughter, is genuine; she wants to know everything.

My gaze skims the men. Bastards. Each and every one of them.

They are all the same, just like my father. I drink some more until I gain Dana's attention.

"You're drinking?" She leans forward while folding a napkin. Her attention is focused on the napkin, like what she's saying isn't important.

"Just the one." My voice sounds defensive, and I curl in on myself when I gain Liam's attention. I hate how he looks at me. I glare at him as I drink, getting a bit braver. How I'd love to call him out on the cruel things he said when I was a child. I should laugh at him and say, look at me, sitting at your table, eating your food, pretending to fuck your son.

Jack's hand touches my leg, and I know the hostility is pouring off me. I swallow my pride and look up at Jack with a smile pressed to my lips. It's a smile that is keeping all the pain in, and I won't let it go because I fear that if I do, I will fall apart at this table. Considering right now, even though I'm angry, this is perfect. Sitting here with Jack as my boyfriend, enjoying food with his family and Dana, my best friend. I'm surrounded by a darkness that presses on our backs. Within these four pillars, it's like we are safe, encircled in fairy lights. It makes me think of my bed-time prayer that my father said with me every night.

"I lay my body down to sleep, I pray the Lord my soul to keep, and if I die, before I wake, I pray to God my soul to take. All four corners of my bed, all four corners of my spread, Matthew, Mark, Luke, and John, bless this bed that Maeve lies on." My father's voice whispers in my ear, and pain lances my heart. I used to picture the four angels, each holding a corner of my bedspread.

Jack leans in slowly, and presses a kiss to my lips that I accept. I need something to anchor myself into right now. I reach up and touch his cheek. The kiss is short, but it sucks all the anger from my system, leaving me dizzy with longing.

"So maybe after, we can go and check out the 'Viper'?" Dana's words pierce through the veil that Jack's kiss seems to have placed around me.

"That sounds like fun," Shay speaks up with the sweetest smile on his face. No matter what, I don't like him. I don't like the intelligence that lies behind his eyes as he speaks. I feel he's speaking one thing but completely thinking another. It's a weird assessment since I haven't been around him much, but that's how I feel when I look at Shay.

"You're coming." Dana is leaning over, making sure I hear her.

"It's up to Jack." I take another drink, and like how it makes me feel. Jack still holds my hand, and it's nice. The warmth that radiates from him is different from the warmth the drink is creating. I know the drink is false somehow, but his isn't. I feel it from the tips of my fingers all the way through me.

"Whatever you want." Jack smiles down at me, and I don't know if it's the small lights that seem to flicker around us, or the liquid that flows through my system, but his smile seems real. Heat rushes to my cheeks, and I dip my head, not wanting him to see what I really feel for him. "I think it would be fun," I say, looking up from under my eyelashes.

Jack faces forward. "It's settled; we will go to the Viper."

"I might pass," Cian speaks up. He's been quiet most of the night; I keep sensing his gaze on me, but each time I look up, he's eating. Maybe this is what comes with drinking, a sense of paranoia.

"Your mother and I will pass." Liam's voice carries that note of authority, and he always sounds like he thinks he's above everyone else. Above humans, above the law, even above gods.

Svetlana laughs. "I wouldn't dare dream of it."

She's still stunning and would attract a lot of attention, but she's looking at Liam like he's everything she could have dreamed of. I don't get it. Do I look at Jack like that? I take another drink to find the bottle empty.

"Would you like another?" I'm surprised at Liam's offer. I'm surprised he even noticed. I should decline.

"Yes, thanks."

"I'd spin you around the floor," Shay smiles up at Svetlana with a sickeningly sweet smile on his face.

"Such a charmer." She's smiling back.

Shay's gaze skips to me, and his smile falters just a little. I wonder if he can see the dislike I hold for him. The only two people at this table that have ever shown me kindness are Dana and Cian.

"You should come," I say to Cian, hating that I haven't made an effort when he has done so much for me.

He pauses eating. I don't know how he still has any space in his stomach for food. It's like a bottomless pit. "I just might do that, Reilly."

I hate it when people use my second name as my title.

I don't dare look at Jack, his anger is practically rolling off him, and it's nice.

He's jealous. I didn't think that was possible. Liam places a bottle and a fresh glass in front of me.

"Thank you." I have to force the words out, but I also will remember my manners. No matter what he might think of me, I was raised to have respect for people. I most certainly would never speak ill of a child like he had done about me.

"You don't have to stay. Go on now and have fun." Svetlana is speaking to Dana, but she smiles at me too. "Thank you so much for coming, Maeve."

Her kindness has always been there. How she ended up with Liam will confuse me until I'm covered in clay.

"Thank you for having me."

Svetlana rises and starts gathering up the plates.

"Are you ready to go?" Jack releases my hand, and I take a good few mouthfuls of my drink before I nod. I know Dana is watching me, but I refuse to meet her eye.

"Let's go."

Shay is still seated along with Cian. Jack pauses.

"I want a quick word with Liam. I'll follow you." For the first time, Shay's voice sounds real, gritty, and he carries violence around his shoulders like a weapon. He could strike, and he wouldn't think twice about it.

"See you later, then." Jack doesn't ask why Cian is still sitting.

"Are you coming?" I can't leave him out. Jack reclaims my hand in his.

Cian hesitates, and I have no idea what's running through his mind. But he finally stands to his full height, towering over everyone else.

"Yeah, I will." He's grinning, and I'm aware of Jack's hand tightening on mine.

Jack finally stops eyeing Cian, and we leave the table. Svetlana walks us to the door, and her goodbyes are filled with hugs and promises for us to come again. I hang on to her a little longer than I should, but for me, this is really goodbye.

I want to thank her for always having been kind to me, but if I start speaking in full truths, my smile will slip, and words that I'm keeping in will pour from my lips.

I get in the back of the jeep with Dana. Cian turns up the music the moment he gets in. Jack is the last, and he turns it off. Cian doesn't dare turn it back on.

"You have to tell me how this happened?" Dana's gaze is glazed over from the drink. She isn't drunk but merry. She's pointing at the back of Jack's chair.

"It's a long story." I reach for the stupid line that needs to be removed from the English language. Nothing is ever that long of a story. It means either I don't have the energy to get into it, or it's none of your business. Doing that to Dana isn't right.

The jeep starts to move, and the silence is stretching out like the road before us. "I met Jack at the Viper."

Dana grins. "What the hell. I never thought you'd go there."

She's right. I wouldn't. Partying isn't my thing. "Yeah, well, Declan had an episode."

Dana's smile falters, and she nods as she gets what I'm saying.

Telling the truth, in a sense, makes me feel less of a bad person. "So I went to the Viper to blow off some steam."

I know Cian and Jack are listening to each and every word I speak.

Dana rolls down the window before sitting back while letting the breeze catch dark strands of her hair. "Well, I'm glad you did." She turns her head, so she's facing me now; her eyes are half closed. "You both always fancied each other."

The child in me that kept that hidden, dies a little. I'd never confessed to Dana how I felt about her brother, so now I know I must have been

172

obvious in the way I looked at him or acted around him. Her words sink in, and she had said both.

I snort. "Hardly."

"You didn't fancy me when we were kids?" Jack moves the rear-view mirror so he can see me.

"You were a dick," I say.

Cian sniggers from the front seat.

Jack's lip tugs up slightly, but his eyes dance with humor. I want him to look away from me. "I might have been a dick, but you liked me."

"God, you're so full of yourself. You always had a thing for her, too." Dana says as she slowly starts to roll up the window.

My heart jumps a little as I deny it in my head.

"Yeah, I did." Jack meets my gaze in the rearview mirror, and I don't want him to play with my heart.

"You sure had a funny way of showing it." The words are a growl, and I sit back, trying to control my emotions. I need more drinks, or maybe the drink is doing this.

"Like you said, I was a dick." Jack's acknowledgement, I hate. He can't act like the good guy.

"You still are," Cian speaks under his breath, but we all hear it. I'd love to know why they are at loggerheads.

We pull up at the back of "The Viper."

"Well, no matter what, I'm glad you guys did the ugly, and you are now my sister-in-law." Dana's excitement is misdirected, and I glance at Jack. He can smash his sister's heart.

I can't even answer, so I get out, and Dana dances around the far side of the jeep. I don't wait for Jack but follow Cian into the club. I want to get lost in the mass of people. I want to be sucked in and spat out later tonight when I'm too drunk to remember the things that I would do.

Tonight I would drink and give my virginity to Jack, so I could walk away from him for good before he did any more damage to me.

The club is packed, the air is warm, and I shrug out of my jacket. Cian glances at me over his shoulder, a cheeky smile on his face as he reaches back and takes my jacket from my hand. "I'll put it somewhere safe."

"Thank you," I mouth the words, and he's ready to walk away, but I grab his arm. I might not see him for a while, and right now, while we are surrounded by sweaty bodies and pulsing music, I drag his large form down to me so I can whisper in his ear. "Thank you for helping my brother. I'll never forget it." I brush a kiss to his cheek; the stubble rubs against my lips.

"I know about you and Jack."

I pull away as my body seems to jerk.

"I know he's forcing you to do this. Pretend to be with him."

"He told you." Fear clings to my words. "Please don't tell Dana." Or anyone I want to add.

"I won't, but if you're in trouble, I can help you."

I laugh, but it's short-lived. I wasn't going to borrow from Billy to pay Bob when they were two sides of the coin; no matter what, they were O'Reagans.

"I'm good." I finally tell Cian.

Fingers twine with mine, and I know it's Jack as he moves me away from Cian. Jack's smell circles me as he brings me deeper into the crowd. He spins me around, and when our gazes clash, I hate him. I hate him for what he is making me feel. Pulling me closer, I stumble into his wide chest, and he moves us slowly. I have no idea what is running through his mind. He holds my gaze before lowering his head to me. No matter what, I can't resist Jack, and that's what makes him dangerous.

The sultry music has my hips moving. I leave Jacks' arms, breaking the kiss, and continue to sway. His arms circle my waist as he drags our bodies back together. His hard chest at my back has my heart beating rapidly when I think of his body on mine. His fingers dance along my neck as he drags my hair aside and places a warm kiss that has me exhaling loudly. I continue to sway, knowing my ass is rubbing against his cock, that's growing rapidly.

His hot kisses are setting my body on fire. I step away from him again and move through the crowd. I need a drink. I need to fuel my body with bravery or sugar coat what I'm about to do. I reach the full bar and try to get the barman's attention, but he's overrun. A warm body presses beside me, and the moment the bartender sees him, he approaches us.

"A Bud and..." Jack looks down at me.

"Vodka." I've never drank it.

"What mixer?" The bartender leans in so I can hear him.

"7up."

He leaves, and the music blasts across the room. Strobe lights bounce off every surface, and everyone looks so happy. So alive. They sway and smile and drink and laugh while I'm being dragged under the current, and only getting bubbles of air before being dragged back down again. I know right now he's watching me with those ice-blue eyes. I get a tiredness in my heart at trying to keep upright. My gaze clashes with his, and I want to confess what I feel, what he's making me feel, and maybe he would give me a real chance. His large hand trails up my arm, firing off my nerve endings. I'm a mess around him.

Don't sleep with him. He'll destroy you.

I drown out the voice of reason when my vodka arrives. I drink the liquid in three large gulps as it burns my insides.

I land the empty glass on the counter, and Jack's laughter nearly undoes me.

"That's not how you drink vodka." He speaks through his laughter.

My body buzzes, and I'm feeling a little braver. I step closer and lick my lips. His laughter stops. "That's how I drink vodka." I don't know why I said that. It isn't sexy, but Jack's gaze darkens with what I note as lust. So, maybe it was sexy.

Jack leans in, and as I fall into his eyes, I know directing him into his office and giving myself to him will be the easiest part of all this.

I know if I do this, I'll be willingly stepping into the waves to be gobbled up and spat out by Jack O'Reagan.

CHAPTER TWENTY-ONE

O'REAGAN
AN CHLANN

MAEVE

His lips are warm on mine, and I sink into the kiss that's fueled with lust and vodka. My hands wrap around his neck, dragging him closer.

"Jack." Cian's voice breaks the hold that Jack's kiss has on me. When I slowly step back, Cian is standing way too close. My foggy brain takes a second to let the idea that Cian is standing here looking all kinds of pissed off, demanding Jack's attention.

I'm widening my eyes at him, trying to ask him what the hell he's doing, but he doesn't acknowledge me.

"A word."

Jack's hand still touches my sides. "I'm busy." Jack's fingers sink into my skin, and I'm expecting Cian to look away. A muscle clenches in his jaw, and his gaze swings to me before it returns to Jack.

"It won't take long." Within Cian's gaze, I can see he's going to say something about me.

I want to step in front of Jack and tell Cian everything is going to be okay. Jack's warm hands leave my sides and rise up, gripping my face dragging my attention away from Cian.

"I'll only be a moment." His promise is sealed with a press of his lips against mine, and then he's gone with Cian in tow. I watch them leave through the door I had come through only a few days ago when I had snuck into the club.

I turn and get the barman's attention instantly—perks of being seen with Jack.

"The same again," I say, and he nods.

I take the vodka, and he slips back down to the crowd of people who are waiting for drinks. I'm not charged, and I turn to the crowd and down the Vodka. The burning seems more intense than the last time, but my fractured system appreciates the numbness it offers. I land the glass back on the counter and walk away towards the door. I don't want to lose my nerve with Jack. I want him in here now so I can do what needs to be done.

I open the door; the hallway is empty. Slipping out of the club, my ears still register the music, but it's like my head is filled with cotton wool.

I hear voices further down. I'm careful with my steps; even in my alcohol fazed state, I'm still aware of my footsteps.

"She's a decent skin, and what you're doing..." Cian's voice has me freezing, and something large slams against the wall, making me stop walking.

"What am I doing?" Jack's voice has dropped a couple of degrees, and it freezes me in place. I've never heard his tone so threatening, and it scares me enough to consider returning.

"Think, you moron. Think carefully about your next words."

There's another bang, and I move my back against the wall like I might be able to sink into it.

"I'm fond of Maeve." Cian's words have me ready to smile, but another bang on the wall has it slipping away as a nervous tingle starts at the tip of my fingers, like I want to reach into the room and see what's making the banging noise. Deep in the back of my mind, I register the hiss from Cian each time Jack slams him into the wall.

"She is with me." Jack's voice is still deadly.

"She's only a piece of pussy to you." I'm pushing off the wall at Cian's insult.

A loud crash has me stopping.

"That pussy is mine."

I'm moving away from Jack and Cian and back into the club as I grabble for air. I don't know what I expected. For Jack to tell Cian not to refer to me like that, or to say he actually felt something deeper for me, and then to refer to me as a piece of pussy, is like a clawed fist tightening around my heart. I rub my chest like I can rub away the pain. I rush into the crowd, who continue to flow around me.

I had said it from the start that he would ruin me all over again, but I didn't think the cut would be this deep or wide. I'm back at the bar, ordering what I hope is my final drink.

The bartender takes a bit longer, but once I have my drink, Jack is beside me. His smile is forced, and the tension in his shoulders would make me think Cian said something to upset him. I plaster on a smile like a hooker layers on makeup, and down the vodka.

I push away all the questions and reasons that I shouldn't do this and focus on one. I want, no I *need,* to get away from Jack O'Reagan.

I reach in and place a hand on his chest; his heart beats fast under my palm. Reaching up on the tip of my toes, I press a kiss to his lips.

"I want you," I whisper against his lips.

His large hand sinks into my hair, and already, the reality of that one touch and the effect it has on me, has me rethinking what I'm about to do.

"I want you now." I press a kiss against his jawline and move my body closer to his. "Can we go somewhere private?" I take a peek up at him.

He's staring at me, and his gaze is swirling with lust, but there is something else that I can't identify. I shouldn't care about what this asshole is feeling. I remind myself of the conversation I had just overheard.

I was a piece of pussy to him, so that's what I would be.

I smile and take his hand in mine. I easily lead him to his office door. He takes a glance around him as if checking to see who's watching. Most people are in their own little bubbles of bliss. I just want him to hurry up so I can have this done and over. The moment he opens the door, my stomach starts to shift, and I hesitate at the door. Jack's reaching for the light switch, and I step in, stopping him.

"Leave the lights off." My voice shakes, and I need more alcohol.

But if I leave here, I don't think I will ever be brave enough to do this again.

I push the door closed behind us and plunge us into darkness. Closing my eyes, I spin, and it's like the turmoil inside me is spilling out into the time and place.

I shiver as his hands land on my face; opening my eyes, I can make him out—light filters in from the window.

His lips are hesitant on mine, but once his warmth starts to wrap around me, I melt into him and return the kiss. It's soft at first but soon grows deeper. My body responds easily. I'm running my hands across his wide chest, his top brushing my palms, and it's like electricity, an undercurrent touching my skin. I want to step away, but I also want to turn it up. Pushing up his top, he breaks the kiss and yanks it off. His hands reclaim my face, his mouth reclaims my lips, and I'm touching his flesh again. My core tightens, and I'm surprised with the level of want I'm feeling for him. I can't see him, and I'm glad because that would make this so much more. To see those ice-blue eyes focused on just me like he's been thinking about having me. Me, Maeve Reilly. Not just another female to fuck.

"What's wrong?" Jack's breathless.

I realize I have stopped kissing him.

"Nothing." I grip his shoulders and drag his mouth back to mine. His large hands grip my thighs, and I instantly wrap my legs around his waist as he carries me back towards his desk. The heat of his chest penetrates my top, and my breasts feel heavier in my bra. He lowers me onto the desk. The light here is stronger from the window. I can make out Jack much more. I close my eyes before I falter and lose my nerve.

I lean back and pull off my top. Jack stands staring at me, and in the dim light, I allow him to have a good look. Reaching back, I unhook my bra. My breasts tumble free.

Jack's hands move, and he unbuckles his jeans, dragging them and his boxers down. His large cock springs free, and I drag my eyes away from it. How the hell is that going to fit inside me? My heart picks up a fast beat, but my fear is extinguished as Jack steps in and starts to kiss me again. Wetness dampens my panties, and I'm shuffling towards his large cock. It brushes my jeans, and everything in me jumps at once. I groan.

My lips leave his, and I'm kissing his neck, sucking in the taste of Jack. His skin is warm, and his cologne lingers all over him. My stomach somersaults as his hands trail down to my jeans. The button is opened, and I press another kiss to his chest, his movements are quicker, and I lean back and lift myself, allowing him to drag the jeans off me. I don't feel cold. I should be cold sitting on his desk in just my panties, but I've never felt such heat. Jack drags me forward, and my core brushes his cock with only the flimsy material of my panties, keeping us apart. Strong fingers reach along the side of my panties, and a tear has the material yanked against my skin; wetness stains my inner thighs as Jack presses his cock at my opening.

I shuffle closer, and his lips move along my jawline before capturing one of my hard nipples. His teeth graze the sensitive skin, and I hiss, and I push myself closer to him. Jack's cock jerks against my opening, and my hands dig into his shoulders as he nips my nipple.

His mouth is gone, and I'm left panting as he grips his cock and positions it right at my opening. With one large hand on the base of my back, he really looks at me and pauses. Alarm has me pushing myself onto his cock so he won't stop. The head pushes in, and the stinging has me freezing, but warmth grows around the stinging, and Jack pulls out before pushing the head of his cock back in. He grips my hands and moves me to the edge of the desk. Bending, he slides his cock in further. His groan into my neck has me sinking my nails into his shoulders. The stinging grows, and I tighten my eyes as Jack pushes in and exhales another loud moan that makes me clench around him. He moves out slowly, and the stinging subsides. I focus on his lips that are now pressed against mine, and this time, when he slowly inches in, I groan along with him. My groans have him pushing deeper, stretching me, widening my tunnel for his large cock. He pulls out slowly, but when he moves back in, it's faster and more urgent. I sink my tongue into his mouth, and his hands grip my face before grabbing my ass.

I'm nearly off the desk as Jack fills my pussy with his cock, and my moans grow loud along with his. His kisses are frantic, and his cock stays in me as he carries us over to the wall. The cold brick against my back sends small shivers racing across my skin. Jack pushes it all away with the warmth of his chest that's crushed against mine. I keep my legs wrapped around his waist. His movements grow faster, and the stinging is so slight now. A sensation of needing more, more air, more of him, is overwhelming, and my legs tighten around his waist as he slams himself into me. My back connects with the wall over and over again, and each time I sink my hands deeper into his shoulders.

Our kisses are sloppy, and I'm panting, fighting for air, as he moves faster. There is nothing gentle in his movements, and the force he slams into me has his moans fast and hard against my mouth.

His pounding grows in intensity, and it's like a match striking and lighting up. The spark in me combusts, and Jack fucks me harder as I cry out as each wave smashes into me and my back smashes into the wall. Jack's release follows mine, and he moans loudly into my mouth, taking the last bit of air from my lungs.

The lights behind my closed eyes flash rapidly and soon die down with each stroke that is growing slower. I take my nails out of his shoulders, and sweat trickles down my back. Opening my eyes, I look right into ice-blue ones that are soft and... I swallow as he pumps a few more times inside me. I see something deeper than a want, but it's my mind trying to salvage this moment. My back stops slamming against the wall, and Jack stops moving. His heavy breaths are against my neck. My hands wrap around his neck, and I hug him. I hug him because I've never felt anything like that before. I've never felt this way about anyone before. I inhale Jack's scent, and one part of me hopes I never forget his smell, but the survivor part of me hopes I never remember this moment.

Girls have said the pain was bad; you bleed after. For me, it may have been uncomfortable at the start, but then it was perfect.

My legs are lowered to the ground, and the shake that enters my body has me releasing Jack and reaching for the wall. He removes himself from me.

"Give me a minute." The moment he goes, he takes all the heat and sensitivity of this situation with him.

Naked against the wall, I feel like a piece of meat. A piece of pussy.

Jack hands me a handful of tissues. His gaze is intense.

"Thanks." I take them and wait until he turns away before I clean between my legs. I take a steady step towards the desk. Jack is there, but so are my clothes.

I pick up my jeans and slip them up my legs. My torn underpants I pocket before putting on my bra.

"Are you okay?" Jack's voice sounds strange.

Picking up my top, I pull it on, feeling a bit more like myself. Turning to Jack, I try not to ogle his bare chest. He's in his jeans, looking like a god who just had a good fuck.

"Yeah."

Jack takes a step towards me, and he runs his fingers through my hair and grips my neck. The kiss he places on my swollen lips is soft and unexpected.

I clear my throat and step back. My stomach roils, and I swallow before raising my head.

"The debt is cleared. I've done my part. So...." This feels wrong, and I hate how my heart trips and falls over itself, but I did this for freedom.

Only, I really believe I've backed myself into a cage that I will never be free from. How could I ever forget him?

Not after that.

"Goodbye, Jack."

CHAPTER TWENTY-TWO

O'REAGAN
AN CHLANN

JACK

Maeve is walking away from me like she thinks that can happen. Having her here has changed everything.

I can't let her go.

Ever.

"No."

She pauses and swings around with fire in her eyes. She's fucking stunning. She's mine. No matter the cost, I'll keep her here.

She moves until her legs are tightly pressed together like she's remembering what we just did. "I cleared my bill." I hate the note of pleading I hear in her voice.

I want to tell her I didn't give two shits about the money. It was so I could have her. The financial cost of having her meant nothing to me. I had spent my whole life wanting her, hating her because I couldn't have her. My father had drilled it into my head that she was an Outsider and would never understand our ways.

"You're not leaving." My words are final. I'll tie her to the chair if I have to. After having her for the first time, I know it's not possible to let her go, even if it's the right thing to do.

"Watch me." Her face tightens, and she spins away from me. Her hand grips the door.

I'm marching across the room after her. "Don't push me, Maeve." I'm half running. My hand connects with the door that she had opened slightly. The force slams it shut, and Maeve spins around, her back forced against the door. Fear takes root in her eyes, and I don't want that.

I take a calming breath.

"I did my part. Now I want to leave." Her words are high and angry.

Is this about Cian? Had he gotten into her head? He had come to her defense more than once. Did they have a thing before? I keep my hand above her head, and my fingers curl into a fist at the thoughts of that fucker touching what's mine.

"I said, 'No.' I want you to stay." My heart races as I say the words that are true.

She folds her arms across her chest. Her gaze continuously dances across my bare chest. I'm too close, I should give her some space, but I can't move.

"I did what was in the contract. There was no part about you fucking me again." She's breathless; her chest rises and falls. Those nipples that were perky and perfect in my mouth, spring to mind. My cock starts to grow again. I divert my gaze back to her face.

The contract, that's all she keeps referring to. She might not feel anything for me now. But in time, she would. I remove my curled fist from above her head and take a small step back and grin down at her.

Her bravery falters as she registers the anger in my grin. She turns to open the door again.

I push my hand heavily against it and tighten my jaw. I need to keep her here.

No matter the cost, I tell myself. She won't turn around, but her body is tense, like she's waiting for a blow.

I stand back, and she glances at me over her shoulder.

"Your brother's mounting debt with the hospital still has to be paid."

Her eyes widen, and I know I've won, but I drive another nail into the coffin.

"If you dare leave, I'll have his ass on the street. His treatment will stop, and he'll be using again." I walk away as that slowly seeps into her mind. "You will come home with me." I pick up my shirt and put it on before turning to Maeve. Even in the dim lighting, I see it. She wants to lash out and hurt me, but she holds her head high.

"You're threatening my brother?" Her growl has her marching across the room.

"It's up to you." I turn on the light on my desk, wanting to really see her.

Her nostrils flare, and she tightens her fists at her side.

"You look like you want to hit me." I take a step towards her; if she lashes out and hits me, I won't stop her. The desire to have her hands on me again has me accepting it in any form.

"I'm not like you, Jack. I told you before I'd never do it again, and I won't. No matter how much I want to."

"Good. As long as you stay, his hospital and recovery will be paid for. You leave..." I finish buttoning up my shirt. Her pale skin has me turning off the light. "Let's go home." She needs to rest.

I reach for her hand; at first, she doesn't react when I wrap my fingers around hers. It's like her body is numb for just a moment. Reality sinks in, and she tugs her hand out of mine.

"Do I have to sleep with you again?" She sounds fucking horrified.

"I won't ever force you, Maeve."

"That's not an answer, Jack."

The office door opens, and Shay pops his head in. His gaze scans the darkened area before they land on me.

"Finn's awake; just thought you should know." Shay's eyes trail to Maeve, and I step in front of her.

"I'm going back to the house if you want to talk there." With each passing moment, Maeve looks paler

"Yeah, I'll follow you." Shay steps out and closes the door behind him.

"Will I have to sleep with him? Or Cian or I don't know, someone else?"

I'm moving and reach for her. I want to cut her words off. My hand tightens on her throat, and she squeals in shock at my abrupt movement.

"You are mine. No one else's." I quickly release her before I squeeze tighter.

"Are we clear?" My voice rises.

Maeve steps away while rubbing her throat. She's nodding.

"I don't want us to have any misunderstanding here, Maeve. No matter your desire. While you're with me, you're only with me. No one else."

Her hand stays at her throat, but she has stopped rubbing it.

"Do you understand?"

"Yes." She blinks, and a tear trickles down her face.

Anger intensifies as I watch the tear fall. "You will share my bed." My anger charges my words until I take another step away from Maeve. "Do you understand?"

"Yes." Her voice sounds like something that just broke down.

I reach in, and she flinches but doesn't move. When I wrap my fingers around hers, she doesn't pull away. Her small hand is warm, and my cock stiffens as I picture her hand stroking my cock. The boom of the club slams into us as I steer Maeve towards the double doors after leaving the office. Once they are open, the noise dies down as they close behind us. I don't let go of Maeve's hand as I walk us down the hallway. I pass the small room that I had words with Cian in. He had pushed me too far, and I had lost my temper. Something my father won't be happy about. I've always controlled my dislike for Cian but seeing him around Maeve and how he looked at her, I couldn't wait to get a drop on him, and I did several times tonight.

The air outside bites my neck. Maeve's sleeveless top has me opening her door first and helping her into the jeep. Her hands shake as she reaches for the seat belt, I take it from her fingers, and she faces forward as I bend around her and clip it in. I want to kiss her, but her lips form a thin line. Her smile is enticing, and I pause at her neck and press a kiss to the slight red marks I had left on her skin.

Her pulse jumps under my lips, and my cock twitches. I lean out and close her door before getting into the driver's side.

"You're tired," I say to her silence. "We'll be home soon, and you can rest."

Maeve continues to ignore me, and I tighten my hands on the steering wheel. I want to hear her voice, but I don't want to force her. I need to be patient. She's had a lot happen tonight; she had a lot to think about. So I would give her time.

When we get home, I take her hand again and lead her upstairs. Lights reflect against the large landing window. Shay has arrived. I'd left the front door unlocked so he could let himself in.

I turn on the bedroom lights and draw the curtains. "I have to have a word with Shay. But you go to bed. I'll be up later."

Maeve seems more together and meets my eyes this time.

"Okay." The word sounds hoarse, but I'm happy she's decided to talk to me. I want to kiss her again but know she needs time.

Shay is in my living room. He's opened a bottle of brandy and is pouring himself a drink. "You want one?" He asks without turning around.

"Yeah." I watch him in the glass cabinet he's standing in front of. It's hard to know his motives in all of this, but I'm aware of Shay.

He hands me a glass, and I take it. "What were you speaking to my father about?"

Shay takes a large drink. "I've heard stories about your Da, from my own. How he smiles when he's plotting your death."

It's a fair assessment, but I don't confirm. Instead, I take a drink of the brandy and sit down.

Shay shrugs out of his tanned suede jacket. He places the glass on top of the piano that is more decorative than anything.

"He smiled at me," Shay speaks while rolling up his sleeves.

"Did he?" I take another drink.

Shay's arms are coated in ink. He picks up his drink and sits down at the piano bench. "Yes, he did. I wasn't sure who would come for me, you, or him. I had assumed him. No offense."

"None taken."

"So I went to him to make sure I am off his shit list."

I liked Shay, and I hoped he had managed to get off my father's radar, but it was doubtful.

"And are you?"

His grin is instant. "I like you, Jack; I like how close you hold your cards to your chest. I have no idea if I'm off his shit list. I told him I would drop my questions about Nan. He seemed satisfied, but you know him better."

Shay is right. There is a good chance that my father might not want him killed, but if Shay backtracks or does anything in the slightest to piss him off, he'll be a dead man walking.

"I'd say if he seemed satisfied, then there is a good chance he is."

Shay studies me for a moment before taking a drink. I have no idea if my words have sated his thirst to be free of my father.

"So Finn is awake." I'm the one who changes the topic. "That's good news." I rest my head against the couch, thinking of sleeping beauty in my bed.

"He might be awake, but he's paralyzed."

My head snaps up. "Fuck."

"Yeah. I'd rather die."

So would Finn. So would any of us. Being confined to a wheelchair is a death sentence.

"He's strong." I lie and take a drink. To me, Finn is the weakest of all the brothers.

"Your Da asked about our progress on the case."

Shay gets up from the piano bench with his drink in hand and walks around the living space like he might own it one day.

"What did you tell him?" I empty my glass, my mind still stuck on Finn. He won't survive this. Who would?

"I told him this is what happens when he puts Cian in charge."

I grin at Shay, like fuck he said it like that.

"Speaking of Cian, he looked pretty roughed up at the club." Shay's asking without asking.

"Did he? Maybe the moron walked into a door."

Shay swings away from me and empties his glass. Placing it on the piano's top, he slowly rolls down his sleeves.

"I'm glad me and your Da have buried our differences. I don't want any bad blood to resurface and keep pouring through each generation," Shay speaks while slipping on his jacket.

"I have no bad blood with you, Shay." That's what he is asking.

He observes me for a moment before stepping away from his empty glass. "Good. I like you, Jack."

I let the humor of his words tug at my lips. "You've said that twice."

"I'm just hoping you hear me."

I rise as he approaches the couch. "I hear you, Shay."

He pulls up the collar of his jacket. "See you tomorrow."

I pick up my glass as he leaves the room and empty the contents. The front door closes, and I lock it as I make my way upstairs.

CHAPTER TWENTY-THREE

O'REAGAN

AN CHLANN

MAEVE

I take a long hot shower before redressing and curl up on the desk chair with his robe thrown across my legs. I refuse to get into bed. I might have to stay here, but that doesn't mean I have to do as he says. I swallow the pain that has concentrated in a slight throb in my neck.

His anger is terrifying. I've never seen that in Jack, and now that I have, I know I'm being foolish sitting here trying to hold on to some control over this situation that I don't really have. So much in my life I can't control; my mother's addiction, my brother's addiction, my father's leaving. I drag my feet up onto the chair and bury my chin into my knees.

When I had thought it was over between Jack and me, dread had tightened a hand on my stomach and squeezed. Going home seemed bleak. Going back to my life and leaving this behind was like being gifted a moment on one of Declan's adventures. Being placed on a Viking ship with waves that should sink us, instead, the foamy water lifts us and propels us through the sky.

The sad truth is, I hadn't wanted to leave him, but the way I'm being kept is like an escort or worse. He had said to Cian I was a piece of pussy.

My cheeks heat at the phrase. I'm not one of those girls. I've clung to my respect my whole life. Watching my mother have more men than Mondays, I just couldn't let a man take from me like that. Or so I thought.

I try to tell myself that this is different.

This is worse.

It's worse because I'm falling faster and harder for Jack. At least my mother knows it's sex, or booze, or money. Not me. My heart is on the front line, and I have no one to blame but myself. I went to Jack, knowing how I felt about him. I went to Jack when maybe I could have asked Cian, but deep down, I did it so I could see him.

The bedroom door opens, and I freeze on the chair—my heart triples in speed. Straight away, I want to dive into the bed and pretend to be asleep. Jack's ice-blue eyes skim over me, and he doesn't look pleased but closes the bedroom door behind him.

"Aren't you tired?" He asks while stepping into the closet and shedding his clothes.

I'm exhausted. Mentally, physically. Seeing Jack has its temptations, knowing how easily I could let myself pretend that we were a couple going to bed. It's too easy to do, like eating or breathing. It would be natural, and I'm thinking of the short term glorification from it, but what about the long term? What about down the road when the debt is paid, and I'm not wanted? This is going to hurt enough already.

"Yes," I whisper as he steps out of the closet in a pair of white boxers. I don't know where to look.

"Then get into bed." His voice doesn't carry the anger or authority it did in the club. I get up off the chair and leave the robe on the back of it. My bare feet sink into the cream rug as I step up to my side of the bed. I don't look at Jack's flesh that is chiseled and crafted to perfection. I get in and drag the blanket around me as I turn my back on him. I've kept my clothes on, not ready to shed any more of myself for him.

The bed dips as Jack's large frame climbs in. I squeeze my eyes tightly as I think of him fucking me. My teeth sink into my lip until a metallic taste fills it. I need to remember his hand around my neck, not him inside me.

I suck in air as his hand grips my waist, and I'm being dragged back to him until my back hits his solid chest. My eyes spring open as his large erection presses against my ass.

His breath teases my ear. "Goodnight, Maeve." His voice is deeper than normal, eliciting a shiver from me like a tongue has run along the base of my spine.

Like hell am I going to sleep like this. I swallow the whimper. "Goodnight."

His breath still brushes my hair, and I shiver, my body moving harder against his, and I regret the movement as his cock twitches against my ass.

His hand on my waist tightens briefly and then loosens as he sinks into the pillows. His breath dances at the back of my head, and I'm staring at the double doors that lead out onto the balcony. I'll keep focused on the halfway mark and wait until the sun comes up.

My eyes blink in and out of focus, and soon, I fall asleep.

I turn and pause as a pain between my legs has me coming out of my sleep. Sunlight filters in as I blink; it takes me a moment to remember why I'm so sore. Jack. I had sex with him last night.

I push up on my stomach as panic at all of last night's events comes racing back. I'm looking for him, but the bed is empty. My fingers run across the space he had occupied last night. It's cold. I let my face sink into the pillow and take in a calming breath. I am back in his house, in his bed.

"How did you sleep?"

My heart jumps, and I'm pushing hair out of my face as I frantically turn at the sound of his voice. He's sitting in the desk chair, in a white shirt that has three buttons opened at the top, the black slacks run along his long legs, and my heart won't seem to find easy ground as it gallops like it's being chased.

"Fine." I brush my hair completely out of my face. Jack's eyes trail to my neck, a muscle twitches in his jaw, and he stands to his full height.

"I want you to join me for breakfast." He shrugs into a black suit jacket.

"I'm not hungry." I gather the blankets around me.

Jack's gaze travels to me, and all I see is indifference. "I wasn't asking Maeve." He steps away from me and into the wardrobe.

This is what happens when Jack O'Reagan gets his way. He took what he wanted, and now I'm to be treated like what, one of his whores who just does as she's told? He steps back out of the wardrobe with a red tie in his hand.

"Why are you still in bed?"

"I'll clean the club, scrub toilets. I'll pay the debt back; you have my word." I'm pushing the blanket aside and kneeling up. I want Jack to know that I won't run. I'll pay back every penny if it takes me a lifetime.

Jack puts on his tie and walks towards the bed, he stops at the foot, and I have to crane my neck back to hold his gaze.

"I know you will, Maeve. But I've already told you the terms."

I grit my teeth, wanting to lash out at him. I climb off the bed and put some distance between us. "You have to at least tell me how long." I hate the pleading in my voice. "I have college, my mother will be worried, I have a part-time job."

I want to pick up something and fling it at him. His face tells me he doesn't give a shit, and he's bored with my complaints.

"I'll see you downstairs for breakfast." He leaves.

I sink onto the bed, and a thought crossed my mind about not moving, letting him seethe downstairs. I know it will do no good; he'd drag me down. I change into a fresh pair of jeans and a black sweater before tying up my hair. Washing my face and brushing my teeth, I make my way downstairs. He hadn't said which room we were having breakfast in, but I follow the smell of pancakes into the kitchen. I'm expecting his chef to be at the stove flipping pancakes. What I'm not expecting is Jack, who has removed his jacket again and rolled up the sleeves of his white shirt.

A bowl with pancake mixture sits on the counter as he flips one that's in the pan.

"Do you like maple syrup on yours?" He asks without looking around.

The breakfast has been set for two. The positions are intimate. My stomach twists as I climb up on the stool. A single rose sits in a small vase between our knives and forks.

"No, I don't want any," I answer, knowing he can't force me to eat. He doesn't stop cooking a large plate of them. He pours out two coffees and carries them to the breakfast bar. I can't look at him as he sets mine down.

He leaves and returns with a plate of pancakes and places them in front of me.

"Please eat." His soft words have me looking up at him. The muscle in his jaw flexes. "We can talk about college."

I pick up the knife and fork, and Jack's shoulders relax as he retrieves his own plate of pancakes and returns to the counter. He's too close, the space too small. I can smell his cologne that wafts over the pancakes.

I occupy my senses with coffee and pancakes. Without asking, Jack places a bit of butter on them and a dribble of maple syrup. I say nothing through breakfast, but I do eat the pancakes and drink the coffee. I sense his gaze on me the whole time, and I spend it trying to control the burn that keeps rising in my cheeks.

"I'll have a laptop for you later so you can resume your classes online."

My gaze snaps to him. "My classes aren't online. I have to go in."

Jack wipes his face with a napkin before picking up his coffee. "I've already organized it with your instructors."

I'm ready to laugh and tell him to stop joking, but he's serious.

"Jack…"

"It's already been done, Maeve. Your teachers are going to accommodate you." He gathers up the plates.

"What if I don't want to do it online? What if I want to go in?"

He pauses and turns back to me, giving me a full stare that would stop a deer in its tracks. "You would prefer to travel to classes, sit with riff-raff than do it from the comfort of your own home?"

There is too much wrong with his sentence. "Riff-raff? Do you mean my classmates? And this…" I point around me. "… isn't my home."

"I give you full permission to treat it as your own."

"So I can go anywhere, pull it apart?"

He flashes me a warning. "I thought you would be happy." He sounds exasperated, like I'm being unreasonable.

I close my eyes as he takes the plates to the sink and try to sort through the panic that keeps shuffling out of my reach. Being able to resume my classes was a relief. Not jumping from one bus to another or freezing during the cold mornings was also a bonus, but still, nothing about this seemed right.

"What did you tell my teachers?" How did he arrange something like this? Money—was the answer. It always was.

"That you wanted to do your classes online." His response sounds bored.

I stand up and shake my head. "Just like that."

Jack takes slow and measured steps towards me. "Just. Like. That." Each word is cut from ice, and I know I need to settle down and stop questioning as if he could turn on me.

"Just say thank you." His hand touches my cheek, and my body, without my permission, leans into his warmth.

I keep my teeth clamped together and my lips sealed. I won't thank him. I hold my head still, and I'm ready to take the repercussions of whatever my defiance brings.

It brings a kiss that he brushes across my closed lips, they loosen under his, and when he leans out, he smiles at me.

"Do you know how sexy you are when you're mad?"

My confusion with Jack just seems to grow exponentially daily. I had no idea what to make of him, but his words were causing my heart to thrash around in my chest.

"Stop toying with me," I whisper, and I can't help but let my gaze travel to his lips. His other hand takes my cheek, and I'm being held between two solid hands.

"I'm not."

His words ring true, but I'm shaking my head. Can't he see what I want him to say? Can't he see the want I have for him?

He leans in and kisses me softly again. His warmth vanishes as he releases my face. "I have to go out for a few hours."

As he steps away, the reality that I'll be alone for a few hours sinks in. "Okay."

Jack pauses at the hope that I can even hear in my one word. He starts to walk back to me. "Maeve." The warning in his voice has anything brave in me shriveling up.

"Lawlor will be here. If you leave or do anything, I won't punish you." Jack once again takes my face in his hand. His thumb strokes my cheek. "I'll hurt him and make you watch." He releases me, and I can't seem to fucking breathe.

Where the hell had this monster been hiding, and why had Jack allowed him to come out now. A final kiss is pressed to my forehead and Jack, the monster in disguise, leaves me with a withered sense of hope and a whole lot of confusion.

CHAPTER TWENTY-FOUR

O'REAGAN
AN CHLANN

MAEVE

Lawlor makes an appearance only a few seconds after the front door closes behind Jack. I'm still standing in the kitchen when he pokes his head in. Distaste, that's what twists Lawlor's sharp features as his gaze starts at the tip of my toes and moves up purposely slowly until he stops at my eyes. He takes a step into the kitchen. "You put one foot out of line, and I'll break it."

His threat sends fear skittering across my flesh, and I'm tempted to take a step back, but I just want to get out of this room. I bend my head and move past him. His hand grips my forearm, stopping me. He's a lot taller, and I don't look up as he holds me at his side. "You cost Freddie his life."

My head snaps up, and I'm already shaking my head in denial. "He fired him." I didn't like the fact that anyone lost their job over me, but I don't control Jack's reactions.

Lawlor sneers and releases me, pushing me away; my back hits the solid wood door frame. Reaching back, I steady myself.

"I like living, so don't think I won't hurt you."

I move past him quickly, and this time he doesn't stop me. I take the steps two at a time, just wanting to get away from him.

The stairs creak behind me, and I glance down as Lawlor follows me up the steps. His eyes dance with venom, and my legs move faster. I race to the room, but he keeps a steady pace. I am moving almost mechanically up the stairs. His gaze never wavers from me, and once I reach the door, I stop and look down at him. Slamming the door, I'm ready to lock it, but I don't have a key.

He isn't going to hurt you, Maeve.

He just wanted me to stay where he could see me. The door rattles, and I step back as he pushes it open.

"The door stays open at all times."

He doesn't come in but keeps hold of the door handle.

"What if I want to change?"

"I don't give a fuck; the door stays open." He lets the door go and disappears for a moment before he returns with a chair which he places directly at the bedroom door and sits down. He opens his black suit jacket. He's dressed like he's going to a funeral. When he's settled in, he removes a phone from his pocket and starts to scroll.

All I can think is that I'm a prisoner. "I can't leave the room?"

"You can, but I'll sit outside whatever room you're in." He doesn't look up as he speaks.

I want to slam the door in his face but turn away and pick up my bag. Placing it on the bed, I remove my study books. I had lost too much time at college. If I'm trapped here, I should at least catch up on studying. Otherwise, my mind goes to Declan and my mother. I want to see them, but with Jack, it's baby steps. If I request something, I'm sure he will make me pay for it in some form. I open the book to keep my mind from going to Jack.

I'm flicking through the book, the words I keep reading, and yet they won't go in. I start to read out loud, hoping it will let the words sink in, but they don't. I refuse to look at the door; I refuse to acknowledge Lawlor's presence. So I pace while balancing the book in one hand and reading out loud. Not one word goes in. I'm thinking about my lessons in psychology and trying to understand Jack. Maybe if I could understand him, I could use that to my advantage. He's been cruel since we were kids; I don't think he will change. He's thirty-two—eight years older than I am, and in all that time, I haven't seen a softness in him. The pancakes this morning seemed nice, the gesture to allow me to go to class online, that was nice too. Or so he wanted me to believe. I hate the confusion I feel when it comes to Jack. I return to reading out loud.

"That sounds pretty complicated." I close the book and glance at the door as Lawlor stands up. He pockets his phone and re-buttons his suit jacket.

"I'll keep an eye," Cian tells him.

His face is a mess, both eyes are black, and the bridge of his nose is purple. I drop the book on the bed as he steps into the room. Straight away, I feel uneasy. What would Jack say if he knew Cian was in his room?

Lawlor's footsteps grow quieter as he makes his way downstairs.

Cian grins and then winces as a cut on his lip cracks. His tongue flicks out, licking the wound.

"What are you doing here?" I place my hands behind my back and stay standing.

Cian takes in the room with a darkness in his eyes. "I needed to make sure you were okay." His gaze lands on me.

"I'm fine. You don't look too good." I bite my bottom lip, hating the uncomfortable feeling that has me wanting to move, but not move, like I don't want to draw attention to myself, yet I don't like being in this room with Cian.

"You should see the other guy." Cian grins again and stuffs his hands in his brown jacket pockets; the collar is high against his neck.

I don't smile. "I did. He hasn't a scratch on him." I'm not going to pretend with him.

Cian stops smiling, and his tongue flicks out and licks the cut on his lip. "Jack is someone you shouldn't be around. I can get you somewhere safe if he's threatening you."

"It's complicated, Cian." I remove my hands from my back and hate how unsure I feel about him. I've met him before and always liked him, but him being here in Jack's room makes me uneasy. He's Jack's cousin, and I don't believe the O'Reagan's ever turn on each other, especially not for a girl he doesn't know. "Why do you care?" I have to ask.

He shrugs and takes another step towards me. "I don't like seeing you afraid."

I'm afraid now, and I have no idea why. Cian hasn't done anything to cause me to distrust him. "It's complicated and this will do no good, if Jack knows you're here."

He grinds his teeth before continuing to speak. "I don't give a fuck about Jack. You want me to pretend he didn't leave your brother hanging from a ceiling?"

I shift and fold my arms. I'll never forget that. "I'll always be grateful, Cian. I mean that." I would. I will never forget his kindness.

"You want me to pretend I didn't hear him threaten you at his parents' house. I'm trying to put all the pieces together, and to me, I think you owe him for something. Maybe that something is what had your brother hanging from a ceiling?" Cian steps closer, his nearly seven-foot frame towering over me. "I saw you leave the club with him last night."

Now my body grows ridged, my heart starts to race. I see the pieces slot together before he speaks, with a slight bit of horror in his lowered voice. "Did he rape you?"

My face flames at the question and I just want him to leave. "No." I had lured him into that room, knowing my own intentions. I had initiated each move, not Jack.

"But something happened between you?"

I want him to step away from me; he's too close. "It doesn't matter, Cian. You being here isn't helping."

Cian exhales loudly, and I hear footsteps coming back up the stairs. "Something isn't adding up, Maeve. I'm trying to help you here," Cian growls, as Lawlor appears at the door with a red case in his hand.

"Your laptop has arrived."

I don't want the bloody thing, but having Cian bearing down on me is too much. I circle around Cian and take the laptop from Lawlor, who doesn't release it straight away. I have to tug it out of his hand just to get it. He stands back with a grin on his face.

"I think it's best you go," I speak to Cian, with my back turned to him and clutched the laptop to my chest.

Cian doesn't move, and when I turn to him, I can see the conflict growing by the second.

"Now, Cian." My voice rises. I want him out.

He moves across the room and out the door. Lawlor continues to grin at me as he sits down. I don't move until the front door slams. The grin he wears is like when you know your next move in draughts, and you can't wait to make it.

"You're really becoming the town bike. I might take a spin." Lawlor's grin spreads across his face, and I stomp across the room towards him. His words sting so bad. I grip the door and let it fly.

The door slams in his face as I try to control my breathing. His words cut deep. It's how I feel. The door opens, and the warning in his gaze has me pausing.

"Don't do that again." His serious tone and expression have me feeling like a trapped animal. I want to lash out, but everything I seem to do or say comes with a price tag, and the cost is always high for me.

I throw the laptop on the bed. It bounces twice before settling, and I go into the bathroom. The lock turns easily, and I move away from the door, waiting for it to be kicked in, but nothing happens. My breathing comes out fast and heavy, and I'm sinking to the floor. The room shrinks, and I curl in on myself. I'm allowing the pain to come, I'm allowing the tears to come, but nothing happens. Instead of the agony that's rattling my bones, laughter spills from my lips, and it streams along the floor. It grows louder until my body shakes with sobs. Banging at the door has me pushing up onto my knees.

"Open the door." Lawlor's voice is loud from the other side.

I rise to my feet while dragging my sleeves over my knuckles. Pushing my tongue against my teeth, I try to push the emotions away.

"Five fucking minutes," I shout back at him.

"I won't warn you again." His voice is low.

I move and open the door only a fraction. "Happy?"

He pushes in, and I stumble back.

"Keep the fucking door open."

"What are you going to do? Watch me go to the toilet?" I wouldn't go in front of him, no matter what.

"Just keep it open." He steps out of the bathroom, and I wait for a moment. I check to see he's back at the bedroom door, sitting in his chair.

"I want to speak to Jack."

He takes out his phone and ignores me. He doesn't ring anyone, but his fingers move across the screen.

"Are you texting Jack?" I wasn't entirely sure that would be a good thing.

He doesn't respond but stays on his phone.

"I want to speak to him." I take a step towards Lawlor, and he glances up at me.

"No. He told me to keep you safe, so that's what I'm doing."

"You're threatening me like a prisoner."

"What would he think of Cian visiting you?"

I'm shaking my head, hearing the double meaning in his words. "You were here. The door was open."

"I went to the toilet."

"Then you didn't do your job." Two could play his game.

"Any O'Reagan can walk in here. What happens after that is not my concern. But to me, when I returned, you and Cian looked pretty cozy."

"Fuck you," I bark the words.

His laughter fills the room like a poisonous gas, and I need air. I wrench open the balcony doors and step outside into the cool air. I'm really asking myself, what the hell had I signed up for?

Chapter Twenty-Five

O'REAGAN
AN CHLANN

JACK

"Mom?" I call out as I enter the kitchen. The room is still mildly warm from the oven that must have been going all morning. I can smell scones and brown bread. Lifting up the white and red cloth, I find a stack of fruit scones.

"Your father is waiting."

I release the cloth. "Shane, I didn't expect you to be here." I turn to my uncle, who raises both brows. His dark eyes smile at me, but his lips don't move.

"He's downstairs." Shane turns, and I give one final look at the scones. I'll grab one on the way out. Today is trial two, and my father wanted me to meet him to discuss what I had to do. I wondered what other pickups I would have to make, or deal I would be drawing up.

Shane isn't wearing a suit. My father had wanted me to wear mine. He said it would be appropriate for this task. The basement, which is off-limits to us as kids, is where my father is. He had lived down there when my grandfather occupied the house.

My father is seated in a wine-colored leather chair. His gaze slides across me, and I don't sense any disapproval from him, so I take it as approval.

"Sit down." Shane points at the couch across from my father, and I sit on the edge of the seat as Shane sits beside me. I'm ready for this trial to be over. I'm assuming I've passed the first one, even though it was a fuck up. I'm thinking about my mother's scones upstairs.

"When you were young, I used to take you to Dun na Ri park. Do you remember?" My father speaks frankly like he always does.

"Yes." How could I forget his lessons there? I had no idea why he made me take things from young kids and leave them crying. I hated each second of it, but the more I did it, the more powerful I felt. "You used to make me take candy or toys from younger kids."

My father leans forward slightly. "You started to like it." There is a twinkle in his eyes. "I could even tell that you looked forward to it."

I want to touch my neck, but my father is analyzing every tick or movement that I make now, so I sit perfectly still.

"What was it that you liked?"

My father leans back slightly.

Shane pulls up one of his legs and drags it over the other. His hand grips his shoe.

"Power. Knowing I could take from them and not get in trouble. Pleasing you."

My father doesn't blink as he takes in my words.

"That wasn't the lesson I was teaching you. In life, we must hurt the innocent to hurt the not so innocent. Having you take from a younger child built you up to when you had to take from the innocent party."

I nod like I understand, but that wasn't the lesson I had learned. Yet, now as I think about hurting someone to get information, I have done it for the information, not because they were guilty of any crime. So maybe it had dripped slowly inside my moral compass and rearranged the way it shifts and points.

"Today, we will test you on just that." My father rises, and so does Shane. When they turn to a door behind my father, my stomach tightens. We weren't going back upstairs. My father opens the door and flicks on a light. He doesn't look over his shoulder with a sadistic smile on his face like I might expect from the room that I step into.

A man and a woman are gagged and seated across from each other. Their wild eyes dance around the room but don't settle. The woman's hair is plastered to the side of her pale face with sweat. Both look unharmed.

I look to Shane to gauge his reaction, but he steps up to a large pillar and leans against it. My father circles the man who tries to keep track of my father with pure, undiluted fear in his eyes.

"This is William. William lied to me, stole from me." My father stops and places his hand on William's shoulder. A whimper leaves the man's lips. "Not once, but twice." My father releases William's shoulder and steps away from him and to the woman who looks equally terrified. William jerks and groans against his gag.

My father kneels down in front of the woman whose head tilts to the side like everything right now is too much. "This is Sarah." My father reaches out and brushes the hair off her face. She cries out at his touch like he had hurt her. "Sarah is William's girlfriend. She also worked for me. She covered up Williams' deeds."

My stomach hollows, and I look to Shane again, who looks bored. My father rises.

"How would you punish them for their crimes?" My father turns to me and places his hands behind his back. Each step he takes is like small placements are marked out on the floor, so he knows exactly where to stand. He stops in the middle of the floor.

"William stole from you. How much?" I ask, trying to push the uncertainty of this situation aside and think logically. This was a trial, so my father would want me rattled.

"Does that really matter?"

"No." He had always taught me that. If I took one euro or ten, the amount didn't matter; the fact I took it did.

"He did it twice," I speak out loud, going through the facts he gave me. "The first time, was he punished?"

My father moves, taking a step towards me. "Yes, he lost his job."

"So his girlfriend stole the second time?" I glance at Sarah, who's sweating again.

"Yes, she snuck him into the delivery section, and he stole again from me."

"Then Sarah should lose her job."

Sarah's chest rises and falls rapidly, and slowly a light returns to her eyes. She's eager to agree but leans against her restraints instead. My father doesn't take a step towards me, and straight away, I know I've given the wrong answer.

"Kill them both," I say, not sure if it's the right answer.

"Why?" My father takes a step towards me, and I don't like that. It means I'm right, and both of them will die today.

"They stole from you," I answer.

"But why kill both?"

Irritation is starting to climb up my legs and into my hands that I want to squeeze into a fist, but I know every word, every movement is under scrutiny here.

"Because you punished him, and that didn't do any good. So either punish both or kill both."

My father doesn't move. "If you kill them both, then you have two dead bodies. Kill one, and you have one dead body and a messenger that can tell others what happens when you steal from me."

It makes sense.

I look at Sarah and William, who are both staring at me, knowing that I hold their lives in my hands. This isn't like the park, this is taking candy from a younger child, and right now, I know the answer. It's killing the innocent one, Sarah, so William would tell everyone what happened, and he would have to live with the knowledge of causing her death.

That is something that I don't want to do. "Kill William," I say, and my father doesn't move.

"Think of the lesson to all of this, son." My father wants me to get it right.

I'm shaking my head. "I'm not killing her."

Shane moves for the first time, and I hold still and keep focused on my father.

"I'm not trying to turn you into a killer; I want you to make decisions not based on your heart but your head." My father takes a step towards me.

I hate what he's saying. Without blinking, he turns and removes a gun from his jacket, he fires two quick shots, and both Sarah's and William's heads rest on their chests. Bullet wounds ooze blood.

My heart drums too fast in my chest. "You didn't have to kill them both." It's my turn to move. I take a step towards my father as he puts his gun away.

"When you lead, you will make decisions based on what's right for all of us. Never hesitate. You give an inch; they will take a mile." My father steps away from the bodies, and Shane moves forward, unbinding William, who slumps heavily on the ground. Shane moves towards Sarah.

"William didn't have to die today. But you showed weakness in front of him."

My father stops at my side; Sarah hits the floor as Shane unties her. "Help your uncle bury the bodies."

My father leaves the room, and I shrug out of my jacket. Shane leaves, and I stare down at the two bodies. Flesh and bones. That's all it is. If I hadn't refused to kill Sarah, William would have lived.

I wrap the bodies with Shane, and we take them out of the basement through a side door. He loads them into the back of a white van. Blood spots fleck my shirt. There was no way of avoiding all the blood.

"Let's go." Shane gets into the driver's side, and I pull the door behind me before looking back at the house, wondering how much my mother knows about my father's basement.

We don't drive far. Shane drives into the forest that's on our property as far as the trees will allow the van to go, and once we find soft ground, we both start to dig.

"We all have to do things we don't want to but remember, it's for the family." Shane's words don't give me comfort as Sarah's body hits the bottom of the grave we just dug.

Shane drags William's body out of the van. It hits the ground with a thud, and I cringe. Shane doesn't flinch. I don't think he's aware of how easily he drags the body across the forest floor and kicks it into the grave before looking at me.

"The foundation of who we are is stained in blood. And that's okay." He starts to dig, and I join him.

"But too much blood and all of the money will soak it up, and we will be left with nothing."

I shovel the clay on faster, wanting to get away from this.

"If you are to lead us, Jack, you need to separate your feelings from what needs to be done."

I stop shoveling dirt onto the body. "How many people have you killed?"

Shane's eyebrows rise high, and he tilts his head. "That's the type of questions that play with the heart."

He shovels more, and I want to call him out on his lie. My father told me that Shane was weak, he tattooed a black line on his arm for each life he took.

"I could just count your tattoos," I say.

He's moving. My back hits a tree, but I still clutch the shovel.

"I'm not happy about you ruling. Your arrogance is going to get you killed, my boy."

I push Shane away, and he doesn't reach for me again. "It must be a sensitive subject." I fire back, not standing down. I would not show him weakness.

Shane's playing with a ring on his finger as he stares at me. It's like he's trying to control the rage I see in his eyes.

"Too many. Be wise, Jack. Make wise decisions." He returns to covering up the bodies, and we finish it in silence.

Once we stop at the house, Shane doesn't turn off the engine. I climb out, and he drives off, his mood sour since the forest.

I re-enter the house expecting my father to be waiting for me, but he's not here. I don't go back down to the basement but call from the steps, he doesn't answer, so I leave through the backdoor.

I pause at the white and red cloth that covers my mother's scones. I couldn't eat after what I just did. I stop at the back door; my hand tightens around the handle. If I don't eat now, I don't think I ever will.

Show no weakness even when no one is looking.

My father's words haunt me as I walk back to the basket and pull off the cloth. I stand at the counter and stuff a scone into my mouth. I chew without tasting, but I don't move until I swallow it all. Only then do I leave.

CHAPTER TWENTY-SIX

O'REAGAN
AN CHLANN

MAEVE

After spending some time outside on the balcony, my temper dampens. It's like the moisture that's carried on the wind that rolls down the mountains extinguishes the fire inside me. The embers still glow, and I'm tired.

Returning inside, I enter the closet room and change quickly into my yoga pants and long sweater. Letting my hair down, I retie it on top of my head before taking the laptop bag off the bed. Lawlor is still sitting at the bedroom door, with his head bent over his phone. I sit at the desk where I can't see his ugly mug and take out the laptop.

It's brand new, and it takes me a good thirty minutes to set it up. I enter Jack's name and the details I know about him.

Once it boots, it picks up the Wi-Fi in the house and connects. From there, it doesn't take long for me to log onto my online courses. With my books at my side, I jump into schoolwork. I didn't think I would be able to focus, but I'm taking in the content slowly and time moves quickly as I pour over classwork for a few hours.

Lawlor has left me three times, each time I've been tempted to close the door but haven't. I didn't want him to threaten me any more than he already had.

He leaves again, and this time I get out of the chair and stretch my legs, walking back to the double doors. I could never get used to the scene before me. Rolling fields, mountains, the sun hitting spots; the rest shrouded in shadows. If I had any skill with a camera, I would take a photograph.

A noise behind me has me freezing. I didn't hear Lawlor come back up the stairs. Turning around, it isn't Lawlor, but Jack. He's standing in the doorway, his hands hanging at his side. My vision quickly picks up on the blood spots on his shirt again. My heart gallops as he keeps staring at me. He's like a screw that's being wrung, and unscrewing it might not be possible. I'm holding my breath, my survival instinct telling me to stay still and not to do anything abruptly.

The blood. I want to ask about the blood.

Jack steps into the room, and my heart starts a new rhythm that's fast—like I'm in a race car— and we are just about to take the bend. Will we make it, or will we topple? He keeps walking until he's reached me. My breaths are too short; his eyes are too stretched, like he's seen too much.

"Are you hurt?" My gaze dances across the red patches on his white shirt. I want to reach out and touch him, but once again, I'm afraid of this man.

"No, it's a woman's blood."

Fear shoots through me and bounces inside my body before it fizzles, as he continues to watch me.

"Were you helping someone?" The question is stupid.

His smile will haunt me forever. It's filled with sadness and anger and so much violence. "No."

I lick my dry lips and swallow. I don't want to ask. I don't want to know. "Did you hurt her?"

Jack takes my face in his hands, his touch is gentle, but it also drags a whimper from me. Those hands could do so much damage.

"No." His answer has me swallowing a second whimper.

"But I didn't help her either."

My hands automatically reach for his chest, and I'm nodding as my fingers glide across his shirt. My fingers dance around the red patches that are still wet. He's lying to me. My fingers move quickly, and he releases my face as I unbutton his shirt. Panic has me moving swiftly. I don't want him to be hurt. Jack doesn't stop me as I peel the shirt open, and my hands roam across his tanned stomach that shifts and tightens under my palms. It's not his blood.

"Is she dead?" I keep my hands on his stomach and move them up to his chest. My right hand lies over his heart that beats steadily.

"Yes."

My gaze skips up to his. He's staring at me. "Why are you telling me this?" I don't want to know, yet I want the details; I need to know the monster I'm lying beside.

His heart beats faster under my palm, but he doesn't answer me. "What aren't you telling me?" He's hiding something, and Jack steps away from me. My hands slide to my side.

Jack's gaze skitters across the room and zeros in on the laptop. "You did some studying." He clings to those words like a dying man might cling to prayer.

What is he hiding?

"Tell me what happened." I take a soft step towards him, but the moment he looks at me, I know I've lost whatever had prompted him to share with me.

He turns away as he takes off his suit jacket. It allows me to see every stain on his white shirt.

"Jesus."

Jack freezes before he shrugs out of his shirt. His back faces me, his back that's coated in ink. The lion standing up like a man.

It's a weird sensation. I want him to open up to me. I want to understand the man in front of me. I want to understand the pull he has. I need to find his softness or what makes him tick, so maybe I can understand all of this.

"What does your tattoo mean?" I ask.

Jack's shoulders rise and fall, but he doesn't turn around. I take slow steps towards the sleeping giant. I feel like I'm approaching something deadly, but if I do this right, it could be everything.

I stop a few steps away from him as he tilts his head but still doesn't turn around.

"It's a symbol from my mother's home country. It means warrior."

I take another step.

"My mother told me the story about the lion who protected the village from a king. I had always loved the lion in the story and not the king."

My heart jumps in my chest, and I step around him, so I'm standing in front of him. His gaze moves to me; it's the only movement he makes.

"Did you try to protect the girl today?" I ask softly, and it's all wrong.

Jack sneers and reaches out, taking my face in his hands. "I'm not the good person in this story, Maeve."

I hate the sadness I see in his eyes. He might be trying to shut me out, yet some part of him is still letting me see all that pain that's rolled up too tightly inside him.

I'm rising on the tip of my toes, and I press my lips against his. My hands rise slowly until I touch his wide shoulders. Jack moves quickly, and his mouth devours my lips. His hands hungrily tug at my clothes. He isn't gentle. It's like all that violence that I see inside him, is seeping out.

He grips my legs, and I instantly wrap them around his waist as he carries me out to the bed. He stops close to the door and holds me with one hand as he pushes the bedroom door closed, and we are moving again. My back is cushioned by the bed. I don't have a moment until Jack drags my yoga pants down my legs. His long fingers sink into my thighs that he drags apart.

This time if I do this, it's not about a debt; it's about my own needs. I close my eyes and let my head sink back as Jack removes his trousers. When his hands return to my legs, I instantly bring them together only to have him drag them apart. His large frame slides in between my legs as he moves up my body.

My heart gallops, and I open my eyes and stare up into ice-blue ones that drink me in and swirl me around. I'm spinning. I'm drunk on Jack O'Reagan.

I don't want this moment to move. I swallow as panic has me gripping his forearms on either side of my head.

"Tell me something real." My voice shakes, and I hate when my vision wavers. I need something real right now. I know what I'm feeling for him is real, but what does he feel for me? I have no idea how much of his actions are driven by lust or control.

His forehead rests against mine, and he closes his eyes. Dark lashes rest on his cheeks. "I can't show weakness even when I'm alone. But with you…" His eyes open, and I'm holding my breath, clinging to his words that he isn't finishing. His haunted gaze glazes over.

"What about me?" I whisper. His cock is hard against my entrance, and I'm ready to take him. I don't think I've ever wanted anything so much. My fingers dig into his forearms.

"I want you to stay."

His confession confuses me. I was staying; I had a debt to clear. Before I can speak, his lips press gently against mine, his cock pushing harder against my entrance. His kiss turns heavy, and the pressure on my lips is painful. I push Jack back as panic tears at me, and he eases up. His hand leaves my side as he reaches down and directs his cock to my opening.

His body slams into mine, and pain lashes across my flesh. His movements are heavy and hard, and he pulls out before pounding into me. His mouth leaves me as I fight for air. His breath is harsh against my neck as he continues his vicious slams into my body.

I'm clinging to him, confused, and yet his hunger for my flesh has my body responding to his. My core grows tighter. The dampness turns to an onslaught of wetness that coats his cock inside me. I close my eyes against the quickness of his movements, and pain mingles with pleasure. I'm clinging to him, wanting this to end—but not.

Jack's rhythm grows faster, and I think he'll break me, his breaths are like growls in my ear, and he doesn't stop even as he shifts both of us up the bed without breaking his savage rhythm. His face finally leaves my neck as he sits back and grips the headboard.

"Look at me." His growl has fear shooting deep inside me, but I do as he commands.

His pace slows slightly, and his breaths are harsh as he glares down at me. He's frightening looking, but I don't stop him. His anger is spilling over and dripping onto my flesh as he goes faster while looking at me. The headboard is what he holds onto as he drives himself into me over and over again. His face tightens, and his growls are inhuman as he finds his release hard and fast inside me.

My own doesn't come; I'm too rattled with lust and fear. I'm at the peak, but I don't fall over. As he continues to pour his seed inside me, he slows down, and I fight for my own breath. I have no idea what that just was.

I'd seen angry sex in movies, and it seemed to be more slapping and hair-pulling; what he just did was beyond anger. It was something more frightening, but some part of me is glad he unleashed it on me. Jack slows down, and his gaze stays on my face.

It's like he sees me under him for the first time. He freezes, and I swear he's holding his breath. "Did I hurt you?"

I shake my head. *Yes, no. I enjoyed it.*

"Jesus, Maeve, you should have said something." He slides out of me and releases the headboard. He sits back, and I pull my aching legs closed. He's staring at me like I'm a dying animal that he might have to put down.

"You didn't hurt me." I want that look to leave his face.

He runs both hands across his handsome face. When he looks at me again, he pulls me to him. I have no idea what he's going to do, but then he drags me against his chest and holds me tightly.

My hands hang limply at my side, but after a moment, I reach and wrap them around his waist. His heart is frantic under my ear.

"You didn't hurt me," I say it stronger this time. "It was different, but I enjoyed it." I don't need him looking at me like some lamb who's being handed up to the slaughter. I was a grown woman and could have stopped him at any second, but I hadn't wanted to.

His hands loosen around me, and I look up into his eyes.

He searches my face for what feels like an eternity before he finally nods. His head dips, and his lips press against mine. I push my tongue into his mouth, and he opens up for me immediately. The kiss doesn't grow much deeper, and it ends far too quickly.

"Go wash up, and we can have some food together."

I'm ready to get off the bed but pause. Guilt wells up inside me, and it's funny that I would feel that way right now. But since Jack is thinking he hurt me, I use it to my advantage.

"I want to see my brother."

His jaw clenches, and his hands leave me. "Like a trade?" His words boil with anger, and I have no idea.

"Call it what you want." Pain circles my words. I let him fuck me because I wanted him to, not because I wanted to see my brother. I just saw the opportunity, and now I'm regretting taking it.

"Go shower." Jack removes himself fully from me and gets off the bed.

"Now, Maeve." His bark has me moving, and I hate him all over again.

CHAPTER TWENTY-SEVEN

O'REAGAN
AN CHLANN

JACK

I feel like an absolute animal.

After I came and had looked down at Maeve, the fear and shock on her face had me thinking the worst. I had hurt her. I had lost myself to pure anger and hurt the one thing that mattered to me.

I shower in a spare room, unable to face her right now. She wanted to see her brother; she used sex like a bargaining chip, like this is some sterile agreement. I couldn't blame her. I made her believe that is the case, and from the way I just fucked her, what else did I expect her to think? I dry off, and when I go back to the room, Maeve is sitting at the desk, her focus on the laptop. I know she's aware I'm here, but she hasn't looked at me.

The V on her red top shows her perfect cleavage. She's stunning as she bites her thumb, staring at the screen. Her pulse flickers in her neck, and I hate to think that's fear she feels for me. She will never allow me in if I don't show her some kindness.

I step up to her and bend down, placing a kiss on the top of her head. She freezes, making me feel like a monster.

"I'll take you to your brother today."

Her gaze finds mine and jumps from my bare chest to my eyes. "Okay."

I don't want to step away from her, and she's staring at me expectantly. She's wondering what the fuck I'm looking at her like a creeper for. "Maybe we could do something after."

Her gaze dances around the room. "Like what?"

"I don't know. Just think about what you would like to do after seeing Declan."

She nods slowly, and I finally step away from her and get dressed. She's closed the laptop by the time I return, dressed in a pair of jeans and a green sweater; I had to visit Finn today, so I would keep my clothes casual. He's awake, and I can't avoid it any longer. It will be another show of weakness that I can't afford to display.

"When you're ready, come downstairs."

Maeve gets up off the chair, and I leave the bedroom.

Lawlor is downstairs in the kitchen. I sit down and put on my boots.

"Everything went smoothly?" I ask him as I lace my boots up.

"Yes. She stayed in her room the whole time. No problems."

I finish lacing up my boots. "Good." I'm ready to leave when Lawlor stops me.

"Cian came around and wanted a word with her in private."

Every cell in my body grows stiff, and I face Lawlor. "How long?" I ask.

"Ten minutes, maybe fifteen."

"Did you hear what they were discussing?"

Lawlor shrugs and shakes his head. "Cian asked me to wait downstairs."

I'm walking back to Lawlor. "He was upstairs with her?"

I'm ready to lash out, and Lawlor knows it. He looks at the door, and I'm aware of Maeve coming down the stairs.

Maeve steps into the kitchen, and she forces a smile onto her face. She has her black leather jacket on. "Ready?" She doesn't look at Lawlor.

I smile back. "Yeah, let's go."

"We will finish this conversation later," I speak to Lawlor, wanting every single fucking detail. I had no idea what Cian was playing at. My hitting him should have been enough of a warning.

Clearly not.

We go outside, and I can't stop looking at Maeve. Once we are in the jeep, I don't start the engine.

"Was everything okay when I left earlier?"

She belts up. "Yeah. Why? Did Lawlor say something?" The shake in her voice gives away her nerves.

"He said you studied the whole time."

She glances up at me and nods, forcing another smile. "Yep, that's all I did."

I'm staring at her. The little liar. "Nothing at all happened?" I want her to tell me the truth.

She nods and looks out the window. "No."

"Okay." She keeps her focus out the window; her hands rest on her stomach. She's forcing herself to look relaxed as I start the engine.

My temper is like a flickering light, and as I drive, I want to switch it off and think clearer. Confronting her would be an option, but I think of what my father would do. He would play cat and mouse. He would back the person into a corner until they knew they were truly fucked. I'm not going to do that to Maeve.

"How long has Declan been sick?" I ask.

Maeve shifts in her seat but still keeps her focus fixated out the window. "He's been an addict for maybe ten years. He got clean a few times, but he always relapses."

"It's hard living with someone like that."

This time Maeve glances at me, and I meet her gaze before refocusing on the road.

"Yeah, it is." Her voice lowers, and the pain that she tries to hide peeks through.

"Did he ever steal from you?"

I turn into the town and stop at a set of traffic lights.

"All the time." Maeve laughs a little as memories must be bubbling through her mind. "I had to resort to hiding my stuff in the garden. Not that I had much, but what I did have, I tried to protect."

The urge to break her brother's legs has me ready to end this conversation. Her words seemed to have flicked a switch back to my anger. I focus as the lights turn green.

"He must have lied a lot." I get to the point I'm trying to make. "Lying, I think, would be the hardest. I hate liars." I turn down Brews Hill and take a look at Maeve. She's rattled. She wrings her hands together.

This is what my father would do. He would let you know he knows, in such a beautiful, and fucked up, roundabout way.

"I'm not like him." Her voice is a whisper, but I hear her.

I don't answer her and pull up to the hospital gates. Once I enter, she's unbuckling her belt and faces me.

"I'm not like him. I know what you are doing." The bite, in her words, has declared my victory.

"I'm having a conversation with you, Maeve." I finally look at her.

"No, you're not. I might have lied, but you are pretending that you care, for one second, just to drive home the point that I'm lying. It's cruel. You're cruel."

I pull into the parking lot. Once I turn off the engine, I face Maeve. "I was having a conversation with you. Whatever this is, it's in your head."

She's shaking her head, but slowly I can see the doubt start to cloud her eyes.

My father would be proud of me.

"But, if there is something you want to tell me, by all means, do it now."

"I've nothing to tell you, Jack. You don't deserve any truths. All you deserve is lies." Her words bite, and I quickly unbuckle my seatbelt.

A screech is dragged from her lips as I grip her arms. I snap. "What was Cian doing in our room?" I shake her. "Did he touch you?"

Fear clouds her brown eyes, darkening them, but I see when she pushes past it. She tries to break free of me, and I shift my body closer.

"He wanted to help me get away from you." Maeve grins, and it's twisted with bitterness and glee as she flings out her next words. "He wanted to know if you raped me."

I take my hands off her. It's like a blow to the stomach. I don't move away, and I don't look away from her.

Her grin slips from her pretty mouth, and she exhales, looking deflated and hopeless.

My heart starts to race as she doesn't tell me her reply when that little bastard asked her that. "I'll fucking kill him." It's out of my mouth, and her hands grip my sweater like she can stop the onslaught of rage from taking over all my thoughts.

"I told him to leave. I told him I was fine. Just leave it alone."

I can't answer her, and her hands leave my sweater and grip my face. "Please, please don't hurt him."

Everything in me becomes clearer. I reach up and remove her hands from my face. "Don't hurt him." I sneer. She had feelings for fucking Cian.

I move back to my own side of the jeep. Her hands fall limply into her lap. "He was just trying to be a friend."

I take the keys out of the ignition. "Let's go visit Declan." I grip the door handle, ready to leave.

"I'm not getting out of this vehicle until you promise me you won't hurt Cian."

I laugh. "I won't hurt him." I lie easily.

She shakes her head. "You're lying."

What did she expect me to do? He had fucking accused me of raping her. The little bastard had it coming to him, interfering in my business.

"I am." I know I should deny it, but I'm too wound up to play any games right now. It's at moments like these that I know I am not my father's son. I'm something else entirely.

This is a weakness to show anger, to show my cards. I should be smiling while hurting her, but I fucking can't. "I'll make him regret ever going near you."

"I can't be responsible for anyone else, Jack. I've enough on my mind without you adding more."

I don't answer her; I can't. I'm going to hurt him. I reach for the door handle again. "Don't you want to see your brother?"

"Did you kill Freddie?" Fear rattles her words, and I release the door handle.

"No."

"Don't sound so shocked, Jack. I mean, you killed Butcher." Her gaze glazes over like she's back in that room.

"He was going to rape you." The words squeeze out between my lips that I barely move. Maeve decides to go silent.

"Who told you I killed Freddie?" I had wanted to, but I hadn't.

"I'm not telling you. I'm not adding another person to your hit list." Her words are told to the dashboard as she folds her arms across her chest.

I'm tempted to threaten her, but I don't. "I didn't kill Freddie," I say calmly, and she slowly turns her head towards me.

She searches my face, and relief has her jaw relaxing. "Okay."

"Do you want to see your brother?"

This time she opens the jeep door and gets out. I don't stop her but follow her along the path that leads to the main hospital doors.

The hospital is quiet as we walk through the halls to Declan's room. I pause at the large window. Declan is asleep in his bed.

"I'll give you some space." Maeve nods and enters the room. She doesn't ask me to come with her.

I leave and make my way further down the hall to the back of the hospital where Finn is. Shay is already here, sitting outside Finn's hospital room.

"He doesn't want visitors," Shay informs me as he folds a newspaper and gets up.

"Have you seen Cian?" I ask instead, my mind still stuck on the red-headed fucker.

"No, he's been keeping quiet." Shay's eyes question me.

I'm not in the mood. I enter Finn's room. The bed is freshly made up. A wheelchair is parked at the window. Finn doesn't turn to me, but I can't stop the smile that stretches across my face at seeing him alive.

"I don't want to see anyone." His words are hollow.

"I'm glad you're alive."

He spins around in his chair, and I try to keep my focus on his face and not his useless legs.

"You should have let me die."

I didn't blame him. "I thought if I came here, you wouldn't be able to stop thanking me. I expected a lot of ass-kissing." I sit down on the bed.

"Thank you."

I laugh at his words that are ungrateful, and that seems to irritate him.

"Jack." He pushes himself closer to me, and I can see his movements are new. His hands fumbled with the wheel as he pushes himself. "What good am I to the family like this." He points at his legs.

"We always need someone to answer the phones."

"Fuck you." His anger is so unlike him, but that's what I want to see, anything but the look of defeat in his eyes.

"You can get an automatic car and drive. You're still you, Finn." I get off the bed.

"Just please leave me alone." He rolls back up to the window, turning his back on me.

"So that's it, you're going to act like a fucking cripple. An O'Reagan filled with self-pity."

The door opens, and I'm surprised when my father steps in.

Finn spins around, and something worse than defeat coats my uncle's features. He looks ashamed as his gaze clashes with my father's. I don't have to look at my father to know what he's thinking. Finn should be put down—useless. I can assume that's the thoughts that are going through Finn's mind too.

"Liam," Finn says my father's name with hesitation.

"How are you feeling?" My father closes the door and glances at me before returning his attention to Finn.

"Fine." Finn bites out.

"Good. The doctor has explained to me the bullet hit one of the higher cervical nerves that start at the base of the skull." My father steps into the room. "That's what left you paralyzed."

Finn nods while glancing from me to my father. He doesn't move his chair, yet his hands keep gripping the wheels, and then he stops himself from pushing the chair. "Is there any hope of me walking again?"

"None." My father steps into the room and runs his thumb along his bottom lip. "Do you remember anything? Did you see anything before you were shot?"

Good man, Dad. He doesn't hold back asking the questions. I personally would have given Finn a bit more time.

"I was looking at Jack while talking to him..." He grips his thighs. "That was it. The next thing I remember is the pain."

"So, nothing," My father states like Finn is a useless witness to a crime.

"Sorry I can't be more helpful, Liam." I try not to grin at the sarcasm that drips from Finn's words.

My father doesn't pick up on the sarcasm. "That's alright. I will find who did this."

"I will let you two catch up. I better go," I say, not wanting to witness the awkwardness my father always creates when trying to show compassion.

Finn keeps reaching for the wheels as if he wants to spin away and face the window, but he won't show that kind of weakness in front of my father. He shouldn't really care. My father thinks him weak, anyway.

I meet my father's gaze. "I see Shay is outside. Maybe you could give him a lift to wherever he is staying."

In other words, get rid of him.

"I'll do that." I don't look at Finn again as I leave him in my father's hands.

CHAPTER
TWENTY-EIGHT

O'REAGAN
AN CHLANN

MAEVE

Declan has gained weight, and I've never seen my brother more alert and healthy-looking. The hollowness of his cheeks has filled out. His eyes are more vibrant. I do sense a lot of guilt, and at times I see flashes of it, but it's the last thing I want.

When Jack returns for me, I don't delay. I know no matter what, I want this progress with Declan to continue no matter what it costs me. If that meant being kinder to Jack, then that's what I would do.

I try to push our fight to the far corner of my mind, and I'm ready to thank Jack for all he is doing, but another figure looms behind him–Shay.

I dip my head down and keep my mouth shut.

"Are you ready?" Jack asks, and he seems tense.

"Yeah."

The three of us walking to the jeep are beyond awkward, and the time I actually want alone with Jack is taken from me by Shay's presence.

"Did he say anything?" Shay asks in a conversational tone.

"No. My father questioned him, but he saw nothing."

We move to the jeep, and I'm ready to get into the back.

"I have some things to take care of. I'll catch up with you later," Shay tells Jack, much to my relief. Shay's eyes glide towards me, and I hate how calculated his look is. He leaves, tugging his gray jacket around him by pushing his hands deep into the pockets.

I get into the jeep.

"Have you decided where you want to go?"

Jack's question takes a moment to sink in; he had asked me earlier about going somewhere. I hadn't given it any thought, especially after our fight.

"I don't know." I knew I wanted to talk; I wanted to make some peace with him before he did something like killed Cian or threw Declan on the streets. "Is there a park close by?" Being in public could be the safest.

Jack starts up the jeep. "The ramparts aren't far. Or we could walk along the Boyne."

"The ramparts sound nice." Walking along a river didn't sound safe. I knew deep down that Jack would never hurt me, but still, I feared that other side I've been given glimpses of.

"My father used to take me to the ramparts." I stare out the window as the shops of Navan move past. I don't let the hate and hurt fill my heart; instead, I allow happy memories to grace my mind. "We used to go for walks and take picnics down here. It was fun."

"Sounds nice." Jack's voice is stiff, and I keep my mouth closed. Maybe I'm boring him.

The silence stretches out, but Jack finally speaks. "It really does sound nice. I never had that with my father."

I'm watching Jack's side profile, and he appears tormented. "He took me to parks, but we didn't have picnics or go for walks."

"What did you do?" I ask.

"I took toys and sweets from the other children."

"You were only a kid." I defend his actions.

"My father told me to do it; it was part of my training."

My stomach roils, and I'm looking at Jack again, looking for the lie that has to be part of that sentence. "Training?"

Jack stops at a set of traffic lights, but he doesn't turn to me. "Yes, so I would understand how it felt to take from someone innocent."

I have no words. What father did that? In a roundabout way, he was teaching him a good lesson, maybe. Not really.

"I suppose he was just trying to teach you by making you practice the wrong things." I'm careful with my words; we are, after all, speaking of Liam O'Reagan.

Jack pulls into the parking lot that sits just outside the tree line, which leads to the ramparts. Knocking off the ignition, he removes the keys, but once again, he doesn't turn to me.

"No. He was training me for when I had to be ruthless."

My stomach twists again, and this time I have no words. How cruel. How wrong. No wonder Jack was filled with hate and unkind words when we were children. I want to reach for him; I want to hold the child and tell him this isn't his fault.

Dana isn't cruel; these lessons weren't put on her. I didn't think she knew anything of her family's activities. We never spoke of my mother's drinking, and we never spoke of her family's criminal ways.

"Dana doesn't know, does she?"

Jack finally looks at me. "No, and it will remain that way."

I'm nodding quickly. My mind is racing, wondering what else his cruel father taught him as a boy. Did he teach him how to strangle someone to death like he had done to Butcher?

"Of course. I would never tell her," I answer quickly as Jack continues to stare at me. He unclips his seatbelt and moves across the space. He dips his head; his mouth is a hair's breadth away from mine. I swallow as anticipation dances across my skin.

He doesn't kiss me like I expect. "Do you want to be with Cian?" His question has me leaning away.

"What?"

"Just give me an honest answer." Jack reaches up and touches my hair. His words are vulnerable, and some part of me thinks of using it to my advantage. I'd be as bad as his father if I did that.

"No. I don't see Cian in that way at all."

Jack leans his forehead against mine, and his breath dances across my closed eyes. "I can't bear to think of him touching you."

Shivers race along my shoulders at his words. As if anyone could hold a candle to Jack. It would be like trying to keep one lit in the middle of a tornado.

Impossible.

"I can't bear to think of anyone else touching you."

I open my eyes and stare into his—my stomach squirms. My heart races, and all I can think is that I can't bear to think of anyone touching him, either. The words are there, but I don't release them.

Instead, I lean in and kiss Jack. He returns my kiss instantly. His large hands grip my face, and I push my tongue into his mouth. He opens up for me, and his own tongue slides into my mouth. My body is awake and alert; all my senses recognize Jack, and I lean into him, pushing him back until he's on his own side. The kiss is broken, but I don't want to stop.

I get up on my knees and lean across while I kiss him again. Jack doesn't break the kiss, and I hear the shift of his seat as it slides back, his lips slowly leaving mine.

He reaches for me and lifts me until I'm straddling him. His cock is hard and pushes against his jeans that rub against me.

It's daylight, and anyone could see us, but that doesn't stop me as Jack kisses me again. His hand grazes the side of my breast, and I groan into his mouth at the contact.

His cock rises up to my core, and I push down on him; he shifts again, and pleasure bubbles through me as I grip the headrest. I should stop this. Anyone could see us.

Jack's hand finds its way under my top, and everything in me clenches at once from the jolt of pure pleasure. I grind down heavier on his cock and groan into his mouth. Opening my eyes, I look out the window, no one is around, but I'm still aware of where we are. I break the kiss and bury my head in his neck.

Jack's arms instantly leave from under my top, and his hands wrap around my waist, and this feels something like comfort. Like he's holding me. Like, I mean something more than a contract. Like we might be falling for each other. That last thought roars to life and races through me before it bites me hard, and I'm pushing back, needing to see his face. My gaze skims across his handsome features, and I know what I want. I want more of Jack. I want all of Jack. I want Jack.

I kiss him, and I can't control or stop the moan that presses against his lips. He pushes himself up, and his cock rubs against my sensitive area. Sparks of ecstasy fire and ignite until I'm moving faster against him. Jack's hands grip my waist as he guides me, moving me quicker. The fire inside me roars, and I'm almost frantic as I bury my head into his neck and grip the headrest. Lights flitter behind my closed lids as my pussy clenches, and pleasure pours through me as I orgasm on top of him. I'm panting, and once again, I bury my head in his neck.

"I just dry-humped you." Horror coats my words, but soon that horror turns to laughter. Jack's hands tighten around my waist, and his shoulder shakes. When I look at him, he's smiling. My stomach soars at the sight, and my laughter continues.

"Yes, you did." His words are delivered with a huge smile.

And in that moment, a list of what-if's murmur through my mind. What if this could be real? What if Jack always smiled? What if I was honest about my feelings for him? That last thought has the car growing smaller around Jack and me growing larger.

"You were so mean to me when we were kids." I'm gripping his shoulder and chewing my lip as his smile crumbles. My earlier joy turns to something close to panic when his eyes darken.

"I don't recall you ever being nice to me either."

I'm surprised by his words; he sounds hurt. As if I could ever hurt Jack.

"I'm sure you started it. You told me I was scum."

"I don't remember, Maeve." His hands rub up and down along my spine. I'm not sure if he's aware of his movements, but every cell in my body is aware of every inch of Jack. His cock is still rock hard under me, and every small movement sends little sparks through me.

"Your dad didn't want Dana playing with me." I sound childish and petty, but his words had taken such a toll on me as a child. They had managed to gouge their way into my soul and leave a permanent mark.

"My mother wanted Dana to be raised as a normal child. So she was allowed to have friends. My father didn't want that. He didn't want you playing with Dana in case you told her something about us. He wouldn't risk upsetting my mother."

I hear what Jack is saying, but it doesn't erase that day that had changed so much for me.

"I'm sorry, Maeve. I know I was cruel. I was jealous. You were unreachable, off-limits, and yet you were always there with defiance in your eyes." Jack strokes my face and smiles sadly like he's remembering. "Even as a child, you were beautiful. You always had my attention."

I stay still, almost not breathing, listening to each and every single word that leaves his mouth. I'm entranced.

His gaze dances to my lips.

"That day, you told me I was scum and that your dad didn't want Dana playing with me. I ran home." Sweat starts to form on the back of my neck, and my survival instincts scream at me, not to share. I ignore their roars.

"I got home, and my dad left us that day."

Jack's hands still before they tighten on my back.

"He left and never came back." I don't cry, but a wall seems to pulse and breathe inside me like someone is banging on the other side, looking for release that I don't grant right now. I can almost smell the fear and desperation like it has its own unique scent.

"I've blamed you and my mother for ruining my life, and now I'm beginning to think I've been blaming the wrong people." I couldn't hold my mother responsible for my father's actions, no more than I could hold Jack responsible for his father's cruel upbringing. He was a child that was taught wrong.

Jack doesn't speak but drags me into his chest. He presses me close, one hand covering my ear. I stay there, not pushing away as I listen to the thump, thump of his racing heart against my ear; it's like the pitter-patter of rain against a windshield. It gives me comfort, and I close my eyes.

We stay like that for a while, in our own little place of safety.

"I didn't know." Jack's words rattle through his chest.

I press my hand against his heart. "You were just a kid, and I took everything too personally." I stare at my hand over his racing heart.

"I didn't know about your dad."

I want to look at Jack, but I don't move. It's safe here. "I didn't speak about it." It had hurt too much.

"How can I make it right?"

I finally get off Jack's chest. I need to see his face. I smile as I try to remove some of the worry from his eyes. "It's okay." I touch the lines that have formed on his forehead, and he relaxes. "What you have done for Declan, I'll never forget. Thank you." I'm ready to press a kiss to his lips, but he looks away from me, the lines returning.

"No matter what happens, Declan will be taken care of." He doesn't look at me as he speaks the words that rattle me down to the fiber that has strung me together.

"You mean that?" my lip trembles, imagining for one second that his words could be true.

Jack finally looks back at me.

"You have my word." It's like his words are dipped in blood, and they bind themselves in the air above our heads.

I close my eyes and rest my head against his chest. His arms clamp around me, and I'm safe.

Chapter Twenty-Nine

O'REAGAN

AN CHLANN

JACK

We walked down the pathway through the ramparts, and I couldn't look away from Maeve. She spoke of happy times with her father, and I soaked her stories up like they just might be mine. Her hand is small in mine, and there is a sense of freedom in how her free hand flutters while she speaks. Her lips are still swollen from our earlier kisses. My cock jerks when I think of her grinding on top of me. I loved having her body so close. Her hands on my shoulders. Her smell surrounding me and her surrender in that moment.

She had let loose, lost herself in the moment. The moment that I hadn't wanted to end—the moment that had been perfect.

"Have you spoken to your father?" I ask.

Her shoulders tense slightly as she shrugs stiffly. "No. I don't know what I'd say to him, to be honest. I used to imagine him arriving home, with his arms stretched wide, wearing his red cap and a large smile." She glances at me, and I want to grab her and take away the pain.

"But I don't think that's going to happen." Her smile wobbles, and she looks back at the tree line. The carpark comes back into view. We've walked the full circle around the ramparts. We hadn't met anyone, and too many times, my mind had thought about taking her against a tree and burying myself in her.

Her words hadn't stopped flowing. The out-pour of hurt had me holding her hand and listening instead of acting on my urges.

"Could I ring my mother? Just to make sure she's okay."

I don't release her hand until we are standing beside the jeep. "Yeah, of course." I open the door for her and reluctantly release her hand. She doesn't get in. Instead, she rises on the tip of her toes and places a kiss on my lips. It's quick and ends too quickly before she slips into the jeep.

I hand her the phone once I'm in, then start the jeep. "You can ring her now or wait until we are home."

She smiles at me, and humor lightens her eyes.

I reverse out of the parking spot. "What are you smiling at?" I ask, liking the look of it on her lips.

She clutches the phone but doesn't attempt to use it. "Nothing."

She stares at the phone now, the smile leaves her face, and she chews on her lip. I start to drive back into the town when she finally punches in a number.

I can hear the ring and am tempted to turn up the music and give her some privacy. I don't. I want to hear every word.

"Mom, it's Maeve."

I can hear her mother's voice, but I can't make out the words.

"I'm fine..." Maeve stares out the window. Her thumb and forefinger pinch her bottom lip as she listens.

She peeks at me before turning back to the window. She turns her back as far as the seatbelt will allow, as if she's putting up a wall between us.

"I will be home soon. Maybe a few more days." Her voice is low, but I hear the uncertainty.

"I'll ring him. I'll sort it, mom."

Her mother's voice grows louder, and I hear the word eviction and useless.

"I'll ring him. Once I get back to work...."

She's cut off again, and Maeve seems to hunch down. Her mother's words aren't as loud, but I hear some of what her mother is saying. Maeve lost her job.

"Just give me a few days." She bites into the phone.

Silence.

"Mom? Mom?" She's staring at the phone in her hand before she sits back.

"I need to go home." Maeve doesn't speak to me as she still holds my phone tightly in her hands.

That isn't going to happen. I don't want to fight, but I'm not allowing her to go back to that place. She could run away if given the chance, and I'm not going to lose her.

"Jack, I need to sort out some things." She hands me the phone, and I take it. I press down heavier on the pedal as we leave the town and enter the countryside. I'm racing like I can take her away from her mother, whose problems aren't Maeve's.

"No. Tell me what you need, and I'll make it happen." I refuse to look at her.

"No. I've done my part. I've done more than what I signed up for. I want to leave." Her voice wobbles.

My stomach tightens. Everything feels tight, the car, the shirt on my back, the shoes on my feet, the truth of what I feel for her. "I said, no."

A growl that's half a cry pours from her and fills the jeep.

I drive faster.

"What is it that you want? Do you want to destroy me? Make me stay here as I watch everything around me crumble." She's facing me, her hands taking on a life of their own as she waves them in the space above her head.

I take my foot off the pedal and remember my control. "Tell me the problem, and I'll fix it."

She barks a laugh that's short-lived. "You're the problem."

I glanced at her for the first time. I want her to stay. I won't let her go.

"I'll come with you." I give in through gritted teeth.

"No. Jesus. I want a moment, just one fucking moment."

I focus on the road as something uncurls in my stomach, and I'm ready to give in. I refuse to see her hurt by her family anymore.

I drive down the lane that leads to the house. "I heard you lost your job, and I assume you paid the rent?"

She folds her arms across her chest and glares out the window.

I continue my analysis. "Is your mother being evicted?"

"Yes, she is. I need to check on her and speak to the landlord and my place of work. A few hours is all I want." She's pleading.

She didn't get that she wasn't returning to a job, so she couldn't do anything about this.

"Let me help," I say the moment we pull up at the house.

"Help." She laughs, and her brown eyes fill with tears that she doesn't spill. "You mean drag me further into debt to you."

I turn off the engine. "You wouldn't owe me, Maeve." She didn't get it.

She climbs out of the jeep, and I'm on her heels as she moves quickly up the steps. "I'm not some charity case."

We enter the hall, and Lawlor looks up at us. I pass him, following Maeve up the stairs.

"I'm offering help. You say you don't want any more debt, yet you don't want help, either."

She enters the room and picks her bag up off the floor.

Like, fuck, she's leaving.

I close the door behind me, and her eyes flash with a warning. She's panicking. Had her mother said something else? Her movements are tight and tinged with hysteria.

I reach for the bag to remove it from her hand, and she pulls it back. I take a step back from her to allow her to calm down.

"I'm going to make this clear, so there's no confusion."

She's staring at me, and I see the storm that rages in her eyes. One wrong word, and she's going to get completely sucked into the turmoil that's ready to spill over.

"You won't be returning to your job. You have a place here. You can continue your studies from here. That life is over."

She blinks several times before she speaks. "You bought me. I paid that debt."

"I don't give a fuck about the money, Maeve. This is about you. I care about you." My heart jumps, and straight away, I regret the show of weakness. My father would laugh at me.

The bag drops to the ground, and I'm hoping I've won, that my words and actions are finally sinking in.

"Your mother won't be evicted. I promise."

She blinks, and tears roll down her face, but she still doesn't speak.

"I can't keep relying on you for everything, Jack." Her cheeks turn pink.

I close the distance between us. "You can."

She's shaking her head, but I drag her into my chest.

"I can't just stay here like this." Her words rumble against my chest.

I tighten my hold on her. "You can. Your brother is safe; your mother will be safe."

Maeve steps out of my arms. "I want my freedom."

Freedom. She had no idea of the cost of that one word—a price I couldn't even pay for her.

"It doesn't exist in this world, Maeve."

"What does that mean? What do you expect me to do? Stay here and watch you come and go while I'm locked up? What happens when you get bored? What happens if I upset you?" Her words are tripping over each other, it's like her brain is on fire, and she's puffing out the words like she might stop it.

Her questions are valid. It's a moment of how much can she take, and how badly do I want to keep her here?

"You can go with Lawlor to your home."

She's already shaking her head. "You're not listening to me. I have a life beyond this. I won't have the likes of Lawlor with me."

"Lawlor is skilled at what he does. I'm trying to be fair here, Maeve." I hold back the frustration that claws at me. I want to end this conversation that is spinning out of control.

She isn't leaving.

"I'm not some average guy." I sound like a pompous prick now, but she needs to know. "I'm next in line to take over from my father."

The color slowly drains from her face, and I think I'm getting somewhere.

"I will rule over them all." I feel the weight of my words like armor around my shoulders. "I will be their King. Their leader."

Fear circles in her eyes, and I hate it.

"I never show weakness, Maeve. So what do you think you will become to them? My weakness. You will never be safe. Your family won't be safe."

She takes a step back and plops down onto the bed. Her gaze is fixed on me, and her chest is still.

"Take a breath." I approach her.

She holds up her hands, stopping me. She inhales deeply. "I'm a target? My brother?" Her words are choked.

I shove my hands into my jeans pockets. It's a cruel existence. But she needs to know.

"You dragged me into this knowing I could end up being a target?"

"You weren't exactly sitting with your eyes closed, Maeve. You came to me, knowing what we did."

"I didn't know this." Her lip trembles and she stands up but takes a step away from me.

"I would never hurt you." The fear in her eyes doesn't leave.

"I would never hurt you," I repeat and take another step towards her. She ducks her head like she's afraid.

"I just want you to understand why I can't have you running around the place. In time you can have more freedom, but with Lawlor guarding you."

Her hands rise, and she joins them together before pressing them against her lips.

I reach for her, and she doesn't stop me as I pull her into my arms. "I can keep you safe, but I need you to listen to me."

My hands tighten around her small frame, and I feel the slight tremble that pulses through her body.

"Do you understand?"

"Yes." Her confirmation has me pressing a kiss to the crown of her head.

I might become a King, but she would become my Queen. In time she would adjust.

I tilt her head back and force her to look at me. Her nostrils flare, but she holds my gaze.

"I want you to stay with me."

She swallows a torrent of emotions before she nods, but one or two tears escape the prison that she's fighting hard to keep it all locked away in. I can almost hear the click of the cell door, the screech of the hinges, and the onslaught of her fear as it continues to open slowly.

I don't know how to stop it. I don't know how else to make her see that she's mine.

Chapter Thirty

O'REAGAN
AN CHLANN

MAEVE

He's looking at me like I'm cracked glass in his hands, like he's waiting for me to shatter everywhere. Fear grips my throat and keeps me rooted. I knew they were criminals, but kings of the criminals are something entirely different.

My insides tremble with the knowledge that's too heavy. I can see it in Jack's eyes. I wasn't leaving. His head bends, and he presses his lips to mine while dragging me closer. His hold on my body is painful. It's like spending too much time outside in the cold, only to enter a hot kitchen. The sting of the warm air pokes and stabs at your face painfully.

Conflict tears through me as Jack continues to kiss me, and I'm clinging to him. His kiss makes everything hazy, and I know if I give in, I can find peace in his arms. It won't last forever, but it might give my heart a chance to find its rhythm again.

I would never hurt you. His words had been pulled from the trenches of his own insecurities and handed to me. I had wanted to cry. I knew he wouldn't hurt me. Yet, he's larger than life, bigger than my dreams, and as dangerous as a misfired gun.

He would never hurt me. His hand is gentle on my back now as it slips under my top and drags it over my head. His ice-blue eyes consume me, and he's opening up slowly, maybe for the first time in his life. I try to picture that young boy whose father taught him wrongs. That young boy who never was taken to the park just to play, or brought for a picnic, just to eat.

I touch Jack's handsome face and crack a little further. I'm clinging to his earlier words, hoping he isn't lying and that I mean something to him. My own fears of him leaving me, getting bored with me, replay on and on in my mind.

He will abandon you eventually, just like my dad.

I don't want the thoughts, so I grab his sweater and tug it up. My movements are quick, and he stops me, covering my hand with his, forcing me to look up.

My heart ricochets across the surface of my own pain and confusion as he takes his sweater and top off. His bare chest fills my vision, and when he leans in, our flesh presses together. His kiss is so soft, yet I've never felt anything so crushing on my soul.

I let him lead me to the bed. I'm waiting for him to press me back, but he doesn't. Instead, he peels off his boots, socks, jeans, and then his boxers. His cock springs free, and I swallow.

I can't seem to look away or move as he reaches for my jeans and strips me down. Removing my boots first, then my jeans, and finally, he looks at me as he pulls the band of my panties. Goosebumps break across my flesh, and my eyelids flutter closed. His fingers run the length of my legs as he drags my panties down.

I shiver when his chest brushes mine, and he reaches around to remove my bra.

My heart storms in my chest, my mind clouds, and I'm ready to just give everything to him.

"Look at me." The command carries more power than I've ever heard before. I open my eyes and look at a King, who most certainly has my heart.

"I'm looking at you." My words sound strange to my ears.

Jack's jaw tightens, and he holds my face while his gaze soaks up whatever he sees. It could be my fear, my want for him, or my show of my heart.

My body vibrates and swells at my core as I wait for his touch.

His lips find mine again, and when he moves me back, I welcome the cushion of the bed. I automatically spread my legs and allow his large frame access to me. He climbs up on the bed as I move back, giving him space. His hands grip my thighs, stopping me from moving any further, and I don't look away as he positions himself at my opening. The head of his cock dips in, and I'm ready for him—wet and willing.

He slides further in as he moves down over my body until he's hovering over me with his cock filling me up. His hands slide into mine on either side of my head, and he moves himself out before refilling me.

I can't keep in my groans, and I don't want to as Jack continues his slow rhythm, and I realize what this is. I might not have the experience, but I've seen it in the movies. I know what my body and heart are telling me. He isn't fucking me. He's making love to me. I tighten my fingers around his, and it's like he knows I know, and he sinks deeper in-between my legs.

A long moan brushes my lips from his mouth. I tighten my legs around him, wanting him closer, but it's not possible. He drags our joined hands closer to my head as he pumps a bit faster, but with each stroke, I feel like I'm a canvas, and he's painting me. I know the end result will leave me breathless.

The muscles on his forearms flex under the strain of his movements that grow faster. He doesn't look away from me, and I'm ready to stop him. It's too much. He's too much. Yet, I've never wanted to see the ending so badly through his eyes. Like sitting and waiting for a sunset. A groan rips from me. Jack moves faster. His body is straining under the pressure as he brings both of us to a new height, one I've never reached before and one I never knew existed. I'm looking into his eyes as I call out his name on my orgasm, which keeps going even as he pours his seed inside me.

I'm spinning and feel like he has cracked me wide open, and he sees everything. My breaths are harsh as I look away, and Jack dips his head into the crook of my neck. His breath is warm against my skin, and everything that I don't want to think about comes flooding back.

I might be falling in love with Jack, but I'm a prisoner here. Talking to him doesn't seem to work, and I am not going anywhere with Lawlor. Jack lifts his head up, and I keep my eyes closed, not wanting him to see the turmoil that coils itself deep in my stomach. Like a snake waiting to strike.

And I will strike.

His lips press against my jawline, and he extracts himself from me but doesn't get off the bed. Instead, he drags my body into his side and wraps a heavy arm around me.

"I liked going to the park with you today."

His words rattle the peace and surety I felt only seconds ago. His voice is open, vulnerable, but I have to think of the Jack who won't let me leave.

The one who will be King. The one who is ruthless, like his father. That's the Jack I need to picture if I'm going to do this.

"Me, too," I whisper. It isn't a lie. It was the first time I felt anything close to normalization. Jack falls silent and doesn't speak for a few beats before he presses a kiss to the top of my head. I lie still, knowing I can't stay here, yet leaving is like going against my nature. My fingers trail along his inked back, and I can't picture a life without Jack in it. Walking away from someone like him isn't possible.

But I need to make sure my mother is okay. I can't have something like that taken from me. Not my family. No matter our issues, they were my family. No matter how many bottles she poured down her throat or how much debt Declan ran up. They were family. They were what kept me fighting for years. Keeping them alive kept me alive. We shared a lot of laughter and happiness too—especially Declan and me. No matter what, my mother brought me into this world, and I won't let her shrivel up and die without trying to help.

"I'm going for a shower." I look up at Jack as I speak. His eyes are closed, and he smiles slightly. "Okay." His lids are half-open, and I kiss him quickly before he releases me from his hold. I'm waiting for him to turn and get off the bed, but I make it to the bathroom and turn on the shower.

Brown eyes that are glazed over stare at me. I nod at my reflection before getting into the shower.

The shower gives me more clarity of what I need to do. I wash quickly, and once I step out, I don't turn off the shower. I leave it running long after I've gotten out and dried myself.

Opening the door quietly, Jack's back is to me, and from the rise and fall of his shoulders, he looks to be asleep. I hold the towel tighter around my body and slowly close the bathroom door behind me before entering the closet, where I dress quickly.

He would be pissed, but if I got to see my mother and made sure she was okay, it would be worth it. Stepping out of the closet fully clothed, I stare at Jack's frame waiting for him to spin around and catch me. The noise of the shower in the background might keep him asleep. I leave the bedroom and carry my shoes downstairs. The evening is moving in, the sky darkening outside as I enter the kitchen. There is no sign of Lawlor. The jeep keys are on the hall table where Jack must have dropped them when we arrived home.

It's too easy, I tell myself.

My heart starts to dance in my chest as my hand tightens around the keys. I make my way out to the garage. Flicking on the lights, my heart stops. The jeep isn't here.

I slip on my boots as I return to the kitchen and tip-toe, remembering we pulled up at the door. I smile as I open the front door and see the Range Rover parked outside. I take one final glance at the stairs, ready to slip out of the house, when my gaze clashes with Lawlor's.

He's wearing a smile like I've really and truly fucked up. My first instinct is to scream for Jack. Lawlor looks like someone who wants to hurt me. I move quickly and pull the door closed behind me as I scramble to the jeep. It purrs to life, and I peel down the driveway. My hands start to sweat each time I look back at the house. Lawlor is running flat out after me, and I hit the locks on the jeep. I'm waiting for Jack to burst through the front door, but the house disappears as I round the corner and drive up to the closed gates.

"Fuck." I search around the gear stick for a zapper, but there's none. I don't remember seeing Jack hold anything. I glance in the rear-view mirror, knowing I'm wasting too much time as Lawlor sprints around the bend, extracting something black from his jacket pocket.

Is that a gun?

The keys.

My fingers tremble as I run them across the bunch of keys before coming across a round disk with a button in the center. I press it, and the gates start to open. A thump at the window drags a scream from my lips, and I'm staring down the barrel of a gun.

"Open the fucking door." Lawlor holds the gun steady, and I'm staring at him for what feels like an eternity as the gates inch open painfully slow. I don't need them fully open, just enough to drive through.

I take my hands off the wheel and hold them in the air. Lawlor's dark eyes don't leave my face, but he lowers the gun. I'm still reeling that he pulled a gun on me, but it amplifies how serious this situation is. My foot takes on a life of its own, and I'm tearing towards the gates. My hands clamp down on the steering wheel, and I'm hunched over, waiting for the gun to be fired.

CHAPTER
THITRY-ONE

O'REAGAN
AN CHLANN

MAEVE

The moment I pass the gates, I push my foot to the floor and tear down the road. I'm still hunched over, still waiting for a rain of bullets to tear the jeep apart, but that doesn't happen. I slowly raise my head and glance in the rear-view mirror, but no one is following me.

Once I'm a few kilometers from Jack's, I slow down, so I don't attract attention. I would be arrested for theft, driving without a license, and driving without insurance. The list would be pretty endless. My hands tightened and loosened on the steering wheel constantly. I'm already questioning if running was the right thing to do, but Jack left me with no choice.

He would do anything to keep the ones he loved safe. That is something we have in common.

The estate is growing dark. The street lights blink on as I slow down. No one is hanging out on the lawn in the center of the estate. It looks abandoned. It normally does, but this evening it feels different. Maybe it's me who feels different. I pull up outside my home, and embarrassment turns my cheeks red. The house looks derelict, and even more so with the boarded up front door. No lights are visible from the front of the house.

What Jack must have thought when he came here for me that first time—that didn't matter anymore. I get out and lock his Range Rover. It's a huge target. It doesn't belong here amongst the council houses.

I don't approach the front door. I already know there's no point. Instead, I walk down the side of the house and push down the backdoor handle. The door opens, and I don't forget to prepare myself for the smell. Filling my lungs with one final mouth full of fresh air, I enter the dark kitchen.

I can see the outline of the clutter, the movements of the cat amongst the dirt. He lands close to my feet, but I don't stop. Closing the door behind me, I'm ready to leave the kitchen.

"What are you doing?" My mother's voice comes from a chair that I had thought was a pile of laundry.

My heart bounces but slows down quickly.

"What are you sitting in the dark for?" I walk past my mother and flick on the light switch.

"Power's off." Her voice is hollow. Her outline is becoming clearer as she raises a mug to her mouth.

"You bought alcohol instead of paying the bill?" My words are pointless as I root around in a drawer for the six-pack of tealights and a lighter.

"I can live without lights."

I light the candle and carry it to the table; I push it as close to my mother as I dare. The light casts shadows on her thin face; she looks frightening.

She pulls her cigarettes out of her pocket and lights one. The red ember burns brightly.

"What are you doing here?" She asks again.

"I wanted to make sure you were okay." I can't move, but watch as each drag of the cigarette lights up her gaunt features.

"Since when do you care?"

"Why do you drink?" I ask my own question that I've never dared to ask.

She sneers and picks up her mug, like my words are a reminder that she's an alcoholic and needs her drink.

"It tastes nice."

"No. I mean, you didn't always drink." I'm thinking back as far as I can remember, and I don't think she always drank, like Declan wasn't always an addict. It's there floating in the recess of my mind. Falling into cracks and crevices, but every once in a while, it balloons up, and this time I'm not ignoring it.

My mother's breath wobbles, and there is a second I fear it might be her last, but she inhales her cigarette. "Why are you so interested now?" Resentment, hurt, and so much more is rolled up in her words.

"I think I've always wondered, but I feared the answer," I answer honestly as a lump forms in my throat.

My mother smokes again. "You didn't want to see your father in a bad light. He always was your hero."

My heart squeezes, and the pain is real. Too real. She's right. This is what I feared, that he played some part in it.

"I got tired, Maeve. Tired of being the bad one. Tired of picking up the pieces after him. Tired of the other women, tired of never being good enough—not for your father." My mother's eyes bore into me, and I see the depth of her despair. "Not even good enough for you or Declan."

My eyes sting along with the back of my nose. This is why I came here today, not just to make sure she was okay, but to face what I've been avoiding all my life. My father isn't the innocent one in all this.

My vision blurs, and tears spill as I take her hand. It's cold and thin, and the shock sobers me. "I'm sorry."

She's still stiff, and once again, I'm wondering if I am sitting here talking to a ghost. The roar of a motorbike has me releasing my mother and standing. The curtain parts slightly, and I watch as Lawlor climbs off a shiny new black bike. I swear he looks right at me, but that's not possible; he couldn't see me in this darkened room. I release the curtain.

"It's not your fault, Maeve. You took care of Declan..."

"Shh, mom, stay quiet." It was silly, pointless when Jack's jeep was parked outside. I had no idea what Lawlor would do. He had threatened to hurt me before. What would he do now?

My mother's smoking sounds loud and even louder as she extinguishes the cigarette. A knock at the front door has her standing.

"Is it that boy, Jack?"

The way she says it would have made me smile if I wasn't so afraid. Jack isn't a boy.

"No. It's his bodyguard."

"Is he here for you?"

I nod, but realize she might not see me in the darkened room. "Yes. I just wanted to make sure you were okay. You won't be put out on the streets, mom. I'll make sure of it." I'm walking to her, wanting to hug her, but she wraps her arms around her tiny waist.

"I'm not your problem, Maeve. Go live your life. Take care of your brother."

She won't look at me. "Sometimes I used to hear you row with dad. I remember you hitting him." My vision blurs again as I confess what used to tear me apart. Lawlor no longer knocks on the front door, and I know I'm running out of time.

"You want to blame me for that, too. Go ahead." She still won't look at me.

"I'm not blaming you, mom. I know he was with other women." She looks at me now, and pain fills her washed-out eyes.

The back door opens, and Lawlor steps into the darkened room.

"I'm coming now. I want five minutes with my mother." I rub the falling tears away from my face, and when I feel Lawlor's hand on my arm, I yank it out and spin towards him.

"You fucking touch me again, and I will make sure Jack kills you. Not like Freddie, but you will be in the ground for good. Now give me five minutes." I'm shouting, snapping, breaking, and all my truths are pouring out of me.

Lawlor doesn't touch me again, but in the flicker of the tealight, I see the anger that's growing into rage at me calling him out. I don't stand and wait to see what happens with him. Instead, I go to my mother and grip her folded arms.

"I'm sorry. I really am. I should have questioned things sooner. I should have..."

My mother cuts me off. "You were a child, Maeve. I could have told you, but I didn't." Her voice carries no emotion as she returns to the table and picks up her mug. She looks over Lawlor.

"Is Jack good to you?" My mother asks while glaring at Lawlor.

That didn't matter. What mattered is getting her somewhere to live and helping her to deal with her demons. "Yes. Don't worry about me, Mom."

Her laughter has no joy in it. "I always worry about you and Declan." She places the cup on the table and walks to me. Lawlor's heavy breathing has me knowing I need to end this soon.

"Declan's in rehab. He's doing great." I want to leave her with some comfort, because right now, the thought of leaving her here alone is too much.

"We have to go." Lawlor's words are a growl and I have to work with him. He's been as patient as he's going to be.

"He's always been so strong and brave." Her smile is slight, but I see pride in it, and it warms my heart.

I try to hug her again, but she keeps her arms at her side. She's tiny in my arms, and my heart hurts again. "Come with me," I whisper in her ear.

Her laughter has me releasing her. "I'm happy here, Maeve."

I blink, and more tears spill. "This isn't happiness."

"Maeve." Lawlor sounds ready to snap.

"Go. I'm fine." My mother reaches out and squeezes my arm. It's the only form of comfort I've gotten from her in a long time. I'm nodding as she releases me and steps away.

"Give me the keys." Lawlor opens his hand the moment we step outside, and I place the keys in his palm. He unlocks the jeep, and I get into the back. I wait as he pushes the black bike down the side of the house. The curtain moves slightly, and I press my hand to the window. "Mom." One word that tears me open. I should have tried to help her the same way I had always tried with Declan. The curtain falls back into place, and Lawlor gets into the front of the jeep.

A phone rings, and he takes it out of his pocket. "I have her. She was with her mother. Yes. Okay."

The phone is passed back to me. I don't ask who it is as I take the phone.

"Are you okay?" Is the first thing Jack asks.

I'm tired. "Yes."

He exhales heavily. "What were you thinking? I told you I'd take you or Lawlor." Anger propels his words down the phone.

"I didn't want anyone with me, Jack. I wanted to talk to my mother in private." Lawlor starts the jeep, and I'm driving away from my mother with a pain in my stomach at the thought of leaving her there.

"I can't protect you if you run off." His words are low and clipped. He isn't alone. I know by how he's speaking.

I sit up straighter in the jeep. "I won't abandon my family," I admit.

He exhales again. "I have to go. Lawlor will take you back to the house."

Lawlor glances at me in the rear-view mirror. "Are you not there?"

"Maeve. I'm asking you, please just stay in the house until I get back. No more running off."

"I just wanted to see my mother," I repeat. I had no intentions of leaving again, but I wanted him to know that my family meant a lot to me.

"I'll speak to you later." My stomach tightens. Would I be punished?

It didn't matter. Seeing my mother and telling her I am sorry was worth it.

I hand the phone back to Lawlor.

"I will. I know. Yes." Lawlor hangs up after a moment. He doesn't speak as he drives me back to the house. I'm waiting for him to threaten me, but that doesn't happen. He doesn't pull up to the front door but drives into the garage.

I get out of the jeep and enter the kitchen. I don't want to go to the bedroom, but I also don't want to be around Lawlor. He follows me up the stairs but stops at the door that I know to leave open. He doesn't drag a chair over but stays standing.

The part of me that has manners wants to thank him for giving me that time with my mother. "Thank you for letting me speak to my mother."

"Let's hope Jack is as forgiving."

"I'll talk to him." I want to add, 'just this once.'

Lawlor doesn't look hopeful. My mind becomes consumed with what might happen to him. Have I put another person at risk?

I plop down on the bed and slowly lie back. I couldn't keep piling on responsibility like that. Closing my eyes, I allow memories that I have kept at bay far too long. Memories of my mother accusing my father of smelling of cheap perfume; memories of red lipstick on the collar of his shirt. Fights. So many fights over women. He hadn't been loyal to her. It must have broken her heart. Once we had been happy, but I can't remember exactly when it fell apart.

I get off the bed to find Lawlor looking in at me. I sit up straight, and he looks away. Folding my arms across my chest, I want to close the door. His stare was too heavy, carried far too much weight.

The front door opens and I'm standing up as footsteps race up the stairs. My stomach stirs, and I place my hands behind my back. I would defend what I did. I'm not abandoning my family. This is the mantra that I keep on repeat in my head as I wait for Jack to enter the room.

It's not Jack. It's Cian.

"You can't be here. Jack was pissed the last time." Lawlor blocks him. Cian flashes a glance at me before refocusing on Lawlor.

"Why don't you go downstairs and have a cup of coffee. That's a fucking order, Lawlor." Cian's voice has dropped to something deadly, a sound I've never heard before, and when Lawlor throws me one final look before leaving, I know something is wrong.

"What? Is it Declan?" I meet Cian halfway across the floor. He doesn't look at me as he passes me and pulls open the balcony door. He juts his chin towards the door, and I follow him outside. It's nearly dark now, and it's cold.

"What is it?" My patience is fraying and my heart isn't doing so well, either.

"You need to leave with me." Cian doesn't speak until the balcony door is closed. I'm looking around the small space, wondering what the hell he's talking about.

"Did Jack send you?" I fold my arms across my chest.

"No, Maeve. You don't belong here. I have somewhere safe you can hide. You just need to trust me." Cian turns and grips the door like I'm going to follow.

"I don't trust you. I don't even know you."

I can see his reflection in the glass door. His jaw is tight, and his eyes narrow before he turns back to me.

"Do you really want to be kept here against your will?" His large frame bends as he tries to meet my eye.

"Why are we out here?" I ask, instead.

"There are cameras in the house, and I wanted a moment in private."

All I can think of is that there are cameras in the bedroom. My face grows red.

"Just come with me. I'll keep you safe." Cian reaches for me.

I step back, my lower-back hitting the rail. "I don't want to leave, and I don't think you should be here."

Cian steps up to me. He makes the balcony shrink with how large he is. He drinks up all the air around me as he leans in. "Don't make me drag you."

"What is this really about?" He was lying. He wasn't trying to protect me. Something more was happening here.

"I'm a friend."

I'm already shaking my head at his lie. "No, you're not. We barely know each other. You're risking a lot, and I don't understand why."

Cian and I flirted sometimes, but what he was doing was really putting himself in danger, so this isn't adding up.

"Do you know who he is?" His growl has him stepping way too close, and all my personal space and air vanishes.

"Yes." I try to move, but Cian keeps me pinned against the rail.

"You're a distraction he doesn't need."

My head snaps up. "Are you going to kill me?" Fear grips my throat and shakes me to the core.

"No." That one word disturbs me, and I'm trying to push past Cian. He's lying.

"Maeve, calm down." Cian doesn't sound calm. He sounds panicked as he grabs my arms and shakes me. "If you just come with me, lay low for a while, you can start over somewhere else."

He had lost his mind. "Get off me." I try to get out of Cian's hold, but his grip tightens.

"If you don't come with me, he'll send someone else."

The words are growled and freeze me to the spot. "Who will send someone else?"

The air is robbed from my lungs as Cian half closes his eyes. "Liam."

"Jack's father wants you to get rid of me?"

Cian's moment of regret passes, and he drags me towards the door. "This is my trial, and I'm not fucking failing it."

His determination is consuming every instinct in Cian. I reach back and grip the rail with every ounce of strength I have. Cian releases me, and for a moment, I think he's leaving me, until he wraps his arm around my waist.

I try to fight him, but he's too strong. A scream tears from my throat and seems to carry across the mountains. The sound is cut off as Cian clamps his hand over my mouth. I sink my teeth into his flesh until my mouth fills with blood. He roars and releases me, I spin and push him, he's off-balance, and I watch in absolute horror as Cian sails over the side of the railing.

CHAPTER THIRTY-TWO

O'REAGAN
AN CHLANN

JACK

I'm running towards Maeve's screams. It sounds like she's outside. Shay has withdrawn his gun and is heavy on my heels. I can't slow down. I can't think. Her scream was filled with so much fear. I round the side of the house and stop dead in my tracks. Below the balcony is Cian, lying dead in a pool of blood. Immediately I look up and into a pair of brown eyes that are wide and filled with horror. She's shaking her head, and when her gaze meets mine, her lip trembles, and she disappears into the room.

I'm aware of so much right now. Shay is right beside me, watching everything. There are cameras everywhere, and Lawlor must be close.

Cian's hand twitches, and he gurgles, blood gushing from his open mouth. I'm looking at Finn all over again.

Shay places his gun back in his waistband. "His neck is really and truly fucked." Shay bends down and inspects Cian like he's a dying animal. I'm looking back at the balcony.

"Stay here," I say to Shay and race into the house. I'm taking the steps two at a time, my panic driving me to the bedroom. I stop at the door. Maeve is against the wall. She's still shaking her head, her hands covering her mouth. She looks like a trapped animal.

"I'm so sorry. I didn't mean it." The words tumble from her lips. Her gaze dances around the room and refuses to settle on anything; her gaze is as frantic as her mind.

"I just pushed him away. I just wanted him to stop." She's reaching for something, and her hands press against her chest. I step into the room, and my movements have her eyes drift towards me.

"I'm so sorry. Please, Jack." She tilts her head as tears fall from her eyes, and the closer I get, the smaller she tries to make herself. "Don't hurt me. I'm so sorry. I didn't mean it." Her head rests on her chest, and I don't understand why she would think I'd hurt her. I'm pulling her into my chest, knowing this is a fucking mess, which I'm not sure I can clean up.

Shane will order her execution.

I grip her tighter, and she breaks in my arms. Her sobs turned to loud cries that I try to hush, but it does no good as hysteria eats away at any self-preservation that she might have had moments ago.

The sound of a gunshot has me releasing Maeve, her sobs gone, and I'm opening the balcony door. Shay looks up at me, his gun still in his hand.

The hole in Cian's head is right between his eyes.

"I just put him out of his misery." Shay's gaze moves behind me, and I stiffen as Maeve steps up beside me and looks down at Cian. A sob tears from her. I look to Shay again, wondering how much time I have.

"Can I have five minutes?" I ask for the grace period.

Shay glances down at Cian before he smiles up at me like I'm asking for more time to get dressed. "Take your time."

I don't like it one bit, but I need to talk to Maeve. She comes easily as I direct her back into the bedroom.

"I need you to listen to me." She won't meet my eye, and I grab her face.

"Focus, Maeve." I hate raising my voice, but she blinks away more tears and focuses on my face.

"I know you didn't mean it." I wanted to know what the fuck he was doing here again, but right now, that didn't matter.

"But right now, I need you to stay calm. Can you do that for me?"

She nods, but there is no calmness in her eyes. Her gaze focuses on me, and her nails dig into my arms. "Jack. Is he dead?" She's pleading with me to tell her he's alive like she didn't just see him with a hole in his head.

"Yes."

Her head rests on my chest, and she starts to cry again. I can't give her much more time.

"Maeve. Shay's here." That is a loaded statement. He knows. He saw. He's after intervening. But I keep so much in.

When she leans out, I see the understanding in her eyes.

"I won't let anyone harm you. I swear it." I wanted that fear gone. "But right now, I need you to be strong and stay here. Okay?"

She nods again. This time I can't stay. I close the balcony door. "Stay away from the door. Stay in this room." I look to Maeve to reinforce my words, but she's not focused.

"Maeve, look at me." I grip her arms again, and her gaze snaps back to me.

"Where was Lawlor?"

She swallows and shakes her head as if she's trying to remember past the horror of Cian's dead body.

"Cian told him to have a cup of coffee."

I press a kiss to her forehead. "Okay, stay here and don't leave this room." I let her go reluctantly and make my way back downstairs.

Shay is still standing over Cian. "He had it coming." Shay takes a pack of cigarettes from his pocket and lights one up. He keeps looking up at the balcony. "If they find out Maeve did it, they'll hunt her down like a dog," Shay tells me what I already know. I don't have to wait long until he reveals why he's telling me. "We could help each other out of this mess." He blows smoke into the night sky.

"How's that?" I step up to Cian and start going through his pockets. Removing his phone, I open it, but it has a password on it.

"I'll help you bury this. No one has to know." I rise with Cian's phone in my hand.

"What's the cost?" I ask him.

Shay grins. "Does the cost matter?" He glances up at the balcony, and I know he's speaking about Maeve.

Did it matter? No.

I nod at Shay. "I need to kill the cameras, and one of my bodyguards is here."

"Don't kill your bodyguard." Shay looks down at Cian and tilts his head. "You and Cian were talking, just like you and Finn, when a shot was fired, killing him. If we have two dead bodies here, it will be harder to explain. You can get him another time." Shay finally looks at me. "I was in the kitchen when the shot was fired and came out to find this."

It would stand. Shay had been at my father's with me, we had all been called in, and they knew who shot Finn and Connor. It was a revenge kill from my father's past. My father had recognized him from footage outside the pub he had been spotted at before. So Shay being here would work.

"That's a different bullet lodged in his brain." I run my hands across my face.

"They won't look at that until everything calms down. All that this will do is send them hunting for John's son; once we have the story out, and they're busy, we can deal with the rest."

"What if they catch John's son before us, and he denies killing Cian?" What Shay is suggesting is risky.

Shay grins again. "Then we better catch him first." Nothing about this sits right with me, but I don't have any options.

Shay finishes his cigarette, crushes it on the ground before he picks up the butt, and puts it in his pocket. I'm staring at him.

"It has my DNA on it," He explains, and I still don't get it.

"It's a habit from up North. Leave nothing behind in case it becomes a crime scene."

"So, what do you want?" I ask before we ring this in.

"You're next in line to rule the East. Let me rule beside you." He pauses to let that sink in. "A panel of us."

I see movement in the house and spot a black suit; it's Lawlor. He hasn't come out to investigate—maybe he knows he's a dead man already.

"How many?"

"Four. Four rulers. We choose one more each. We rule equally."

275

"What about the North?" That was his. It only had four counties, but they were large.

"We would rule the North and the East together, and you never know, we could take over the rest of Ireland."

I look back down at Cian. If Maeve hadn't confessed to pushing him, and Shay hadn't been with me, I'd believe he planned all this.

"Right now, we need to ring this in."

Shay lights up another cigarette, the only sign that he's nervous. I take out the phone and dial my father's number.

"Yes," He answers almost immediately.

"Cian has been shot." I look at Shay, and he nods at me before turning away and walking back to the house.

"Is he dead?" My father's words carry no emotion.

I glance down at Cian. "Yes. It was a headshot."

"Where are you?"

"I'm at my house. It was the same as Finn," I say the lie that he can surely tell. Silence. "Should I ring Shane?"

"No. Let me." I'm glad when he offers to ring Shane.

My father hangs up and I go into the house. Lawlor is in the kitchen with Shay.

"Go home, Lawlor. I'll contact you later."

Lawlor looks ready to speak, but I give him one final look, and he leaves. I don't linger but go into the security room under the stairs. All TV's are on, and one by one, I power them off before removing the small chip that would have today's footage on it. I slip it into my back pocket and lock the room behind me. Shay's standing outside.

"My father knows. He's ringing Shane now."

"He's going to question you. Are you ready for that?" Shay holds my stare, and I feel he's asking me more than he's saying.

"You mean is Maeve ready for this?"

Shay runs his hands across his beard. "I'll back you, but just make it good. Shay takes his gun out of his pocket. "Anywhere I can stash this?"

I don't want to touch it. So I lead Shay into the living room. I press down on the third floor-board away from the wall, and it clicks, popping open. I push aside the cash and passports and stand up. "Go ahead."

He grins again as he puts it in. "Afraid to get your prints on it?"

When he stands up, I stand on the floor-board, and it clicks into place. "Of course."

He sneers. "You go and deal with your woman. I'll stay outside with Cian's body until they arrive."

Maeve is sitting on the bed. Her lips are moving like she's talking to herself. The moment I enter, her head snaps up. I know we don't have much time.

"My father and Cian's father will be here soon."

Any color that was left in her cheeks disappears, and she starts to rock back and forth.

"They are going to question us. So this is what happened."

I walk to the bed and sit down to make sure she pays attention. "You were studying up here. You heard a gunshot, looked out the balcony window, and saw Cian's body. It will explain the state you are in."

"Why can't you just say I wasn't here?" She blinks more tears. "I don't want to talk to them. I killed him."

I grip her arms. "Maeve, it's not safe to say something like that. You were studying, you heard a gunshot, and that's it."

She looks away from me and I hate frightening her anymore, but she needs to see. "If they EVER find out it was you, you will be executed, and I won't be able to stop it. Do you understand?"

I'm not sure if she's going to throw up, but she nods.

I drag her into my arms, and she's never felt so far away from me. I hate not knowing what will happen next, but no matter what, I'll do my best to keep her safe.

I hear the rumble of a vehicle along the ground outside. I release Maeve and go to the balcony doors. It's Shane who's running across the lawn. He collapses to his knees and lifts Cian's head into his lap. He's a different man who watched two people being shot without blinking. His roar has me stepping back. Maeve starts to sob. "They're here."

I'm helpless right now. I can't show weakness. I turn to Maeve. "You stay up here until I come for you."

Tears stream down her face without her saying a word. I grip her face and kiss her. Her salty tears wet my lips. "I'll protect you," I say the words against her lips before leaving the room and dragging the door closed behind me.

Chapter Thirty-Three

O'REAGAN
AN CHLANN

MAEVE

I can't breathe. All the air has been sucked from the room. I've bent over and placed my head, in-between my legs. The world tilts, and I'm okay with that. I tighten my eyes as the memory of Cian grabbing me fills my vision, my stomach somersaults, and I'm shaking my head like I can shake the image right out of it. Like I can see him rising above the rail and walking back into the room. Like I might be able to rewind time.

I sit up straight as a roar that feels like it rattles the walls has me covering my ears. It's so filled with pain, and I cry when it starts up again. I stand up, and against my better judgment, I walk slowly to the balcony doors; I have no idea how my legs are carrying me. I cover my mouth with both hands like I might keep the sob in.

Shane is pacing in front of his son, his hands in his hair. He half bends and roars again like he can release all the broken pieces, the vision of him wavers, and I blink him back into focus. I'm caving on the floor.

I took his son from him.

The image disappears as I sink to the floor and cover my ears as he roars a few more times. When he stops, I finally take my hands away from my ears, only to hear a vehicle drive around the side of the house. I crawl to the window and stay hidden as Liam O'Reagan, dressed in a black suit, calmly walks across the lawn. His sharp eyes take in the scene before me. He stops when he reaches Cian's body; he assesses it, and no one seems to speak. He finally looks at Shane, who walks up to Liam and clings to him.

I'm surprised to see Liam hug him back. I'm surprised the man has any compassion. He sent Cian here; I wonder if Shane knows that. If he does, he would know Cian was sent to retrieve me, and his body is right under the balcony. When they do a post mortem, the fall would have done some damage. It would show up. They would know what I had done.

My heart stops when Liam looks up. His sharp eyes meet mine and it's like he knows. He knows I had some involvement in this. I'm crawling backwards like I can outrun this. Like I can outrun what I just did.

Cian had said it was part of his trials; I hadn't thought to say any of that to Jack. I was so sure that Jack would kill me. I still don't believe for one second I'm safe. You didn't take the life of an O'Reagan and simply walk away.

I hear the footsteps on the stairs, and I get up off the bedroom floor. Blood roars in my ears as the door opens. I don't know what I am expecting, but it isn't Liam. A whimper that I try to swallow unsuccessfully slips out.

He opens the door fully before stepping in. "Do you have a minute?"

His question is fucking bizarre as I try to breathe. "Yes." My voice squeaks, and I want to look out the balcony doors to see if Jack is still down there, or did he send his father to kill me because he couldn't do it himself.

Liam walks into the room, and I want to scream, but I hold still as he steps closer. He stops at the balcony doors. The night is nearly fully here. "It's quite the view."

My breathing is too heavy, and spots gather like a band of guilty dots in front of my eyes. "It is," I answer Liam.

He doesn't turn. "You can see a lot from this window." He turns to me, and my legs give out. I'm close to the bed and land heavily on it.

"You look pale." Liam moves away from me and slowly walks around the room.

"I've never seen anyone die before."

Liam glances at me. "Really?" He sounds surprised. "What were you doing up here?"

His eyes touch everything in the room, and I try to remember what Jack said. "Studying."

He stops at the desk and opens the laptop that hasn't been powered up.

"My books," I say. My frantic mind—for a moment—can't see them on the desk, but when I do, I'm pointing at them like it's a victory.

"Tell me what you heard and saw."

Now Liam faces me. "I heard a gunshot, and I raced to the window. Cian was dead."

"You raced to the window after hearing a gunshot? That seems a very unusual thing to do. Most women would hide."

"I panicked. I didn't think."

"Did you see anyone?"

"No." I shake my head for extra emphasis.

"You never spoke to Cian?"

My heart thumps against my chest. I fear it will tear through the wall of my chest and land at his feet.

"Not today." I fold my hands into my lap, and Liam's gaze flickers to them like he can see the blood on them. I tighten my hands into fists.

"So you have spoken to him before."

"Briefly. At your house and at the club."

"But never here?"

I know not to lie. If Liam had sent him this time, then he had sent him before. "No. Sorry." I frown and stare at the floor like I'm trying to remember. "He was here before. A few days ago."

Liam nods. He doesn't ask me what we spoke of. He already knows.

"Thank you, Maeve." He nods, and the fear of God is in me. Did I pass? Am I going to be executed? He stops at the door, and I'm praying that he just leaves me alone.

"I will find the person responsible." He turns to me, and I see it in his eyes, he knows.

He just knows.

I can't speak, and he finally leaves me. My body slumps, and I don't think I could get up even if the house fell down around me. He makes no noise as he moves down the stairs. All I hear is a static sound and the roar of blood that gushes violently in my ears.

I don't move. I don't know how much time passes. The room grows darker, and I'm repeating what happened over and over in my head, watching Cian fall to his death. His huge limbs flailing like he might find something to cling to or stop his fall.

The noise on the stairs brings me back. The bedroom door is still open from when Liam left. I glance up as Jack steps in and flicks on the light. I close my eyes against the harshness that threatens to burn my eyes.

"Maeve." Jack kneels down in front of me. "You're doing great." The smile is forced, and he looks pale. "Just one more small hurdle." His voice is low, and he glances at the door. I've never seen Jack nervous before. His hand takes mine in his.

"Shane wants to ask you a few questions."

I'm already shaking my head. "I can't."

I'd break. I'd confess, seeing all that pain.

Jack's hand tightens on mine. "You have to." His words are low but fierce. "Last round. I promise."

Did I have a choice?

Jack rises and keeps my hand in his. As we leave the safety of the bedroom, it's like I'm being walked to my death. A horrible image of being brought outside, and standing up against the wall, fills my mind. I see Shane with a gun in his hand. I pause on the stairs. Jack looks back at me and squeezes my hand.

We move downstairs and into a sitting-room. I think it would be anyone's worst nightmare. Liam stands at the unlit fireplace. Shay is standing, looking out the window, and Shane is pacing. The moment we step in, his bloodshot eyes focus on me. Old and rusty barbed wire tightens around my chest, and guilt so severe squeezes me. The room tilts, and I lean into Jack.

Every man in this room is a killer. I'm scrambling for control of my frantic mind as Shane's mouth moves, and I can't hear. I look at Jack, and he squeezes my hand.

"Just tell him what you saw." Jack reaches up and touches my face, and I want to slip through his fingers and disappear.

"I was studying in my room," I tell Shane, and he takes a step towards me. His eyes, black eyes that hold too much wildness, like something untamed, stare at me like can see deep into my soul. My words are his clues, and he has them under a microscope.

"I heard a gunshot and went to the balcony window." I'm aware Shay is watching me too, and I take a peek at him. His gaze makes me shiver, and I look back at Shane.

"I'm so sorry for your loss."

"Did you see anyone else?" He ignores my sympathies. He's in survival mode, but it's not working correctly. He's stepping closer to me, his body tight to the point it might break.

I shake my head. "No. I'm sorry, I'm not more helpful."

Shane finally releases me from his gaze and turns to Liam. He runs his hands across his face and shakes his head. "This is going to kill Una."

"It is the sad part of our profession." Liam's unapologetic words rip me from my turmoil.

"Not. My. Son!" Shane's roars are towards Liam, but I'm moving back. Everything in him is amplifying and growing, manifesting, and the air grows too thin.

Jack jerks my arm, stopping me from leaving the room. I hadn't been aware that I was even trying to leave. I blink, and tears spill. I want to beg him to let me go. But the words are stolen from me as Shane roars again. He races towards the wall. His fists smash into concrete, and Shay is moving. Jack releases my hand as both of them try to peel Shane away from the wall that is smeared in his blood.

I glance away to find Liam watching me, and it's all too much. I'm out of the room and running up the stairs. I make it into the bedroom. My knees hit the tiled floor of the bathroom hard, and I bring up the contents of my stomach.

The bedroom door closes. "I just need a minute," I plead, wanting to be left alone. A shadow fills the bathroom door, and I know it's not Jack.

"Your life isn't the only one on the line." Shay doesn't step into the bathroom, his voice is controlled but I can hear that undertone of his annoyance, like he would prefer to squash me then have this conversation.

I wipe my mouth with the back of my hand and look up at Shay.

"If they find out that Jack and I are helping you, we won't just get a slap on the wrist. So we need you to keep it together."

I was under no illusion that Shay was helping me. He was doing this for his own reason. He steps in and holds out his hand to help me up. I don't take it, but get up off the floor.

"You mean a lot to Jack. He's put everything on the line for you, so I suggest you repay him by not attracting attention to yourself."

I nod. His words hit me hard. He was right. What had Jack sacrificed to lie to his family?

"Good girl." Shay smiles and steps out of the bathroom.

A car starts up outside, and I walk into the bedroom.

"Shane is gone, so you won't be questioned again by him."

I'm cold and tired, and all I can manage to do is nod.

"But once anyone is around, you can't draw attention to yourself like that ever again."

I want him away from me. His words might hold truth, but I didn't need a fucking lecture. "I heard you the first time."

He half sneers before making his way to the door. "Good. Heed it."

CHAPTER THIRTY-FOUR

O'REAGAN

AN CHLANN

JACK

She's asleep on top of the covers. Her knees are curled up towards her chest. Too much brandy makes my steps noisy as I make my way to the bed. The moment I land on the mattress, Maeve stirs.

"Jack?"

I reach for her, following the sweet sound of her voice has me smiling. "Yeah, come here." I drag her body closer to mine, and instantly I want her. I inhale her scent deeply before brushing her hair aside and pressing my lips against her warm skin.

"Jack." Her voice shakes and I turn her towards me, her breath brushes my cheek, my cock grows harder as her hands reach up and press against my chest.

"I need to tell you something about your dad."

I trail kisses down her neck and let my hands slip to her legs. I didn't want to talk about my dad or anything else. All I wanted was to bury myself inside Maeve.

She pushes me softly. "He sent Cian here to get me."

The brandy had made me warm. Maeve made me forget. That information makes everything flee and I'm climbing out of the bed. I need to have Maeve repeat herself, only I want to see her. Flicking on the lights, she's sitting up, her knees dragged up to her chin. Dark circles under her eyes make me slow my demands down.

"What do you mean he sent Cian?"

I crawl onto the bed and she grips her knees tighter. Her knuckles turn white. "Why do you look so afraid?" My question comes out in a growl.

Maeve quickly looks away. "He's your dad."

I reach for Maeve and her gaze flickers to me. I soften my features to try to make her understand as I touch her face. "I would never hurt you. You don't hurt the people you love."

She blinks, and tears fall before she spills into my arms and sobs. "I'm just waiting for you to change your mind and kill me."

I hold her tighter. "My mind is made up about you. You have to know that by now."

She snivels into my neck. "Yeah, I'm starting to see that."

I kiss the crown of her head. "Tell me what happened."

Her sobs cease, and she slowly comes out of my arms. "Cian said your father had sent him here to take me away. That I was a distraction to you."

287

I'm ready to dismiss what she's saying as Cian's way of making her go with him.

"When I fought Cian, he said he wasn't failing his trials."

I'm staring at Maeve, her lip trembles, and I sense she isn't telling me everything. "What else?"

"Your dad knows it was me."

I drag Maeve back into my arms, I want her to stop.

"No. He would never suspect you," I say, pressing another kiss to the crown of her head.

"Jack, when he was up here questioning me, I just knew it."

What if she is right? What if my father sent Cian? I can't ignore what she is saying. I want to. I want to push it all aside.

"Tomorrow, I'm going to the coroner, and I'll make sure Cian's death is pointed at the sniper."

"How?" Maeve's voice is filled with disbelief. "He must have broken bones."

"That won't go on record." I cut her off.

She leans out to look at me. "You can do something like that?" She sounds disturbed and I don't blame her.

"Yes."

"Have you done this before?"

I don't want to answer her. I don't want her to know too much. It's dangerous. "All you need to know is that this will go away."

Her eyes tell me that she will never forget, but I know in time it will fade. "Let's get some sleep."

I release Maeve and start to pull back the covers as she scurries under them. As much as I want her, she looks exhausted and having all that on her mind about Cian and my Father didn't help. I flick off the lights and get into bed beside her. She instantly wraps her small frame around me and I spend the next while fighting the urge to take her.

"Shay will be staying with you." I get into my suit and make my way downstairs as Maeve fights her case.

"I don't like him. I don't want to stay with him."

Her not liking Shay was one reason I would gladly leave her with him. I knew nothing would happen between them when I left. Also, he was the only person I could trust right now. Lawlor had to be dealt with, but first, I needed to get to the coroner and arrange everything before Shane got there.

"I won't be long."

Shay's vehicle rolls up along the front of the house. "He's here, so be nice," I say to Maeve.

"Nice?"

When I turn to her, she's folded her arms across her chest. I pause for a moment, thinking of how stunning she is, and if leaving her here is wise.

The front door opens and Shay steps in.

"I'll just grab a cup of coffee." He points at the kitchen and closes the door. "Do you want one, Maeve?" His voice is sweet, like how he talks to my mother, only my mother eats it up. Maeve's face grows stern, and she glares at him. "No."

I lean in and place a kiss on her lips. "I won't be long."

She unfolds her arms and exhales as Shay goes into the kitchen. "I know you have a lot on your mind, but I still need to see my mother."

I did, and her mother was at the bottom of the list, but I can see from the sternness in her gaze that I needed to move her mother up.

"I promise when I get back, we will talk about it."

Shay's rattling around in the kitchen loudly, and I think he's giving me the signal to leave.

"Okay." Maeve gives in.

I give her one final kiss before going into the kitchen. "I won't be long. If my father comes around, text me."

Shay grins up at me, but I see the question there. "No problem." He pours himself a coffee, and I'm hesitant about leaving Maeve, but I need to get this done now.

David is bent over a body when I enter his workroom. A man in his fifties, naked and gray, had David's attention. A light on the top of his head is pushed back as he straightens.

"Mr. O'Reagan."

"David. I wanted a quick word."

He drops the scalpel in his hand and removes the gloves while glancing at the door.

"William let me through," I explain. He isn't used to dealing with me. It's something I need to rectify.

"Do you have the report on Cian?"

He removes the light from his forehead and places it beside the body on the silver tray. I look away from the body as he takes a file out of the filing cabinet and opens it.

"Let's see. His neck was broken from what must have been a fall. It damaged his lower spine, and a rib that broke, punctured his lung. If he wasn't shot in the head, he would have died within two minutes."

I walk to David and remove the file from his hand. Taking out his report, I fold it. "He was shot in the head," I say.

David nods. "He was shot in the head."

"The bullet that was extracted from Finn's neck is the same bullet that you extracted from Cian. That bullet will arrive here tonight, so you can present it to his father."

"I understand," David answers as I stuff the piece of paper into my jacket pocket.

David scratches his thinning hair. "Your father wants a full report. I'm assuming I can give him the information I just gave you?"

"My father was already here?"

David looks unsure now and closes the filing cabinet. "Yes, yesterday."

"What did you tell him?"

David stands straight. "I hadn't completed my report but told him he would be the first to know."

Relief has me nodding. "You tell my father he was shot. That's it. That's all you tell anyone."

His gaze dances around the room. "Mr. O'Reagan, no disrespect, but lying to Liam isn't wise."

I take a step towards him. "Liam is stepping down, and who do you think is taking his place?"

I don't allow David a moment to answer. "Me. So I am your boss, and going against me isn't wise. Do we understand each other?"

He's nodding vigorously.

"Tell Bernie and the kids I said hi."

David holds his head high, maybe used to the threat that no doubt my father made countless times.

I leave, and once I'm outside, I remove my tie and get back into the jeep. Checking my phone, I have no messages from Shay, but I still ring him.

"Hello." Soft music plays in the background, and it sounds like he's frying.

"Are you cooking?"

"Yeah, I fancied a fry-up. Maeve is here in the kitchen with me. She's fine." It sounds like he moves. "No sign of your Da."

"I shouldn't be much longer, but all's been tied up."

"That's a load off."

I had no idea if Shay was being smart, but right now, with my father's betrayal, I had nowhere else to turn.

I hang up and make a few more phone calls. I had bought into some investment properties in the Navan area a while back and I need to secure one for Maeve's mother. It doesn't take long before the management company finds one that is vacant, a small bungalow on the outskirts. Telling them to make sure it's fully furnished and ready for her to move into, I make my way back to the house.

I'm halfway there when the phone rings. A message from Shay. "Your Da is here."

"Fuck." I drive faster, wanting him as far away from Maeve as possible. The moment I pull up into the drive, I want to rush into the house. Wisely, I pull up into the garage and turn off the jeep. Putting my tie back on, I take the piece of paper out of my jacket pocket and leave it in the glove compartment.

Entering the kitchen, my father is seated at the table drinking a cup of coffee while Shay makes a meal of his fry-up.

"Where's Maeve?" I ask, not seeing her.

"Studying in her room. She's fond of the books." Shay swings around, and the serious look in his eye has me sitting down.

"I came around to see how you were doing?" My father's words are stiff.

I sit down. "I'll be a lot better when we catch John's son," I answer.

My father pushes away a mug in front of him. "There is still no sign of him, but don't worry, we will get him."

"You never really explained why John's son had a vendetta against you." Shay cuts a sausage up like it's the finest meat and places it in his mouth. His chew is as slow as my father's answer. I wonder if he knows how close he is to pushing my father.

"It's history. His father worked for me. Later he went into the army. Then he came back home. We met briefly and shortly after, he overdosed. His son must blame me."

Shay cuts his egg, and the yellow pours out onto his plate. "Why would he blame you?"

My father doesn't shift in his stance, and he is someone you should study when given the opportunity. He's a masterful liar, and you couldn't guess what he's thinking.

"That is truly a mystery, one I don't care for. All I know is that it's him, and it's the only reason I can see for him coming after my family."

Shay shakes his head. "Crazy Cunt."

"How is your father?"

All this chit chat would lead somewhere I was sure of it, but right now, all I can think about is Maeve and what she told me.

"Recovering. He's as strong as an ox." Shay sounds proud.

My father has no love for his father. My father nods and rises. He pauses and his attention falls on me. "I was meaning to ask, it's not important, but it was for my own records. What was Cian doing here?"

I could say anything I wanted right now, and he'd have to take my word for it. Since he fucking sent him. I hate thinking my father would betray me like that.

"He wanted to be given the chance to take part in the trials." I lie as fluently as my father.

"Interesting. Did you grant it?" My father pushes in the chair as he speaks.

"I don't have the power to do something like that. I told him to go to you. But now we will never know the answer." I stand too, wanting to call him out on what he did. I want to know why he did it. Maeve was important to me. I want to ask him if it was Mother, what would he have done?

"I'm curious what you would have said?" Shay is still eating, listening, learning. He's far cleverer than we give him credit for.

"It doesn't really matter now, does it?" My father answers.

Shay returns to his food.

"I'll let myself out." My father gives Shay and me one final look but pauses again.

"I'm off to the coroner, so I will let you boys know the results."

"David said they would be ready this evening."

My father looks at me, and for the first time, I see surprise in his eyes. "You went there?"

"If I am to rule, I think finding out who killed my cousin takes priority."

My father doesn't answer, and I stay standing as I wait for the front door to close.

"You want to tell me what's going on?" Shay asks from the table, and I will share everything with him, but just not yet.

CHAPTER
THIRTY-FIVE

O'REAGAN

AN CHLANN

MAEVE

The clock moves, but time seems to stand still for me over the next three days. I'm numb and I want to remain that way. I've been to Cian's parents' house for the wake. Jack had tried his best to shield me from the grieving family, but I had still shaken hands with Cian's family and offered my condolences.

Jack's reminder to me, whenever we were alone, was that Shay killed him, not me. That he would have lived if Shay hadn't pulled the trigger. Part of me clung to his words and prayed that they were the truth.

The church moves past in a blur, and now I'm standing in the graveyard, sensing someone watching me. I don't want to look in case it is Liam. He is the one person I have avoided intentionally. When I look up it is Shay.

It's been three days since I've seen him. Since Jack went to the coroners and I was left in Shay's care. He nods at me—and out of manners—I nod back, knowing that someone else is surely watching. Stuffing my hands deeper in my long black coat, I face forward as the priest says kind things about Cian.

No one cries except for Una. Shane holds his wife, and he isn't the man I watched fall apart a few days ago. He's strong and put together. To an outsider, they might think he doesn't care. Jack's at the front with his father. I didn't want to stand shoulder-to-shoulder with them. Dana looks back and gives me a watery smile. Guilt churns in my stomach. She's another person I've been avoiding. So many lies I've had to tell her. So many more I'm sure I will have to say. Having a friendship with her has never been more complicated. She's been talking about returning to Italy soon, and I know Svetlana is encouraging her to go. She doesn't want Dana involved in any of this, but I think it's only a matter of time.

"May he rest in peace." The words pull me from my thoughts as Una wails, her legs buckle, and Shane supports her as the coffin is lowered into the ground. I look away from the heartbreaking scene before me and focus on the sky. The dark clouds that are forming over our heads, threaten to open and soak us with tears from the heavens. I hold onto the knowledge that Jack gave me. Everyone thought Cian had been shot by the same man who also shot two of Jack's uncles. He said no one would ever look any deeper into it. That knowledge I had to cling to, I had to hold on to like my life depended on it. I suppose in some ways it did. My sanity depends on it.

Once again guilt rolls through me because I felt relief knowing I would get away with it. The crowd starts to disperse, and I keep my eyes on the ground now, not wanting to meet anyone else's grieving gazes. I didn't need any more watery eyes, or turn downed mouths to become my focus.

"Are you coming back to the hotel?" Dana's voice pulls my gaze from the gray stones that crunch under the footfall of the many people here, there must be hundreds. I didn't think Cian was that well-known, but by the looks of the clientele, it was more for the O'Reagans. I'm looking across the crowd for Jack, but of course he would be going back. "Yeah."

She exhales loudly and steps up beside me, linking her arm with mine. Dana rests her head on my shoulder. "I'll miss him."

"Me, too." My gaze clashes with Jack's and his features soften further when his eyes glide towards Dana, who's still holding onto me. He looks so handsome in his dark suit and jacket. He kisses Dana on the head before pressing a kiss to my lips.

"That was lovely for him." Dana straightens up but doesn't release me.

Jack smiles. "Yeah, he got a good send off. Come on, and we'll have a drink on him."

Jack's ice-blue eyes settle on me and he takes my hand in his. Dana releases me and we walk to Jack's jeep.

"Did you drive?" Jack asks Dana.

"No. I came with mother and father. Let me tell them I'm going with you."

"Okay. We'll be in the jeep."

Dana leaves, and Jack pulls me closer. "I'm so proud of you," His voice is low, and he leans into me as he speaks. "You are doing fantastic."

"So are you." I look up and meet his gaze. He stops walking and takes my chin in his gloved hand before leaning in and pressing a kiss to my lips. It's soft, but like all things with Jack, no matter how small the touch or word or gaze, I feel it all the way down to my toes.

Jack releases me as one of his uncles walks beside us.

"How's Finn?" Jack asks him.

"He's still here. I think him seeing Cian has made him realize he should be fucking grateful he's above ground."

Darragh. That's his name. I had met him at Shane's house. He looked just like Finn, who was in a wheelchair.

"Yeah, I think it's a reminder to us all that we aren't invincible." We stop at the jeep, and Jack unlocks it.

Darragh lights up a cigarette. "Some of us. Others think they can walk on water and turn piss to wine."

Jack laughs.

Darragh winks at me. "See you at the hotel."

Jack opens the door for me, and I climb in. The moment he's in, he turns on the engine and starts the heat.

"Who was he talking about?" I ask. I didn't really care, but sitting here and seeing all the grieving people move past, didn't entice me one bit to keep my focus on them.

"Shay and his dad, Connor. They are a different breed."

I turn to Jack as he shrugs out of his jacket. "But he's your cousin."

Jack loosens his tie like he's about to take it off, but stops. "He is, but they're up north and do things differently than we do."

Dana races towards the jeep. My gaze trails behind her, where Liam and Svetlana stand. I hate the sight of Liam, so I smile at Dana as she passes my window and climbs into the back.

"I don't think I will ever get used to seeing you riding up front."

I smile for the first time. "Me neither."

Jack waits until Dana is buckled up.

"Well, get used to it." Jack's words have me looking at him. I see so much in his eyes, and my own feelings are reflected in them.

I love him.

I love every part of him, and I know that love is new but will continue to grow. I think I've always loved Jack O'Reagan. Throughout my life, it was a different kind of love.

When I think of all he has done for my family and me, my mom now has her own home, and Jack and I are going to go for dinner one of these days soon. Declan is out of the hospital and at home, continuing his rehab. I couldn't be prouder. I still can't see them, but Jack promises I can soon.

"I thought Richard would come home." Dana pulls me out of my thoughts.

"I rang him. He couldn't get out of work." Jack's voice is deep, like he's repeating words he doesn't believe.

"Family is family. An Chlann," Dana speaks, and I want to see her face. I wonder if she understands the power that term carries for her family.

"How's Declan?" She asks after a moment when the talk of Richard stops.

"He's out of rehab." I half turn because I know she will share my joy.

"I'm so happy for him. And you." She reaches and grips my hand.

"He's looking so well."

"He's always look well to me. I wouldn't kick him out of bed."

I'm tempted to look at Jack, but don't. I wouldn't encourage a relationship like that. I simply wouldn't want my brother involved with Liam.

One of us is enough.

"No love interest in Italy?"

Dana's grin tells me there was.

"You girls can chat at the hotel." Jack turns down the street of Kells.

Dana rolls her eyes at Jack's statement, and I turn around, facing forward again.

"I'm picturing some hot Italian stallion," I say, just to get a kick out of Jack. It's nice to joke, and when he looks at me, he flashes a warning.

"Dana, tell Maeve she's wrong."

"Yeah, Maeve, you're wrong."

I can picture Dana rolling her eyes. Our banter stops as we pull up at the hotel. No one moves, and Dana clears her throat.

"So... I'll see you inside?"

"Yeah." Jack doesn't answer, so I do, and Dana gets out.

As she passes my window, she gives me a half-smile, and I hate how dishonest I've been with her.

"Are you ready for this?" Jack asks as he watches people enter the hotel.

No.

"Yes."

Jack turns fully to me, and I want to reach across and kiss him. My stomach squirms as his intense gaze doesn't waver, even as the seconds pass between us.

"When we bring women to outings that are exclusively for us, it's a signal to everyone."

I bite the inside of my cheek.

"It makes this more official than you can imagine." Jack holds the steering wheel with one hand while watching me.

"How official?" I ask.

His smile has everything in me turning to mush, and I get it when girls freak out over a guy. I never did before, but with Jack, staying with him is the only option.

"Really official." His smile accompanies his words.

His words raise all the hairs on my body, and I'm ready to sign my soul over to him in blood.

"So, if I don't go in?" I ask, knowing I will, but there is a vulnerability in his smile that makes me want to see what happens. He doesn't show this much, and I'm pushing, wanting to see more.

"I'd hate to drag you in and start off our life together on such a bad foot."

I bite my cheek but can't stop the smile that takes over my features.

I dip my head, feeling ridiculously in love. Jack shifts towards me, releasing the steering wheel, and his hand cups my face. He tilts it, so I'm looking at him.

"So which is it?" His playful tone gets lost when his gaze drops to my mouth.

"I think I'll walk through the door."

His smile is back. "Good choice."

His mouth consumes mine, and I get lost in Jack. His smell. His touch.

A rap at the window drags us apart. Shay bends down, his hands stuffed into his coat, and he grins. Jack nods at him, and he leaves.

"We better go in," I say, feeling guilt about kissing him and enjoying myself when Cian was dead.

"I won't leave you." Jack places one final kiss on my lips.

Once I get out of the jeep, he meets me and takes my hand, giving me strength and hope that after today we might be able to start over.

CHAPTER THIRTY-SIX

O'REAGAN
AN CHLANN

JACK

I keep Maeve's small hand in mine as we enter the main room where the function is being held. A row of waiters stand ready to the left of us. Each time a guest arrives, one steps forward and gives their attention to that guest. That attendant's spot is filled with another keeping a strong line of black clad servers.

It's my father's hotel, so he has held nothing back as far as expense goes. Could he be feeling guilty over Cian's death? I tighten my hold on Maeve's hand at the thought of Cian succeeding. What would they have done to her?

We maneuver through the room that is littered with large round tables. White linen tablecloths cover them all, and in the center of each is a large vase of white lilies. It looks more like a room set out for a wedding, not a funeral. Everywhere I look, I acknowledge the men I grew up around as a kid. Every criminal who has a foothold in the Irish or English country is here, offering up their sympathies, planning, building bridges. It's a dangerous place to be. The five large mirrors in the room are covered in black sheets, normally something you would see in the home of whoever is being waked. My father was really showing respect to Shane and Una.

Gazes trail from me to Maeve. I keep my pace slow throughout the room so they see and make note of her. I want them all to take a good look, so they know she is never to be touched, that she is mine.

"Why is everyone watching us?" Maeve's words are low, and I don't react to her sweet voice. I want to smile, I want to stop and kiss her, but I continue our walk around the large room.

"They are watching you," I answer, while nodding at Noel Murphy. His family has power over the South. He's the eldest of three, and someone I haven't spent much time with. It is something that I do wish to rectify in the future.

"Why?" Alarm mingles with fear in Maeve's voice.

"I told you this is your introduction to our people."

"As what?" Maeve's voice wobbles.

This time, I do stop walking and turn to her. "As my future."

She's holding her breath, and I brush a piece of blond hair off her cheek before leaning in. Her cheeks are flushed from having so many eyes on her, and she looks innocent and pure.

"Breathe, Maeve." A gush of her breath hits my cheek, and I press a kiss just under her earlobe. When I look up, I see my father is watching. I straighten.

"I want you to stay with Dana." I refocus on Maeve.

Her gaze dances around the room before it lands on me. "You're leaving?"

"I have to speak to someone." I don't tell her who and she doesn't ask.

I take Maeve's hand again, and direct her towards Dana— who's sitting at the bar having a cocktail with a small pink umbrella—like this really is a wedding. The moment she sees us approach, she smiles wide.

"I swear, I can't get used to seeing you together." She twirls the umbrella, and I'm tempted to tell her how inappropriate it is.

"I have to say hello to a few people. Will you keep Maeve company?"

Dana rolls her eyes. "Like you have to ask." She raises a hand towards the bartender, who approaches with swagger and a glint in his eye, which dies the moment he notices me.

"Another cocktail." Dana winks. Wisely, the bartender nods and does his fucking job.

Maeve sits up beside Dana. She still looks nervous, but for now she will be safe with Dana. When the bartender arrives back with her drink, I reach in and remove the umbrella without saying a word and pick up her drink. He's still watching me as I brush a kiss on Maeve's forehead. "I won't be long," I say, placing the drink in her hand. She takes it and I give the bartender one more warning look before I search for my father.

I return to where I saw my father last, but he's gone.

Shay is talking to Darragh. They are close to the door and I'm ready to slip past them, but Darragh stops me.

"Your father is looking for you."

"Funny, I'm looking for him too."

I glance at Shay and nod.

"He's out in the courtyard. Acting like he owns the place," Darragh sneers.

"I'd better not keep the King waiting."

Darragh grins and downs his drink. I leave before Shay can question me on what I want with my father. His gaze gives his questions away.

My father's personal security is on the double-doors that lead out to an almost empty courtyard. My father is the only occupant. His back is towards me, his hands are stuffed into his trousers pockets. Seeing him sets a storm off inside me.

The door is opened for me without question, and I step out in the cool air. The sky has a crimson hue to it, like it also senses the foreboding that will surely come with this conversation.

"I decided to wait here for you," My father speaks without turning around, knowing it is me. Knowing I would come.

I walk down the wooden ramp that leads out onto the small seating area that's scattered with wooden chairs and large benches. Umbrellas are closed and nothing is on the tables. Plants are placed around the space, the vibrant colors not suiting my mood.

"I see you brought Maeve. You've made your point. She's yours." He continues to speak with his back to me.

"When you were first with Mother, if anyone threatened to hurt her, what would you have done?" My question gets his attention.

"Kill them." He doesn't even fucking hesitate.

Adrenaline shoots from my brain to my fist, and I quickly place my hands behind my back before I act on instinct. I have never raised a hand to my father, I would never dare, but right now he is pushing me to a place

I don't want to visit. "Then should I kill you?" That would never happen, but he needed to know how serious I was.

"Cian came to me. He wanted a way into the trials to be considered for a chance to be King."

I go around to face my father. I'm shocked that he is admitting what he did. A bitter taste pools on my tongue. "A chance that wasn't even real."

"Hope is a good thing for men like us. To see hope in someone else's eyes, gets things done. He said he knew her, that she would go with him easily. I didn't have to encourage the situation."

My father removes his hands from his pockets. He's calm, collected. I'm no threat to him. "Why did you want her out of the picture? What did she do?" Except to want to help her family, and I took advantage of that.

"Nothing." My father steps away from me.

I curl my hands into fists so I don't reach out and grab him and demand a proper fucking answer.

"You never showed interest in women, so I had one arranged for you."

I'd laugh if I didn't know just how serious he is right now. "An arranged marriage?"

"Yes. To a Murphy girl. It would strengthen our control in the South. An easy fix, and the girl is willing to marry you."

This time I clear the space between me and my father. "The only girl I'm marrying is Maeve."

My father doesn't flinch, but his gaze warns me to take a step back. "I see that now. But I have to come up with an alternative to our dilemma."

"You mean your dilemma." I step away from him. I never saw this side to my father. I never thought he would try to marry me off. If I hadn't met Maeve, maybe I would have considered it. It would be for the greater good, but Maeve was right for me. She was mine.

"Does Shane know that you sent Cian after Maeve?"

For the first time, my father reacts. He touches his chin. "No, and it will stay that way."

I grin. "So he doesn't know that you sent his son to his death."

My father's lip twitches. "His son came to me. I'm assuming since you destroyed the coroner's report that you or Maeve had some hand in his broken neck."

Dread starts to drip down my spine and I remain silent. He knew—of course he knew. The coroner would never lie to him, I was stupid to even think for a second, that he would.

My father nods like he got his answer. "When your mother was pregnant with you, Una took her and hid her from me."

My father has my full attention. "What?" I couldn't see Una doing something like that. "Why?" And why was she still breathing?

"Because she was a threat to the family at the time. It was a silly thing Una did. She could have harmed you or your mother."

My father never talked real, so hearing his past has the arranged marriage, Cian's death, and all the rest falling away for now.

"What happened?" I still don't understand how Una is breathing. It isn't like my father to allow someone to live.

"Shane loved her. He claimed her. So she couldn't be touched. Otherwise, I think he would have killed her himself."

My father turns fully to me now. "Maeve will never be touched, you have claimed her. What conspired must be buried here today."

That's why he told me. He was gaining my trust by giving me a fucking sob story. If he wasn't my father, I'd consider having him killed.

"Shay knows everything." It's a small lie. He knew of Cian but not about my father sending Cian. For the second time, I caught him off guard.

He raises a brow. "I didn't think you were stupid."

His insult has me grinning at him. "I didn't think you were ruthless." I meant how he had tried to get rid of Maeve and he knew it.

"Shay wants to have control over the East."

This time my father laughs and it stills the space around me. It's a warning like you have fucked up, and he's about to unleash the consequences on you. Or it's like the strike of lightning that's a warning of the rattles of thunder that will follow.

I plow on, knowing this will be my only chance to make any of this happen and keep Maeve safe. "He suggested a table of four Kings, to control the North and the East equally."

My father's laughter cuts off and he's snarling at me. "You think he will rule equally?"

"I don't know. It's hard to know who to trust these days. But, I'm willing to make a change. I'm willing to give him my trust." At that moment, I realize I trust Shay, and ruling with him wouldn't be a bad idea. "For the first time in history we would have control of the North." I'm taking a step towards my father with excitement that he clearly isn't feeling.

"His position in the North is temporary." My father reminds me.

"It won't always be, like my position here will change soon." It's a subtle reminder that I will be King one day. "You can't stop this. One day I will rule." I didn't want to use Shay going to Shane with the truth about Cian as an incentive to my father. Threatening him never worked, so maybe a reminder that I'm his son and will rule one day will work.

"And may I ask, who will occupy these two other seats?"

"Shay will select one and I will select the other."

My father's face twists like he's in pain. One of the double-doors open, the security man is ready to speak.

"Close the door." My father's raised voice has the security man gripping the door handle, but the door doesn't fully close.

"Excuse me." It's my mother who steps through the door, and I watch my father transform.

"I didn't know it was you. I'm sorry I raised my voice." He steps up to my mother and kisses her cheek.

My mother's brown eyes swing to me. "Are you okay?" She frowns.

I force a smile for her. "Yeah. I'm fine."

"Is there something the matter?" My father asks my mother, redirecting her attention back to him.

"Shane was looking for you. He didn't want to leave Una." My mother's gaze grows heavy with sorrow. "I said I'd find you so he could stay with her."

I wonder if he would still be looking for my father if he knew that Dad had caused his son's death. I didn't think Shane would hold on to much honor. I think he'd lose his head, and in doing so, try to kill my father.

"I'll be with him in one moment. I'm nearly finished with Jack."

My mother touches my father's face, and the smile that lights her eyes is only reserved for him. "Okay. I'll let him know."

Her smiling eyes land on me before we both watch her walk up the ramp and into the double doors.

"Family is everything to her." My father glances at me. "I'm still the King of the East, so this is what will happen. We agree to Shay's terms."

Relief swims fast and hard through my system. This would bury what happened to Cian. Maeve would be home free. That's all I wanted right now. I'm tempted to thank my father, but there is something in his gaze that keeps me quiet.

"You will continue your trials, a seat will be reserved for you, and I will continue to rule. Shay will be granted a seat; and the last seat—I will decide who gets it."

That didn't sound like Shay's terms. But once again I keep quiet.

"Red Murphy will have to be compensated for his daughter not marrying you. It will cause a war between us and the South, and to renege on such a deal..."

I tighten my jaw. "You should have thought about that before you made the deal."

"I will have to offer another O'Reagan."

I'm shaking my head. "Richard? He would never agree to something like that."

My father's lips curl up in disgust. Richard is a disappointment to him. He doesn't hide it, only to my mother, but the rest of the world knows and that includes Richard.

"Shay. They won't be happier with a Northerner. Red Murphy will decline, but if I sweeten the deal with the chance for one of his sons to rule alongside us, we could really unite the South, East, and North."

For the first time, I see the excitement in my father's eyes. "Maybe this could all work out."

I didn't share his joy. "Shay won't agree to an arranged marriage."

My father exhales and looks away from me like I'm boring him. "Leave that with me. He will agree."

My father steps closer to me, and it's like he pulls in any emotions, or signs that he gave away during this conversation. "I don't ever want to hear anything about Cian's death, only that he was shot in the head. That's it. The rest doesn't exist."

"I'm happy with that," I say.

My father looks at me. "I had better go find Shane then." My father walks away and I watch as the double doors are open for him. His security follows him and I'm left not sure how all that went, or what the future would look like with my father ruling alongside Shay, me, and now a Murphy lad.

I leave the courtyard, knowing I would soon find out.

Chapter Thirty-Seven

O'REAGAN
AN CHLANN

JACK

I leave the courtyard, not entirely sure how that went. The fact that Maeve was safe now from my father was the biggest thing I could take away from it. I enter the corridor and I'm surprised when Maeve rounds the corner and nearly walks into me. She grips my shoulders, dragging me closer and fear grips me as her chocolate eyes hold mine.

"What's wrong?"

"They are going to find out." Her voice is too loud and I glance up to make sure we are alone. We are, but anyone could come around the corner.

I take her hand and push open the ladies' bathroom door.

"Get out." Two women stare at me and I don't have the patience right now. One has half her lipstick on, the other shaking water from her fingers.

"Get the fuck out, now!" The one at the mirror grabs her handbag and ducks as she passes us, the other is a bit slower, she's looking at Maeve. The moment they are out, I step into the bathroom still holding Maeve's hand. I open all four doors to make sure we are alone before turning to Maeve.

"Why do you think that?"

"I heard your father talking to Shane. The guy who they think shot Cian, arrived at some pub."

Fuck!

"Did you see where they went?" I'm asking while releasing Maeve's hand. Taking my phone out of my pocket, I hit my father's number.

"No." Maeve shakes her head. "I came straight for you." Her lip trembles. I reach out and touch her face. "It's going to be okay."

"John's son was spotted at The Hen's Nest pub. I'm on the way with Shane." I want to scream into the phone at my father to keep Shane away from there.

"Who's driving?"

"Me, of course."

I'm nodding as I release Maeve's face. "I'm on the way."

I hang up. "I need you to stay with Dana."

"He's going to tell them he didn't do it." She's panicking. I feel the panic rising in me too, but I need her to stay calm.

"It's important right now that you return to the funeral."

The door opens, and a woman freezes at the door as she takes me and Maeve in. "It's closed. Get out."

She steps out very fucking quickly.

314

"What are you going to do?" Maeve's question is filled with worry. I take one moment and kiss her, pushing aside everything wrong about this moment—and dragging all that is right, forward.

"I won't be long, and when I return we can have a drink." I step back. "Go back to Dana. I won't be long."

Maeve hesitates but leaves the bathroom.

I take out my phone and ring Shay. He answers immediately. "I'm following them."

"You left without me?" I hang up, not bothering to listen to his answer. The blond woman who had tried to enter only moments ago, jumps aside as I leave the bathroom, and return to the courtyard, taking a shortcut down a few steps that lead to the side of the building. I half run along the side, until I come out at the front of the hotel where my Range Rover is parked.

Every scenario is going through my mind now as I get into the jeep and start the engine. I tear down the road to Navan. It will take twenty minutes to get there, and they had a ten minute head start. A lot can happen in ten minutes. A lot can happen in ten seconds.

Shane will torture him first; he'll want to hear how he shot Cian. If he keeps denying it, and admits to shooting Connor and Finn, it's going to look suspicious. My foot's already to the floor, and I can't go any faster. I overtake every vehicle in front of me, but I'm not going fast enough.

My phone rings, and I answer it.

"They got him." It's Shay. "They are taking him to a Beech Mount industrial estate. Shane has a unit at the back, number 32."

"Don't let them question him," I say. Knowing nothing is going to stop Shane, the only person who might have a chance is my father.

"I'll do my best." Shay hangs up this time.

I enter Navan. It's taken me twelve minutes, which is impressive, but I don't feel quick enough as I drive towards Beech Mount industrial estate. It's filled mostly with large furniture outlets that are open for business. I have to slow down as every five meters is a speed bump. It's frustrating, but I finally arrive at the unit and jump out.

Shay's at the side door, and that's not a good sign. I don't ask all the questions that want to pour from me.

"Shane is questioning him." Shay sounds as hopeless as I feel. Why was my father rung first? I had left word that I had to be called, but once again, no one would defy him. I needed to rectify that, so no one would ever defy me again.

John's son is tied to a chair. He's a fucking mess. Already I want to shoot him just to put him out of his misery. Shane's using his face as a punching bag. My father is standing to the side, and glances at me as I enter.

Shane stops heaving, and roars into the man's face. "Admit it."

The man can't even speak, and my father answers for him. "He denies shooting Cian, and also Connor."

I sneer. "Of course he is." I step closer, trying to make out his face. I can't. I just know where his eyes should be, and his nose and mouth. I wouldn't be able to identify this lump of flesh, if I didn't know the structure of a face.

"I don't think he can talk, Shane." I step closer and the man's head jerks up towards my voice. There is no way he can see me.

"He's not lying." Shane's huffing as he turns to me.

Fear shoots through my body, and adrenaline has me ready.

"He shot Connor too, yet he's denying that." My father steps forward while speaking, but Shane can't take his eyes off me.

"What happened to my son?" Shane's demeanor sparks and collapses, and I no longer recognize any part of my uncle. He wants to rip me apart.

"That fucker shot him. Why are you looking at me?" I take a step towards Shane and allow him to see my clenched fists. "What the fuck do you want me to say?" My voice rises, my temper escalates, it's been pushed by pure fear. He can't find out, no matter what I have to do at this moment, I know he can't find out. If it comes down to me or him, I'll choose myself.

"Did you hurt my son?" He blinks, and it's the sign that he's in there behind the wall of pure and undiluted rage that propels him towards me.

I withdraw the gun from the band of my trousers. "Are you accusing me of killing Cian?" I say it, and hold the gun at Shane's head.

"Jack." The warning in my father's voice doesn't penetrate the panic I feel to keep this situation in control. To stop Shane from killing me. I know Shay is somewhere behind me, but I have no idea where he would stand if this gets messy.

"Cian was like a fucking brother to me." My voice rises and I step closer to Shane who's staring at me with a deadness in his eyes. "I would never fucking hurt him."

The tip of the gun presses against Shane's forehead, and I dig it in. Shane opens his arms wide, and looks directly into my eyes.

"Jack." My father issues a second warning.

"I didn't hurt Cian. That motherfucker did."

Too many beats pass as Shane stares into my eyes. Finally Shane starts to deflate, and something close to shame fills his features as he drops his arms. I step back, and he turns to John's son, and I see how his body grows tighter. He's ready to ring the truth out of him even if it takes the man's last breath. I'm all twisted and tight with a fear of him finding out. I move forward quickly and pull the trigger.

317

I don't stop.

The sound roars through the wide-open space as I empty my gun in John's son's chest. I'm still pulling the trigger long after the bullets run out.

My finger relaxes, and I turn to Shane to find him looking at me. "For Cian," I say.

Shane blinks, and one lone tear falls. He takes a final look at John's son's body before leaving the warehouse. He doesn't say a word, and the moment the door closes, my knees grow weak, but I keep upright.

I'm still holding the gun. I'm still staring at the body, not allowing the thought that I pulled a gun on Shane to take over. My father steps up to me and places his hand on my shoulder. I look up, and I see something I have never seen before in his eyes. Pride. He's proud of what I just did. I'm not. I shrug him off and put the gun away.

"Why did he shoot them?" I ask. Wanting to know why I just took a life.

"He was after you," my father says. "It was revenge for me killing his father."

I didn't have to ask if he had killed his father. I want to ask why, but I'm tired.

"You knew he didn't shoot Connor." My father's words are directed towards Shay. I'm still reeling from pulling a gun on Shane; it was a necessary evil that I hope I'd never have to do again.

"A while ago," Shay's voice is directly behind me and I turn around.

"You knew he didn't shoot your father?" The man had been telling the truth. "So the only one he shot was Finn, but I was the target?" I ask my father.

He confirms with a nod of his head, but he hasn't taken his eyes off Shay. "Why did you stay when your father told you it had nothing to do with us? It was a northerner who had shot him."

Shay grins. "I kind of like it here, Uncle Liam."

My father takes another step towards him. "Jack tells me you want to share equal control over the South and North of Ireland?"

I turn back to John's son's body. His head is slung back, his throat on full display. I want to feel a swell of guilt over taking his life, but I don't. I feel guilt over pulling a gun on Shane, and making him believe that he was the wrong one, that I would never hurt his son or cover up his death.

"A panel of four, equal control. I think it could work," Shay answers my father.

"It could. It could be great." My father's answer has me walking over to John's son and untying him from the chair. His body hits the ground hard, getting Shay's and my father's attention.

"I thought you might want to be part of this conversation," My father's voice carries a note of annoyance.

I can't stop the smile that takes over my lips. "I can listen and work at the same time. I think it could be great," I say honestly, imagining an Ireland united. It might be in the criminal world, but it's been divided for over a hundred years.

"I agreed to the terms with Jack," My father lies.

Shay of course looks at me.

"Four chairs. One for me, you, my father, and a Murphy lad," I say.

"So you didn't agree to my terms." Shay glances between me and my father.

"You must enter an arranged marriage. That is the terms." My father fixes his cuffs like he has this in the bag.

I move along the side of the large room and grip a piece of the plastic sheeting that has been left there, no doubt for cleaning up bodies.

"What kind of cunt do you think I am?" Shay has balls.

319

I laugh as I drag the plastic back to the body. My father hasn't met anyone like Shay. Shay has got to know that he could be digging his own grave, one shovel load at a time.

"That's the terms, Shay, or you can ship yourself back up North, where you belong."

I drop the plastic at my father's tone. Shay looks ready to draw a weapon. Mine is empty but if he did pull a gun on my father, I wouldn't hesitate to shoot him.

Shay looks at me, and I know he's thinking about what he did for me, what I promised him in return.

"Do you have someone you want to marry?" I ask Shay, and kneel down, dragging the body onto the plastic.

"No, but that's not the fucking point."

I heave the body. He's heavy, but I get him on.

"It is the fucking point. You either want in or you don't." I know I'm back tracking, but he has to see that there is no room for negotiating. He might accept it better from me than my father.

I wrap the plastic around the body. "You lied to me about your father." I stop working and look up at Shay, feeling pissed over that. "What else have you lied about?"

"I only found out a few days ago and was already knee-deep in it." He says and takes a pack of cigarettes out of his pocket.

"Well, I will let you two talk about it, and I'm looking forward to your answer, Shay. I can assume you can clean up?" My father asks, turning to me.

I nod and he leaves.

Shay lights up his cigarette.

"What is she like? A one-eyed gypsy or something."

I'm glad that Shay's mind is turning to his arranged marriage, even if it's negative. He's thinking about it, and that's what's important right now.

"I have no idea." I don't mention that she was meant for me. That wouldn't sit right with Shay. He wouldn't like anyone's seconds.

"She'll hardly be paraful looking?" He blows smoke into the air.

I straighten." What does that mean?"

"Paraful?"

I nod.

"Like a stunner. A head-turner."

"Would that matter to you?" I ask and point at the body. "Help me lift him."

Shay throws the cigarette on the ground. "I won't be with a gypsy." He says, crushing the cigarette under his boot.

I grin.

So he's considering it.

He picks up the butt, and puts it in his pocket before helping me.

"Out back." I jut my chin towards the back of the warehouse.

"What age is she?"

"I don't know." I grin even as the weight of the dead body has me moving faster towards the door, wanting to get the body out of my hands.

I hold the body with one hand and push down on the handle. It's still bright outside. A large silver bin is already open.

"On the count of three," I say to Shay.

He doesn't wait, but heaves the body into the bin, nearly making me drop it. The moment I'm free of it, I close the lid.

"Clean up will get rid of him later and tidy up the warehouse." I tell Shay as we go back inside.

"I should have told you about my Da."

I stop and nod. "Yeah, you should have."

"I honestly didn't think your Da knew, and I wanted to stay. I really want to unite us all."

"If we are going to work together, there can't be any lies. No secrets."

Shay nods. "Aye."

"My father sent Cian after Maeve. He wanted her out of the picture," I admit.

"Honestly, it doesn't surprise me." There is silence as we stand looking at each other.

"You're not like him, Jack."

I'm not sure if that's a compliment or an insult.

"You're a cunt. But not a cunt like him."

I grin at Shay, only he can use a word like that and get away with it.

"We need to get back." We had been gone too long.

"What you did with Shane. It had to be done. I can't imagine it being easy."

I appreciated Shay's words, but I didn't need either of us going soft.

"Taking a life is never easy. Even the ones we love." It's a warning, one I hope I will never have to use.

Shay nods again. "Aye." A flash of irritation in his dark eyes has me wanting us to leave this behind and start fresh.

"It's all behind us now. We can move forward." We leave the warehouse and I pull the door behind us.

"So are you going to get married?" I ask him.

He lights another cigarette. "I'll think about it."

"What if she's as ugly as a dog's ass?"

"Then you and your father can fuck right off."

I laugh as I get into the jeep but roll down the window. "See you back at the hotel. We could have a drink."

Shay grins. "An Chlann."

His words have me starting the engine. "An Chlann," I repeat back, because that's what we are. A family who will rise together and die together.

Family isn't what keeps us O'Reagan's side by side; it's the lies and secrets that's like glue, that ties us all tightly together.

"An Chlann."

Epilogue

O'REAGAN

AN CHLANN

MAEVE

TWO WEEKS LATER

I'm so caught up in the look on my mother's face, that everything seems to swirl around me and blend into a blur of color. She's happy.

"Are you ready for this?" She asks with a smile that has been missing for years. I nod, afraid that if I speak, she will hear the emotion in my voice. She opens her bedroom door and steps in. Pride shines from her eyes.

"It's beautiful." I have to look away from her, and I take in the contents of her room. A large double bed, the duvet has a pattern of pink roses, the color is soft, and the pink is carried throughout the room. Everything about the room is gentle and ladylike.

"I love it here." She's looking around the room with me like it's her first time seeing it. She's been here a week, and I can't get over the change in her.

Jack's voice drifts up the stairs as he talks to Declan about the recent football game. Everything feels so perfect.

"I can't thank you enough." My mother's gaze fills with that old sadness that I want to magically make go away.

"You can feed me. I'm starving."

The magic works, and she's leaving the room. "The roast is nearly done." I watch her as she descends the stairs of her new home. My mother is cleaning and cooking, and she looks good. My mother enters the kitchen and I'm about to follow her when Declan's voice flows from the sitting room as I'm about to pass.

"Maeve, you never told me we had a traitor in the camp."

I step in. The sitting room is small but cozy. The gray couch the boys sit on is new, and I love the cream cushions that are scattered across the couch and armchair.

Jack's grinning, and my stomach tightens, and his gaze drifts to me.

"He supports Dublin." Declan's voice carries a tinge of outrage.

"I support the winning team, and Dublin wins every year." Jack defends his decision.

"You're not a Meath man at all." Declan shakes his head and looks back at me. "You will be mom's least favorite now."

My mother is a huge Meath supporter, always has been. I grin. "I don't think so. I think I'm ranking pretty high in her eyes."

Declan sits back. "I think this could be a deal-breaker."

I laugh as I leave the sitting room and enter the kitchen to help Mom. The sun dies slowly as I watch her pick up a glass of wine and happily drink from it as she stirs the gravy. She had reduced her drinking, but she hadn't stopped.

I have to take joy in the small things, and I do, as I step into the kitchen. She turns and smiles at me while placing the glass on the counter.

"I'll set the table."

"Thanks, sweetheart."

As I set the table, I can't stop the thoughts of my father arriving back and making this a perfect picture. Yet, for the first time, I wonder, would it really make things perfect, or is that just the idea that the grass is always greener on the other side?

A hand on my hip has me smiling. I don't have to turn around to know who it is. "I can't wait to get you home," Jack whispers into my ear, and I jut out my hip, pushing him away as I continue to set the table. I loved being here at my mom's with him, but I couldn't wait to go home with him.

"Can I do anything, Jane?" It's so weird to hear Jack speak to my mother.

Her eyes grow even softer as she looks at Jack. "You have done enough. Sit down. Dinner is almost ready."

Jack does as my mother says, but his gaze never leaves me.

"Declan. Dinner!" My mother calls like this is normal for us to sit around a table and have a meal. This is the first in years, and once all the dishes are on the table and we are all seated, I do something I haven't done in a long time. I take Jack's hand in my left hand and Declan's in my right. They do the same, joining hands with my mother, and I thank God for the food on our table, our health, and mostly our family. I look up as I speak the last line to find Jack watching me. I don't think I will ever get used to how he looks at me.

I hope I never get used to it.

"Amen," I say and release Declan's hand. I hold on to Jack's just a bit longer before my mother tells us to eat, and we do.

"I also wanted to thank you, Jack." My mother's voice shakes a little, and I'm not sure if it's that she is about to thank someone for something or it's the topic. "For helping Declan, for getting him out of trouble."

"Don't mention it." Jack glances at me, and I'm wondering what I'm missing.

My mother puts down her knife and fork. "I contacted Jack about the legal case with Declan and asked if he could help."

I wasn't happy with my mother doing that, but I listen.

"All charges have been dropped against Declan. I don't think we can ever repay you, Jack."

Jack waves it off, but my mother is right. I don't think we could ever repay him.

"You did that?" I'm looking at him like he just appeared.

"It was only a phone call. The whole thing was just a misunderstanding," Jack says the last part to Declan, who nods, but has a tightness in his shoulders.

"Well, thank you," I say, and we fall into an odd silence.

"I know how you can repay me," Jack speaks after a bit of silence. He isn't looking at me but cuts into his meat.

"Anything." And I mean it, I would do anything for him.

"Anything?" He questions and his serious tone reminds me of the old Jack, the one who would frighten me.

I hold my head high. "Yes."

He nods and returns to his dinner. "Tomorrow, we can come here and watch Dublin destroy Meath."

Declan snorts.

Relief floods my veins.

"You will wear a Dublin jersey." Jack finishes.

And that is how you cause an argument in our house.

"That will never happen," I say, and we laugh.

We eat and laugh, just like a family would do, for the first time. It's the closest to perfect I think I will ever feel.

It's close enough.

THE END

I hope you enjoyed *Mafia Prince*.

Mafia King is the next book in the Young Irish Rebel Series.

Read Shay and Emma's story.

You can scan the code below or get your copy HERE:

https://author-vicarter.com/products/mafia-prince

Or read on for a sneak peek!

MAFIA KING:

O'REAGAN
AN CHLANN

PROLOGUE

The air is too thin. I can't breathe. It's like a swollen storm that's all caught up inside me—rose-red blood blossoms on my once white wedding dress. My fingers play along the destructive substance as I drag air painfully into my lungs. The dress had been designed just for me. Every inch of the trim was done in lace, each stitch done by hand. It was truly a masterpiece that was smashed to pieces.

The room tilts, and I dig my hands deeper into the soft fabric to keep myself on the small navy stool. I focus on the white piano in front of me, the cover open, the white stool at an angle like it's waiting to be played.

My vision blurs, and I close my eyes as I drag another breath in; it hitches on a sob that I can't hold in any longer.

It's their screams and panic that still pierces my mind. Hundreds of people fighting to get over each other, with love flying out the window, protection didn't exist at that moment, as each person fought for their own safety.

Yet, all the while, he had stood at the altar staring at me. Knowing who was behind this.

It's the look of absolute betrayal in Shay's eyes that I will never forget.

Bending my head, I seal my lips together, so the scream doesn't erupt from me. He hadn't run like everyone else; he didn't dive to the ground; instead, he stood before me in his dark suit, looking like a King that had just climbed off his horse, only to find out that there was nothing at all here for him to rule.

Footsteps pound along the wooden corridor, and I tuck my head deeper into my chest. *Keep running, check other rooms. I'm not here.*

My memory is filled with brown eyes widening before narrowing, while guns released countless rounds of ammunition. Hysteria reached its peak as everyone scrambled across church pews. Large golden candle holders collided with marble. The impact rattled the ground, but nothing rattled me like Shay.

Another sob has me slipping from the stool, and my hands touch the dark wooden floor. My polished nails drag along it as my mind grows more frantic as I replay the pain in Shay's eyes. He no longer was a god with a shield around him. No, he became a man, made of flesh and bones. The moment he hit the ground, I knew the game was over.

I push my nails a little deeper until they bend and threaten to snap.

Right now, as I sob on the floor, the thought that races through my mind is: What have you done, Noel?

What have I done?

MAFIA PRINCE

Download and read HERE:
https://author-vicarter.com/products/mafia-king-2
Or scan the code below:

OTHER BOOKS BY VI CARTER

THE SIXTH (NOVELLA)

THE COLLECTOR #1

THE HANDLER #2

<u>THE YOUNG IRISH REBELS</u>

MAFIA PRINCE #1

MAFIA KING #2

MAFIA GAMES #3

MAFIA BOSS #4

MAFIA SECRETS #5

ABOUT THE AUTHOR

V i Carter - the queen of **DARK ROMANCE**, the mistress of suspense, and the high priestess of *PLOT TWISTS*!

When she's not busy crafting tales of the **MAFIA** that'll leave you on the edge of your seat, you can find her baking up a storm, exploring the gorgeous Irish countryside, or spending time with her three little girls.

Vi's Young Irish Rebels series has been praised by readers and can be found in English, Dutch, German, Audible and soon will be available in French.

And let's not forget her two greatest loves: ***coffee and chocolate***. If you ever need to bribe her, just offer up a mug of coffee and a slab of chocolate, and she'll be putty in your hands.

So, if you're ready to join Vi on a wild journey with the mafia, sign up for her newsletter and score a free book! Just be warned - her stories are so **ADDICTIVE**, you might not be able to put them down.

What Readers Are Saying

Editorial Reviews

"Vi Carter has once again blown my mind with another outstanding story. She never fails to create a masterpiece with memorable characters that leap off the page. This book is complete perfection."- USA Today Bestselling Author Khardine Gray

Vi is one of those authors who never disappoints. She weaves **LOVE** & **DANGER** effortlessly. ★★★★★ stars

I definitely recommend this book. It is **SUSPENSEFUL** and exciting. I enjoy reading Vi Carter's book. ★★★★★ stars

How to Keep in Touch with Vi Carter

Visit Vi's website: https://author-vicarter.com/
Join the newsletter: t.ly/yZWbX
Or scan the code below:

On Facebook, Instagram, TikTok and Youtube @darkauthorvicarter and on Twitter @authorvicarter

Or scan the code below:

ACKNOWLEDGEMENTS

I'm very lucky to have such amazing readers and Beta Readers. I want to thank the following people who worked with me on this book.

Editor: Sherry Schafer

Proofreader: Michele Rolfe

Proofreader: Cassie Hess-Dean

Blurb was written by: Tami Thomason

Beta Readers

Amanda Sheridan

Laura Riley

Lucy Korth

Tami Thomason

Paula Rhodes

Teresa Doherty

Megan Corbett

Patti Shaw

Tonni Brown

Cindy Kemp

Printed in Great Britain
by Amazon